Vampire League

Book III
Children of Midnight

Vampire League

Book III
Children of Midnight

by Luiza Dobrzynska

PAPERBACK ISBN: 978-1-7353456-2-8

EPUB ISBN: 978-1-3938965-9-3

***

WRITTEN BY LUIZA DOBRZYNSKA

PUBLISHED BY ROYAL HAWAIIAN PRESS

COVER ART BY TYRONE ROSHANTHA

TRANSLATED BY RAFAL STACHOWSKY

PUBLISHING ASSISTANCE: DOROTA RESZKE

***

FOR MORE WORKS BY THIS AUTHOR, PLEASE VISIT:

WWW.ROYALHAWAIIANPRESS.COM

***

VERSION NUMBER 1.0

PART 1

African Magic

Everyone later agreed on one thing - Fronda was not guilty of anything. It has happened more than once that everyone traveled to the assembly point from a different side and no one saw anything strange about it. They were adults, they had experience, and they didn't need each other to avoid getting into trouble. This time, however, one of those unpredictable things happened that ruined the best plans and could become deadly.

They were to go to the Republic of Congo to find a man named Delaney Robbins who was missing in the impenetrable forests. Octavio had no idea why Delaney went to areas inhabited by primitive African tribes. He wasn't part of his research team, he was quite secretive and hardly anyone knew anything about him. However, it was known that he needed help, since - remaining in constant contact with sister - one day this contact broke off without a word of explanation. It was his sister, Tomira that came to Octavio begging for help she couldn't give.

All what di Mauro could pass on to Never's investigation team was the location of the base to the south of Brazzaville, the address of some Shani Batawi, a check for fifty thousand, and a picture of a dark-haired man in sunglasses. The money came from Peg Robbins, the owner of the silver mine and several companies, as well as a relative and caretaker of Delaney and Tomira. She was almost ninety years old and had only her pupils, so she agreed with what they had become.

"I really don't know why some vampires are as poor as we are, and others are luxury," Gladiator sighed, looking at the check in disbelief.

"Because that's how it is in the world. The capitalists would like to keep everything for themselves, at the expense of those who develop their wealth," Gerard replied pompously.

"Communist... You start with this again?" Never snorted mockingly.

"Why a communist?" The blond highlander got interested.

"You don't know anything? Our star of cinema, theater and more, he sympathized with communists. Fortunately, not with the Soviet, but with the French. He met with Fidel Castro, he went to Moscow, and who knows what more..."

Gladiator opened his eyes wide and looked at the actor with explicit scandal. He shrugged.

"I wanted social justice," he murmured.

"Yes? Did you not know what communism looks like? Haven't heard of the labor camps, UB torture chambers and other similar matters? Were you blind or just a fool?"

"Okay, Yanek, it's not time for ideological training," Never interrupted Gladiator's tirade. "Many were deceived in those days, not just him."

"I just... anyway, why do I explain myself?" Gerard was angry this time. "It was my life! I wanted to devote it to doing something for people and I did! I fought for a dignified salary and good treatment of extras, I took part in work to improve the lives of the poorest and prevent overt injustices! Is that a sin?!"

"He's a little right," Oggy suddenly took his side. "Some are choking on gold and they don't know what to do with it anymore, while others are selling themself for a slice of bread or dying of hunger and disease in the streets. This most perfect of the worlds is beautiful, heh."

"Some have a lot of money and some have nothing. It is like that and always has been. It is good though that the first ones give earnings to the latter sometimes." Never took the check from Gladiator and placed it carefully in his wallet. "Tomorrow I will realize this valuable paper in the local bank, today it is too late. Money will come in handy, because we need equipment, and we don't have too much. Since Robbins was missing in the wilderness, you will have to look for him there. It requires equipment, supplies and so on. As soon as Fronda lands, we will go to the local base. Maybe they already know something there?"

"What time does his plane land?" Oggy asked anxiously. "Poor Theo doesn't like flying..."

"It should be here just after midnight," Never looked at the clock in the hall. "He's off with a girl again, let him tire himself a little. He will be fine."

Oggy looked around the airport hall, poorly arranged, as she judged. At one point, she pulled Never by the sleeve.

"Rajah, look at the board," she said. "No aircraft will arrive today."

"Don't bother with it. It's a private airline that has an agreement with this airport," Never patted her on the fragile shoulder and looked around too.

The hall of the small, suburban airport was almost empty, except for a few service people, yawning with fatigue. They were also waiting for the private DC-10 to land, so they could check in and finally take a nap. Only the controllers visible behind the large window looked brisker. They couldn't afford to be tired.

Meanwhile, Fronda sat in his chair, digging his elbows into the railing and clenching his teeth nervously. The DC-10 was old and clapped-out, and though none of the people in it showed any anxiety, he was feeling nervous, as always when he was several thousand meters above the ground. He hated it, but he had no choice. The sea journey would have lasted two weeks, far too long, while the flight was only a few hours. He had to overcome himself and did it, but he counted the minutes to land. Unlike other passengers, he didn't even try to sleep - he knew he couldn't do it anyway, he was far too nervous.

"Miss, when do we land?" He finally asked the stewardess passing by, an elderly lady who should have been retired for a long time.

"Soon, sir. Please calm down." The woman answered politely, giving him a dazzling smile. Like everybody of her age, she treated the word "miss" as the greatest compliment.

Her words didn't calm him at all. The bulbs under the ceiling blinked yellow, the fuselage creaked dangerously, sometimes there was a slight turbulence, causing his stomach to run up his throat. He definitely didn't like flying, and this plane probably remembered the Second World War. Suddenly something happened that made him forget his fears. A passenger sitting nearby, opened the bag on his lap and pulled out a shiny steel-black object.

Fronda jerked forward just as the man shouted:

"Nobody moves!"

Theo couldn't stop and fell on him with his whole body. There was a bang, then another one. An armed desperate fought with the madman's fury, so that even the vampire's strength could not overpower him, the passengers screamed, and the great magnum shot time and again, hitting it out the window, then at the wall. The hysterical scream of passengers intensified the horror of this scene, which seemed to have no end. Finally, Fronda managed to knock the madman off his pistol, and overpower him with a blow.

"Calm down, it's over!" He exclaimed at his fellow passengers, tying the unconscious man with belts torn off the seat.

When he finished, he stood up and looked around to assess the extent of the damage. The flight attendant was wounded in the shoulder, but one of the passengers, probably a nurse, had already taken care of her. The fuselage was pierced in several places, and maybe that's why the plane began to jolt dangerously.

"Get attached to the seats with everything anyone can!"

Holding on to the seats, Theo headed for the pilot's cabin to calm down the probably scared aviator, but before he reached it, he saw, to his indescribable horror, a trickle of blood flowing out from under the door. He opened it with a sharp jerk and went numb. One of the bullets had to break through the cover because the pilot was sitting in his chair with his head tilted back unnaturally. The autopilot lamp on the control board was illuminated, apparently the man had turned on the device before he lost consciousness. Instead of the co-pilot, Theo saw a uniform dummy sitting rigidly in the chair. Headphones hung from his neck, from which the monotonous calling of the control tower could be heard:

"Flight 504, come in!"

Fronda stood for a moment, chilled with what he saw, then slowly took headphones and put them on his ears. He suddenly realized that he was probably the only man on board who could bring the plane down. The flight attendant could not replace him, her wound looked serious and the woman was clearly shocked. Most of the passengers were a group of elderly from the Cairo Active Seniors organization, going on an annual trip. They all came from a poor Cairo under a government aid program, and one could predict in advance that there was nothing to count on them.

Theo understood that he was unaided, facing a task that surpassed his strength and skills.

"Houston? We have a small problem here." He said with an effort into the microphone of the headphones.

He didn't know where the stupid words came from. Perhaps subconsciously, he tried to reduce the tension slightly choking him.

"What? Who is there?" The controller voice worried in earphones.

"This is flight 504," he replied, not knowing his own voice. "Terrorist on board, currently overpowered. Pilot killed, flight attendant seriously wounded, fuselage shot in several places, decompression. The second pilot was replaced by a mannequin. We're flying on autopilot. It jolts like hell, passengers are hysterical. Me too."

He removed the pilot's body from the seat and sat at the controls himself. He didn't know why - he was shaking like jelly and was sure he couldn't do anything. He stared into the darkness outside the windows, wondering in panic how to find the way when the controller spoke again in the headphones:

"504, listen carefully. We'll bring you down, but you have to buck up..."

"There must be Rajah in the hall," Theo interrupted. "Sinclair Radhjaleah. Call him. Say Fronda calls him. I want him to be there."

The flight controller removed the headphones from his ears. He looked at his colleague, as horrified as he was, and shook his head in desperation. Opening the glass door, he shouted:

"Is anyone here called Rajah?"

Never made eye contact with his friends.

"It's me," he volunteered.

"Please, come inside. This is serious, there is no time to hesitate!"

Never hurried to the control center, and the rest followed, though without an invitation. The controller handed the spare headphones to the Indian and put on a second one himself.

"The pilot is dead, they are decompressed, and someone completely just off the boat is at the controls," he whispered, and said aloud. "Flight 504, Rajah at the microphone."

"Never, I'm at the controls. I am alone here. I'm afraid like never before." Said Fronda in trembling voice. "The passengers are screaming; the wind is blowing on the plane. On the dashboard I see a lot of different widgets and I have no idea which one it can be used for. I can't bring this piece of metal scrap to the airport."

"Yes, you can do it," Never said firmly. "Buck up and stop acting like an old woman. Listen to the instructions carefully and take heed."

He looked at the controller, who nervously adjusted the headphones and covered the microphone with his hand.

"Are you crazy? Someone who has never flown cannot put DC 10 on the runway and not break it by the way."

"No? I saw a movie like that..." Oggy interrupted.

"For God's sake, it's just fiction! There was no chance that such a thing would succeed! The plane is not a small motorbike! And now, at night..."

"Don't yell, sir," Never rebuked coldly. "It worked or failed, irrelevant. Now he must succeed, and you will bring my friend back to the ground. Is it clear?"

"You don't have much way out," Gerard added. "This plane will crash anyway. Theo can save it, but he can't do it without you."

"The guy is right," said the second controller. "If we do nothing, we will be accused of being passive about the disaster. We have to do something."

The first one shrugged angrily and took his hand off the microphone.

"Can you hear me? How much fuel do you have?"

"How do I know?!"

"The pointer is straight ahead. Such a rectangular display. Please read the numbers."

"One and half?"

"One and a half tons. Little. We have to hurry. First of all, please turn off autopilot. It's a red lever next to the throttle on your right. Immediately afterwards grab the control column and pull towards you until the drawing of the aircraft on the indicator next to it rises above the artificial horizon line."

"What is the throttle? I don't know anything... Oh, on the right..."

Theo moved the miniature lever and grabbed the controls as the plane flopped. A scream escaped him that no one had ever heard before. He jerked the control column toward himself while squinting at the indicator dial. He felt as if he had no power in his hands, his teeth clang like castanets. He wasn't sure how long this tension would last, and he just wished he could sit down on the ground. It was not that difficult to keep the plane on course, but his hands were shaking anyway.

"Now be careful," said the controller. "You must keep the aircraft on the display above the artificial horizon line. We'll be watching the plane on the radar and we'll tell you when something goes wrong, like when you're off course. Now you will control to the airport and then you will end up."

"I do not know if I can..."

"That's an order!" Never bellowed furiously into the microphone. "Put your French ass on the landing strip, or you will be in trouble!"

"Relax," the controller pushed him away impatiently. "Listen to me carefully, I will guide you through the whole procedure. Now we will lower the flight because the machine is too high. Slowly. Be careful..."

In a calm and even voice, he began to give more instructions.

"I see two rows of lights," Fronda reported after some time.

"It's an airstrip. You have to steer the plane between these lights. Please keep flying, not too fast."

The glowing spot on the radar screen was falling slightly. They watched him holding breath.

The machine is right above the airport. Now extend the landing gear. It's like a leverage. It is in this place as in the car the gear lever, and next to it a red lamp light. When the landing gear is extended, it will glow green."

There was silence for a moment, then Fronda's trembling voice suddenly sounded in the headphones:

"It doesn't come out at all. God, it's blocked!"

"Try again," the controller advised him anxiously.

"Nothing... God! God save me!!!"

The controller put his hand over the microphone again and looked at his colleague."

"He must land on the belly," he said quietly. "Damn, at night, and layman... Call the security services, let D80 begin pouring onto the landing pad."

"And what is that?" Gerard asked distrustfully.

"Glidant. We have to reduce the friction, otherwise we'll have a flambée here. We have to take a chance, now we don't have other option. Hey, 504! Stop yelling for a moment and listen to the wiser than you. You need to taxi for a moment before you sit down. Can you hear me? Buck up!"

"What?!"

"Not your wally, plane!" Never joined.

Unlike his friend, who was only terrified by the fact that he was sitting at the controls and responsible for twenty passengers, he knew well how great the danger was. Theoretically, after a landing gear failure, the aircraft could land on its belly, but friction against the landing surface would cause instant ignition. The glidant was the only salvation at the moment, but it did not guarantee success.

"Can Theo land? What do you think?" Oggy asked quietly, trembling like a leaf.

"He must. Still, there was no accident that the plane remained in the air. Of course, the question is whether it will remain in one piece, but do not worry for days. Our Fronda is a tough guy."

Never spoke as if he wanted to believe his own words. He knew Fronda's fear of flying well and had no doubt that his friend was now experiencing real torture.

The controllers spoke to ground staff, and their voices sounded like a funeral threnody. They also did not believe in the success of the action. Finally, the second of them switched headphones to aircraft communication again.

"Flight 504, landing pad prepared," he said. "Release up to fifty knots. Fly exactly between the rows of lights and slowly push the control column so that it goes down."

"I'll try."

"There is no time for rehearsals. You must land on the first try, you are already flying on the fumes."

"I'm going down. Can you see me?"

"All the time. Now close the throttle. It's the lever next to the autopilot, all the way. You did it? Good. Warning! Now push the control column with all your strength and don't let go!"

"Close your eyes if you're afraid, but don't you dare to fail," Never added, menacingly.

Everything was to take place in a few minutes. Fire trucks, patrol cars and ambulances called by the airport staff were ready. Technicians constantly poured a strongly foaming to airplane lane. The DC-10 lowered the flight and finally, after a moment of waiting, which seemed endless, touched the belly of the landing pad. It drove inertia for some time, scrubbing its belly over the surface covered with the lubricant, in clouds of steam and foam. Finally it stopped. Poured by streams of water from fire hoses, it evaporated violently, making it look like a huge storm cloud, and then rescuers moved into action.

Someone, presumably a wounded flight attendant, left the gangway, on which trembling passengers, intercepted by paramedics and policemen, began to run down. Two rescuers carried the pilot's body, covered with a green cloth. Never and his crew were not allowed behind the police cordon, but from outside they watched everything happening on the landing pad and their nervousness grew. Their friend was not among the people on the plane. It was strange because everyone was talking only about him as their savior. Finally, Never could not bear it. He pushed hard through the cordon and, despite the opposition of dark-skinned policemen, ran onto the plane.

"Where is he?" Oggy asked tearfully, who followed him without hesitation and followed him onto the plane.

Never answered. He looked around the inside of the machine, devastated by bullets and a struggle with the terrorist, then headed for the pilot's cabin. It was empty, except for the uniformed mannequin still sitting in the seat. There was a pool of blood on the floor and a few candy wraps. Never leaned over and picked up one of them.

"Oh no..."

"What is it?" The girl asked anxiously.

"Sugar cubes," answered the Indian almost desperately. "If Fronda sucked sugar, it gave him a good kick, but it could also disturb his sense of reality for a long time. Pure sucrose acts on the vampire's body like amphetamine on humans."

"Okay, but where is Fronda?!"

"Who knows? He will always cause trouble for everyone..."

Never looked around the cabin again, shrugged in resignation, and left, hurried by impatient and inventing policemen. The fact that Fronda had disappeared from the booth in an unexplained way did not surprise him, his friend did such numbers, but where was he? In a state of extreme stress, he often run where his eyes took him, and Never had to hunt him down like a professional detective. The problem is, they have never been here, Fronda did not know this place and could easily get in trouble, especially now when people were looking for him as "the hero of 504 flight". And yet vampires are not suitable for heroes for wide masses.

"Does Fronda know this area? He had probably been to Africa before..." Gerard asked anxiously when Never explained what had happened.

"Yes, in Egypt, but never here."

"Well, we have a problem." Gladiator muttered and added a few words in Polish, as you might have guessed, not very decent. He spoke English quite well, tried French, but he cursed exclusively in Polish.

Taking advantage of the confusion, friends managed to search the airport, and then get out of the police without embarrassing explanations. They even smuggled into the open savanna of a rented jeep. However, their situation was still miserable. They were in Brazaville without a guide, without an auxiliary address, and finally without the most important team member. Only Fronda knew Shani Batawi, who was recommended to them as a "contact", without him there was even nothing to dream of establishing conversations with the local base.

Seeing no other way, friends began to methodically search the area around the airport using the "eagle method", which consisted of making a wider circle around the place where the search began. It would be difficult to find a hideout here. The moonlit savanna looked empty, and apart from the sparsely scrub bushes of mimosa, there was nothing to hide behind. It also seemed to be the last place to get lost. The dry grass crunched under the wheels, sometimes a nocturnal predator flashed somewhere. It was about ten kilometers to the city in a straight line.

And yet Fronda disappeared. He somehow got out of the pilot's cabin, penetrated through the double cordon of guard and police, and literally dissolved in the air. Friends swept the area around them with flashlights, Oggy sniffed eagerly, even though she knew that vampires did not emit any peculiar smell. Not only that, their emanation effectively suppresses any fragrance that could stick to their skin. Finally, more than two miles from the airport, Never's flashlight shone into a dark shape, curled under a barbed bush. The Indian breathed a sigh of relief and jumped out of the jeep.

"Theo, I'll kill you someday," he said, coming over. "You could have mercy on us. Why are you sitting here? You look like something the cat dragged in. Get up."

A friend looked at him with numb eyes. He was shaking clearly even though the night was hot.

Never leaned over him, concerned.

"Did something happen to you? Are you hurt?

Theo shook his head.

"Say something, knight. You can talk?"

The same move.

"So you are speechless," Never nodded and grabbed his arm. "I wanted to live to this moment. Now get up and walk. We have to find some shelter from the dawn, because you and Gladiator don't like the sun, and we better avoid it as sharp as here."

It was a very reasonable statement. Vampires, even "martens", can't stand strong sunlight, so there should be less of them in the tropics than elsewhere. However, only in theory. In these countries they are simply hidden deep in dense forests. The sun sifted through the leaves and branches of tropical trees seems to harm them relatively little. Despite this, among the representatives of the indigenous African tribes, living as they did centuries ago, there was not a single vampire. For a simple reason - even if a vampire was interested in preserving a relatively primitive, uneducated man, he would not be able to convince him.

All African vampires came from cities, from the upper classes, and when they hid in the woods, they kept their civilization habits. Half-naked hunters treated them with superstitious fear, especially since they noticed that they are not aging and can survive despite wounds that would kill every human being. However, in this part of the world there were few. There were only two bases in Africa, with a dozen or so permanent crew members, and maybe twenty who used it from time to time. And another, which is actually a kind of private club, only for members.

It was better in Egypt, but they were only there passing by. In their time, they easily tracked down a small nightclub where Egyptian bloodsuckers met. The club was called "Luxuria" and was an official entertainment venue. However, it did not play the role of an operational base in the strict sense, like the one next to Brazaville, which is intermediate between a scientific institution of an unspecified profile and a detective agency. This base had to be found now.

*****

It took some time before it became clear that the shock had caused Fronda permanent damage to her voice. He couldn't speak, only whispered. As Oggy said, it was very sexy but nevertheless troublesome on a daily basis.

"Acquired aphonia. Paralysis of the vocal cords as a result of mental shock." Never announced after careful examination of his friend, but if he could make a diagnosis, he turned out to be helpless in the matter of treatment.

Theo, after shaking off despair, reconciled with his condition, without having much choice. He actually remained what he was before - a cheerful, spontaneous guy, but now he was as quiet as a ghost. Oggy regretted it very much because she liked it when he sang in carefree moments, but, like him, she had to come to terms with the facts. Anyway, Theo immediately got to work, in which the lack of voice did not bother him. First of all, he contacted a journalist, Italian, about the appearance of a gangster. The journalist worked for a magazine in his homeland, and for everyone who paid well.

"If he is a naturalist, and he is not here on behalf of any institute, then ask Gloria Webson," he said after hearing Fronda's whispered tale. "I will give you her address, but I warn you that you must not be surprised at anything." Gloria suffers from agoraphobia and anthropophobia, in other words she does not leave her fortress at all. It's a villa in the center of Brazzaville, equipped with probably every type of security and alarm. The girl works at home and orders everything she needs online. She can't stand the sight of people or their company.

"Nice freak. So, is she so omniscient?" Fronda looked at him questioningly.

"She collects data from every available source. She will definitely have some information for you. You don't want to look blindly for this guy? Africa is quite big."

The argument had its weight. Theo knew that with only a photo, name and a vague idea of the purpose of the search, they were left blind. In this situation, any information could prove to be important.

It was not difficult to find Gloria Webson's house but standing in front of the gate friends felt a bit helpless.

"This could look like an abandoned Frankenstein residence," Gerard said, looking incredulously at the bizarre house glistening with electronics, but surrounded by a terribly deserted garden.

Never pressed the button at the gate. A small speaker strainer next to the button creaked, then a female voice said from it:

"What is going on?"

"Mrs. Gloria Webson? We've got a case. We will pay well for some information." Never said.

The wicket grunted, dodging slightly. After passing through a garden in which no one had probably moved a pebble for the past twenty years, they found themselves by a porch resembling a double airlock. Somewhere here a second speaker must have been hidden, because they heard the same voice:

"What information is it about?"

"Our friend wanted to find a black orchid and went missing. We want to know where to look for him."

"Wait a minute."

Friends sat on the porch railings, because the mysterious Gloria apparently did not intend to let them into her loneliness. They tried to imagine her leaning over the computer keyboard, which is its only connector with the world, and introduces key words searching for the answer to their question. What could she look like? What age is she? The voice from the speaker was quite nice and suggested thirty years at most, but the appearance could not be guessed from it. Was she pretty? Or maybe just so ugly that she was afraid to leave?

A quiet discussion was finally interrupted by the jaws of the flip door opening.

"Twenty-five dollars," a voice said from the speaker.

Never put the required amount into a small box, which immediately slid under the flap and disappeared.

"Thank you. The black orchid does not exist, but there are rumors that it was seen in the heart of the forest, south of here, where the town of Makidu is, a local tourist attraction. Land of the people of Gangoulou, Teke and Loshi, as well as the more primitive than others strain, Tonga. Virgin forest, hardly explored, admission at your own risk."

"Not bad," Gerard muttered with an involuntary shiver.

These revelations were not impressive to Theo, only that he made some adjustments to the previous plan. Friends from Cahville base, friendly with Octavio, couldn't help them, because they lived much further and more to the west. The area around Makidu was not their territory. One had to go to the Hardygran base, which they had been told about before, about where they heard that would not get help there. This, however, was Fronda's role. He knew two locals, Shani Batawi and Ernie Ford, with whom he had a quarrel for death and life long ago. So he preferred not to address him directly.

After resting a little, he visited Shani and convinced her that she should help them. She was wary, but she agreed to meet the whole group. The girl's apparition surprised those who had not seen her before. She looked more like Hawaiian than African and dazzled with her beauty. Her behavior was also quite surprising. After a short, very substantive conversation, she suddenly left, leaving them in mid-word.

"Take it easy. She knows what she is doing." Fronda whispered to them as they looked at him for an explanation. "We're waiting now."

"For what? She is human," Oggy growled.

"Yes, but not common. She is a "sensor".

The word "sensor" meant a man with developed psychic abilities of the receiving type. He can't "signal" like Gladiator, but he can sense things well. He always knows if someone is telling the truth or lying, and what his mood is. Somehow, probably taking advantage of her unusual talents, Shani infiltrated the local vampire subculture. She was trusted without reservation, to such an extent that she did not check the newcomers in more detail.

It was also partly influenced by the fact that the base director, dark-skinned and dark-eyed Lilias Maureen, who looked about twenty-five years old, knew the series about the fictionalized adventures of Theo. Not only that, she was his passionate admirer. Immediately after the casual greeting, she ceased to be interested in the rest of her friends and absorbed herself in a lively conversation with Fronda.

"I will never understand what these women see in him," Never murmured with dissatisfaction and began looking around the base and getting to know its inhabitants.

It wasn't particularly big. A dozen small, terribly dirty rooms in which the employees lived, an outpatient clinic, something like a small natural museum, and that was all. Ernie Ford, deputy of Lilias, was an avid naturalist and he was doing some of his private research. Lilias had a different passion. She was a writer - she wrote books under several different pseudonyms, and although she was far from famous, her novels were read willingly in many countries. Several nurses, a midwife without a diploma and an herbalist ran an outpatient clinic for the local population. As they figured out, almost only women lived here. So, it was more surprised that this place was at such a deplorable condition.

"They could clean up here, though from time to time," Oggy muttered, looking around in disgust. "Lots of cockroaches and other vermin here."

"Not worth it. In this part of the world, you will not get rid of house insects, unless a column of sieve ants walks through your home," Never told her. "You just have to make sure that you are not at home then, because these damn things are dangerous even for people."

"I understand cockroaches, but these Afrikaners are really slobs. It's all sticky here," Gladiator ran his hand over a shelf and heavy wooden sculptures standing on it to show his reasons.

"Why bother? Life is hard, and then you die," someone's voice said from the threshold. "What's the difference, is it clean or dirty around? You can't respect abnegation. If you want to live in a sterile environment, check in at the infirmary."

Ernie Ford crossed the room and collapsed in his shoes on a bed that was unmade. All his neglected and gloomy appearance testified that he avoids bathing as carefully as cleaning.

"You're right. If you all want to live in a landfill, it's your business," Never agreed with him. "Just tell us if you know anything about Delaney Robbins and we'll leave you alone."

Ernie pushed back his long, greasy hair.

"Del came to see me." He said thoughtfully. "If I think so, I can actually see that he has not returned... Although this was to be expected. Nobody comes back from the Dark Backwood."

"From where?" Gerard was surprised, stopping contemplation of incredibly dirty, but no less interesting sculptures, of which there were plenty in the room. They took literally every corner. If not for cockroaches crawling on them, they could be a decoration of any museum.

"Dark Backwood is a place in the middle of the forest," Ernie explained lazily. "Del went there looking for black orchids."

"So they exist?"

"Are you crazy? Of course not. Well, but these are at least dark purple. This species is so rare and so valuable that no museum has a single specimen. Apparently, some billionaire has a dried flower in his private herbarium, but I don't know who it is about. Del is possessed by the thought of getting not only the flower, but also its seedlings."

"Are all vampires crazy?" Oggy asked helplessly. "Put yourself at risk in order to pick a flower, even very rare?"

Theo put his arm around her.

"See, dear, long life makes people bored," he explained softly. "So they search for some goals, even senseless, and then achieve them. One of my friends and compatriots, Choderlos de Montpellier, has been hiding in a Buddhist monastery for two hundred and thirty years. He is looking for the meaning of life, although I wonder if he is eating there since he became a Buddhist."

"Gee," Ernie raised his head and looked at him with interest. "What do the monks say?"

"Nothing. They respect all life forms, including us. They still believe that it does not seem who one of the venerable brothers is. Can you imagine what a scandal would be?"

Theo chuckled silently at the memory. The trip to Nepal was one of those he made without friends and hardly anyone knew what really happened to him then. He rarely talked about his lonely adventures, which was strange when you consider how much he liked to brag.

Never shrugged. He got bored of talking to Erni, and the dirt was pessimistic. His countryman, those whom he knew personally, liked cleanliness and order, so that what he found here struck him twice. It occurred to him that he already knew what he wanted to know and could leave. The location of the "Dark Backwood" could have been shown to them by Lilias, so there was no need to expose themselves to the company of an annoying cynic looking like a 100% prowler.

"And to think that Nuntia is trying to make us a race of lords, higher beings," he muttered under his breath as he left the room. Gladiator, who had had enough of talking to the naturalist, followed him, and Oggy joined them.

The base director was sitting in her office typing at thunderous speed. Fronda was sitting on a padded chair in the corner and looking through the album with clippings. Lilias smiled at the sight of her friends, pushed the machine aside and adjusted her glasses. She had a little short eyesight and the transformation into a vampire did not cure her of this embarrassing ailment.

"Did you find out anything from Ernie?" She asked.

Never looked distrustfully at the cluttered, but much to his relief fairly clean office. "Yes," he replied meekly. "Tell me, Lilias, where are the Dark Backwood?"

The girl became serious. She took a clean sheet from a pile of typewriter paper and began to draw a simplified map on it, using colorful felt-tip pens that reveal cartographic preparation.

"This name is used to describe a part of the forest growing on a not too high mountain, called Khamandi," she explained simultaneously. "It's supposedly an extinct volcano, but I don't know exactly, nobody checked it. The forest is very dense and little known here. The natives do not venture there, considering this place as the seat of evil spirits, the white people also bypass it, mainly because they would not find a guide."

"We don't need a guide, except as a supply of fresh food," laughed Gladiator.

"It's your choice. If you want to go there, I advise you to go to the town of Makidu first, here. You buy mules there, because you would not get by jeep far. Don't be tempted by horses. Mules are more durable and resistant to diseases. Prepare also for fasting, because I don't think you can hunt anything there, and in this climate, you can't transport frozen plasma. I will give you a few cans of blood, preserved by the vacuum method, but treat them as a really last supply, for a rainy day."

"Naturally... by vacuum?"

"Yes, it's such a small patent... This blood is not suitable for transfusion, and for us it is of little value, but better than none."

Never looked at the map carefully. Although it was created very quickly, it was refined in every detail and contained a trail marked with miniature black arrows. Lilias knew her stuff.

"This forest is huge," he said. "And if we get lost in it, there will be a failure of the century. Well, let's see what can be done. Now tell us what to expect there."

"Have you ever heard of a lukundu?"

"I read something," said Gladiator. "The story of a certain White is called "Lukundu" and is quite nightmare. The author claims that he dreamed the whole story."

"Right. Lukundu is the belief system of the Khamala people here," Lilias said, adjusting her glasses again. "The whole tribe only has twenty-three people, so it's more of a strain that is dying out, but it has kept its own language and beliefs. And their own magic. It's really dangerous. Its basis is ancient knowledge about the endemic properties of plant species, primarily certain orchids and fungi. Every member of the Khamala people can make potions that are followed by symptoms of various diseases, for example leprosy or tuberculosis, so deceptive that they can even deceive a doctor. In the short run, of course."

"Interesting..." Never murmured. "And have they something to improve the mood?"

"I did not mention the hallucinogenic preparations they prepared, because here the matter is obvious. They also know very well about parasites and can intentionally infect selected people with them. It is interesting that officially Khamala live in the savannah, and practice in the Dark Backwood."

"It's like voo doo, right?" Gerard asked calmly. Little was able to amaze him.

Lilias shook her head.

"No, no. Voo doo is also New Year's fun for children in kindergarten. Lukundu is much more mysterious and much more dangerous. Fortunately, there is something that keeps them in line. Somewhere in the middle of the Backwood, perhaps at the top of Khamandi, supposedly lives a mysterious creature named Smenkharei. Something like the punishing hand of the gods. Because you never know when and in what situation Smenkharei will show his anger, Khamala are afraid to act too openly."

"You don't know what this thing looks like?" The actor asked. Feeling through the skin that another paranormal adventure is being prepared.

"No, angel with green eyes. Nobody knows what it looks like. If you want to try, you can go to a local psychiatrist and talk to a man named Stiles. Apparently, he saw Smenkharei up close and went crazy from it so thoroughly that they still put on his straitjacket for the night. From this it can be concluded that the idol is not special beautiful."

"Well, not everyone can look like our Fronda," Oggy said dismissively.

"Happily," Never murmured sourly.

The director gave Fronda a warm look and smiled. She also thought that hardly anyone could match his beauty and did not hide it at all.

"Returning to the case, if you want to follow your bane to the Dark Backwood, you must be prepared for many unpleasant surprises," she said. "Darkland magic is not being talked about for nothing. I don't think, by the way, that this is a real magic, just some phenomena that no one has yet diagnosed. But you can get really hot, and not just because it's Africa. Think carefully whether this crazy naturalist is worth the risk."

"He may not, but our money does," replied Gladiator soberly. "We are troublemakers for hire, we earn on such missions."

He joined the group only recently, but he was already acting as if he was at least its founder. Gerard called him in a sharp whisper, but Never just shrugged. Gladiator's insolent behavior was not a problem for him - he never tried to rule his friends more than was actually necessary.

"We'll go there, Lilias," he said. "Someone really cares for Delaney to come back in one piece from his trip for a black orchid, since he pays so much for it."

"Apparently it's his sister and aunt," Gerard reminded him.

"Yes, of course, but I have some suspicion that this is not just about worried relatives. Something's not right. It's just a feeling, but there are things that I rarely get wrong..."

Never shook his head. He couldn't explain where that gut came from, but it was very strong and very unpleasant. Somehow, he stopped believing that Delaney went alone to the heart of the forest only to get some specimen for his collection. It did not match the personality of a typical vampire. He hadn't thought about it before, but now... The longer he thought, the less he understood of the situation.

Lilias didn't bother with it, absorbed in something else.

"Look," she said, pointing to the television in the corner of the room.

On the screen, the dark journalist talked to an elderly lady whose almost white, curly hair clearly stood out from the chocolate skin.

"So, you don't know who the mysterious savior was?"

"I've never seen him before. He got in at the last minute. I remember so much that he was white, very young, and that he had black or dark brown hair... Lord, if not for this boy, we would all have died!"

"That's true." The reporter turned to the camera with a professional smile. "This man can be proud of himself and therefore, if he is watching our program, please call us. I'd like to interview him."

Theo smiled faintly. He was not proud of himself at all, for he knew too well that he did what he did, because it was forced not by courage and nobility, but by the circumstances in which he found himself. He was no more of a hero than someone who escapes from a burning house, and the fact that others will also pass through the passage he chopped out proves nothing.

Gerard patted him on the back. Although it was strange, he understood him best now.

"After all, knight, you can afford this bit of pride," he said. "You managed to pull your nerves together, get a hold of yourself and land unscathed, and that really couldn't be done by anyone."

"Don't butter him up, he is vain like a peacock without it," Never growled.

"Worse, now he can't show himself in front of people because he will expose us all," said Gladiator, sweeping aside the mosquitos. He came to the conclusion that he hated this place and now wishes that they can leave as soon as possible.

Never guessed his thoughts. He also wanted to find Delaney and leave the Black Land as soon as possible. He did not like Africa, with which he had very bad memories, although it was here in Egypt that he met Fronda, the best friend. The sand of the desert, the flared vegetation of the tropical forest, snakes and scorpions, primitive hunters who hardly ever understand anything, all this disgusted him.

"Load the jeep," he commanded. "We're moving. There is nothing to wait for."

"But the sun has not set yet," Theo protested.

"You'll sit in the back with Gladiator. The tarpaulin is lined with a black masking canvas cover, you will be safe." Decided the Indian.

"I'll bring you blood soon."

Lilias ran out of the office and after a moment returned with a full backpack of tin cans. Here, in a sparsely populated region, blood was at a premium, and friends duly appreciated her gesture. She was friendly from the beginning, unlike other base residents who clearly blamed them for "cutting into their lives," one of them said bluntly. I don't think they liked the guests at all.

Equipped with provisions for a rainy day, a handwritten map and a weapon they could go wherever they wanted. The Jeep was very large for this type of vehicle, had four-wheel drive, power steering and a supply of fuel that could last for quite a long time. However, it was better to listen to good advice and not choose it to the destination. The mules were so much better that they could squeeze through every sideways, they didn't have to refuel gas and they didn't have to worry about getting a flat tire.

"Besides, I like riding on top," Theo concluded the discussion.

"It's so human, using poor animals as vehicles," Oggy grumbled. Ever since they left the base, she was strangely depressed and silent. They did not associate it with her visit to the infirmary, which she had checked before leaving - though maybe they should.

Suddenly Never stopped the jeep and gestured for silence. Somewhere nearby, a monkey scream erupted, followed by several shots.

"Somebody's hunting for monkeys here. Probably poachers, as I know life," Gladiator said furiously, jumping out of the cart.

Others followed him. When they crossed the line of trees, a terrible sight appeared to their eyes. Three dead chimpanzees lay on the ground, little ones squeaking with fear clinging to their side. Two men in khaki costumes looked around alertly, weapons ready to fire, then one of them threw the rifle over his shoulder and approached the chimpanzee. He grabbed them and torn them away brutally from the dead female, not paying attention to the toddler's desperate squeak.

"Wild animal dealers," Never murmured, who had already seen such people in action.

"Murderers!" Shouted shrilly Oggy, transforming in the blink of an eye not into a friendly shepherd whom they knew well, but into a huge, shaggy beast with red eyes burning. Even her friends instinctively backed away.

The dealer let out a roar of fear as an unexpectedly snarling monster leaped out of the brush and lunged at his throat. The second of them turned away, but did not manage to do anything, because the accurate blow of the silent Fronda broke his neck like a dry twig. He didn't care about the sun still looking over the horizon, he just acted. It was all over in a split second. Gerard did not think to stop his friends this time. He did not support killing without good reason, but the scene he saw filled him with such disgust that he was able to join the action himself. Theo tossed the dead poacher aside and picked up the weeping chimpanzee. He hugged them to him, trying to calm down.

"Is nothing wrong with him?" Oggy asked anxiously, taking human form and wiping blood from her mouth. "God, poor baby... Monsters in human skin? How can they do such a thing?"

She was so nervous that she didn't even think about getting dressed.

"Unfortunately, my sun, the price of such a toddler in Europe or Asia is about ten thousand dollars," Never said sadly. "And unless the guards shoot poachers like ducks, and the law doesn't severely punish those who buy smuggled animals as mascots, this practice will continue. It's quite a common case when they kill an entire monkey family to capture one small one. Sad. Just what will we do now?"

He paused because the scrub rustled. Several black warriors emerged from them, almost naked, covered in blue tattoos, with javelins in their hands. They looked at the corpses and the living with fearful curiosity. White travelers froze, not knowing what to do. They stared at each other for a moment, and then one of the warriors spoke in broken English.

"Bad man kill our monkey. We see female demon kill bad man. Welcome you. We Teke, hunters. I M'Kudu, head of strain."

"Hello, great warrior. We are from distant country. I Rajah, head of the group. Friends. Demon woman good. Kill the bad, help the good," Never replied him in a similarly simplified way. "Do you know them?"

The black man shook his head vigorously.

"They come and go. Bad man. We don't kill the monkey. Wizard speak, monkey ghost ancestor. White woman and white man also say it's very bad. We believe. They good, heal our children. They speak truth. We listen to them, we don't kill monkey. We now know this to be wrong."

"Wow, what a gibberish. I don't understand anything," Gladiator murmured.

"Be quiet. Where are they, those whites?" Never asked.

"There," the warrior showed his hand. "Big house. They save small monkey and other animal."

"Thank you, friend. May your javelin be always reliable, your belly always full, your woman fat, and your enemies always dead."

Never hurried his friends before him to the jeep. He was very unhappy with this obstacle in travel, and the scene he witnessed filled him with disgust for mankind. That people were killing each other offended him much less than thoughtlessly killing animals. The years spent in the monastery of the goddess Kali meant that he approached these matters completely differently than most people.

Going in the direction indicated by the natives, they easily found the small property they were told about. A small, gray-haired woman came out at the doorbell from a large house surrounded by a huge catwalk. She stared at the arrivals with amazement.

"Jane Goodall," she said, greeting Never with her narrow, hard-worn hand.

"Sinclair Radhjaleah," he replied, squeezing her hand lightly. "We've got a resident for you."

He pointed to the small chimpanzee, which snuggled against Fronda's side, still squealing and wailing like a child.

"What happened? We heard shots here..." Mrs. Goodall said, stammering slightly.

"We even wanted to see what was going on, but the guards who lived with us just went to get supplies."

Two poachers killed the kid's family to kidnap and sell him," Never shortly explained.

Lightning shot from the older lady's eyes.

"And where are they now?" She asked angrily, rolling her eyes at her guests.

"They are dead," Gladiator replied briefly, approaching her. "You don't need to know more. They will never trade anything again, and the world will certainly not cry for them. Fronda, give lady this little boy."

"I feel like I have to give my own child," Theo whispered, handing the chimpanzee Mrs. Goodall with evident regret.

"Indeed, the resemblance is striking," Gladiator remarked harshly. "You have the same low forehead and similarly silly faces. However, I think we don't have the qualifications to raise a small monkey."

"It's really hard work," Mrs. Goodall hugged the chimpanzee. "Thank you and be careful. From now on, the poachers will have hunted you down."

"Please do not worry. We can take care of ourselves," Never said dismissively. "Only one question: wasn't a white naturalist passing here looking for black orchids? His name is Delaney Robbins."

"There was someone here with that name, but quite a long time ago..." The old lady hesitated slightly and added. "He went to the place where they say that he does not return. If he's back, it's not this way."

"That's the problem, he didn't come back. Well, please take care of your toddler, we are going further."

"Never, look how many monkeys there are," interrupted Oggy delightedly. "They are so sportive! I could stay here for the rest of my life."

"Unfortunately, you need to have careful preparation. It is extremely hard and responsible work, but I am glad that you like animals and want to help them." Jane Goodal smiled, but her eyes still expressed some concern.

Even though she herself had the worst feelings for poachers, she was terrified by the realization that these people had literally confessed to her a double murder. Torn between respect for the law and her feelings, she didn't know what to do. Fortunately, this situation did not last long. It is not known whether the visitors really were in such a hurry, or did they understand how difficult they were putting her, in any case they said goodbye quickly and drove away in their jeep towards nearby Makidu.

*****

Mules proved to be quite expensive. Not very beautiful, thick-boned and a bit neglected, they looked really durable. The Jeep was left under the protection of a local head as a pledge for valuable animals and they continued their journey. It was dusk for good, but it didn't bother anyone. Fronda, who was slightly sunburned during the rescue of the chimpanzee, clearly enjoyed the falling darkness, but Africans looking behind the disappearing riders tapped their forehead eloquently. They could not imagine that someone could voluntarily risk a night trip into the impenetrable forest. Nobody intended to explain to them that darkness was the proper element of the expedition's members.

The further they ventured, the denser the forest became. In this thicket of trees one could feel safe even during the day, because the dense crowns of huge trees let in little light. This was especially important for Fronda. His burns were quite superficial, but in advance it could be said that they would heal for weeks, causing unbearable itching and burning. While wounds in vampires heal very quickly, burns are very difficult to heal, especially sunburns.

"That's how it is, my Fronda, when someone wants to be noble," said Gladiator philosophically.

He also suffered some injuries, but definitely smaller, because unlike Theo, he put on a white safari outfit for the day, supplemented by a cork helmet and gloves. It was unbearably hot for him, but it protected him from direct contact with the sun. He gave his friend a tube with a soothing balm.

"Thanks. Sometimes, you know, I forget I'm a moth."

Theo took the tube and carefully lubricated all the burned areas. Fortunately, despite being sensitive to the sun's rays, he endured the heat very well. He liked the forest. He associated the wonderful, wild vegetation with the Garden of Eden, although he was aware that in fact this piece of the world is not like Paradise. It was, after all, a place of ruthless struggle for existence, in which all tricks are allowed, a place where people like them were only intruders and very badly seen.

This was even seen in the behavior of the mules. These patient animals treated their momentary masters as ironic and indulgent as they could, though they were generally obedient. They quickly realized that the company of vampires had their good sides - all predators stayed away, as if enchanted. Even the nagging insects were kind of less intrusive. There was nothing particularly strange about this, considering that vampires do not typically emit any human scent or none at all. Animals simply do not know what they are dealing with and therefore bypass them.

"It's muggy here," complained Gerard. "I feel like I'm in a Turkish bath. I don't understand how a white man can settle here of his own free will?"

"Apparently, if you quench your thirst only with beer in the tropics, you'll never get drunk," Oggy said. "You will sweat alcohol faster than it can get you intoxicated. I am tempted to try."

"Don't you dare," Never warned her, "We don't want to have trouble with a drunken werewolf. Anyway, I forgot to pack a beer. You have to do without it, chit."

Oggy showed him the tongue long its entire length. There was a funny thing about her tongue - it remained doggy even when she became human. This raised the question, how could she speak, but it also looked impressive when she wanted to demonstrate such a tongue to someone.

Never didn't pay any attention to this provocation. Everyone has already noticed that for several hours Oggy is not only depressed and silent, but also strangely aggressive towards everyone. Initially they attributed it to climate change, but now they began to worry. Oggy was never like that. As a quiet girl and attached to friends, at the same time gentle and hard in her own way, and as a friendly and cheerful dog. Something has changed and it's not for the better.

When they camped after an overnight journey to rest during the most dangerous part of the day, Theo decided to take a chance.

"What's wrong, baby?" He asked, forcing the girl to sit next to him while others finished fencing the canvas tent with spiky branches. "You're sick?"

Oggy shook her head, avoiding his eyes.

"So?" He urged her on the loudest whisper he could. "We all see something wrong with you. We will help you."

The girl started to cry so suddenly that the busy men stopped, looking at her uncertainly.

"You can't help me," she sobbed. "It's too hard."

"Or maybe? Confide in the old knight."

"I fell in love..."

"Oh no," snapped Gladiator, but Theo silenced him with an angry look.

"That's even nice," he said, turning to Oggy again. "Who is it?"

"In Shani, this girl who helped us get to the base," Oggy confessed desperately.

Gerard dropped an armful of prickly branches, and Gladiator sighed loudly and sat down. However, he jumped up quickly and rubbed the seat, because he hit the buttocks just on a beam dropped by a Frenchman. Even Theo clutched his head and blushed like in an apoplexy. For a moment they thought he would scream like in the good old days, but even with all the excitement that had overwhelmed him, he couldn't do it.

"Oggy, damn it... Isn't it enough for you to be a werewolf?" He croaked.

Only Never didn't seem moved. As a native Indian, he had completely different views on certain subjects than his associates.

"Do you think I'm ok with it?" Moaned Oggy in despair. "I don't know what to do with myself! But there is something worse..."

"Go on. Nothing will surprise me anymore."

"I think I'm pregnant."

This time, Never even stared at her and was speechless. This news was so absurd and so unexpected that all four forgot about the whole world, even forgot that they were hungry. It is true that they noticed that their friend had recently gained a little weight, but they did not attach importance to it. She always had a good appetite.

"Are you sure?" The Indian asked when he had already recovered his voice.

"What do you think? No, I am not. But I suspect."

"And... who is it with?" Gerard asked after a moment, trying to calm down. "Not with Shani, I think."

"With Wisha... Don't be angry."

The girl lowered her head, wiping the tears still flowing down her cheeks.

"With this Russian bear, beautiful. Oggy, if it got you on, why didn't you turn to one of us? Everyone would be happy to serve you!" Cried Never, shaking his head desperately, until the ruby buckle with which he was pulling his hair slid to the ground.

"It is impossible. I could tear you apart. Wisha was safe."

"It's been a while... Why didn't you tell us earlier?" Gerard asked reproachfully.

Angry flash of lightning shot out of Oggy's eyes.

"I just knew what you were going to say and ask for!" She called out. "And I want to give birth to this child, understand?"

Theo nodded slightly, but his expression clearly showed that he was very upset and even scared of the situation. He didn't know much about biology, but he was well aware of how dangerous a combination of genes like Oggy and Wisha could be. A child who was supposed to be born as a result of their romance could look and behave like a hybrid of man and animal, and that meant incredible problems. Oggy's quirk put them all in a very difficult position, because it was clear that it was case of all of them. They would not leave her in need.

"When this child will be born, we'll all have a lot of work," Gladiator remarked melancholy, who didn't like babies and was a bit disgusted.

"It's not my business, Oggy, but is it safe to wander with us in the various woods?" Gerard asked, remembering how much he cared for his Anne when she was pregnant. He would not let her literally do anything at the time, for fear of something threatening the anticipated offspring.

"Don't worry," the girl snapped. "I can take care of myself."

"Don't worry, yes... and if something happens to you, it will be our fault. Oh, my dear, you can never tell with you ladies," Theo sighed. "Let's go to sleep. There is nothing to meditate, too late for this."

They agreed with him because it was known that they would not come up with anything that day. Silently, the construction of the "zeriba" was completed and everyone lay down in their place, closing their eyes. The sensational news meant that no one could sleep, they only fell into short, intermittent naps, more tiring than watch. Gladiator could not sleep at all. He was the youngest member of the band and he didn't know much about the world as vampires see him. However, he managed to realize how rich he was in things capable of frightening everyone to death. He was just beginning to discover them, but he sometimes had the unpleasant feeling that his comrades didn't tell him everything.

He fidgeted in his bed until he crawled out of his stuffy tent to get some air. Tangled branches upstairs provided sun protection, but it was furiously hot and stuffy like a bathhouse. It was no better outside than under a tent.

Smelling the smell of cigarette smoke, Gladiator crossed over and came across Fronda to his surprise. Theo stood, leaning against a huge fig tree, smoking a cigarette behind a cigarette, choking smoke. His face, usually fair, cream-colored, now strangely grayed, and dark circles appeared under his eyes.

"Since when do you smoke?" Wondered the highlander.

Fronda looked at him with unconscious eyes.

"For several minutes," he answered grimly. "I have to blow off steam... Damn it, we've packed everything and forgot the most important thing. I searched our bags and you can really get mad, not a drop of something stronger."

"And good. With this furious heat, you would be drunk immediately."

"You're not my nanny."

They were silent for a moment, looking at the few sunny spots sifted through dense leaves. The forest around them played a whole range of daily sounds - bird, insect and animal, and they felt like they were in a nature film about the original nature.

"Can't you sleep because Oggy, either?" Gladiator finally asked cautiously.

"I do not know what to do. This is a terrible situation that can cost us a lot, especially her. I like her too much so that I can sleep."

"And I like her too. You won't help her if you will be tired. You must rest."

Silence fell again, then Fronda suddenly turned his head and looked the highlander straight in the eye.

"I hate being responsible for something or someone," he said. "I hate."

"Do you think all responsibility will rest at you?"

"It's always like that, Yanek. Never plays Captain Blood, but in the long run everything is all about me, because this Indian prince of the apes at the least appropriate moment decides that now he wants to hunt alone and leaves me with another nasty thing on his neck. Believe me, it was already like this."

Theo tossed his cigarette butt to the ground and trampled it. Gladiator put his broad hand on his shoulder.

"But get some sleep," he advised. "I'll try too. We cannot afford to lose strength, especially if it is as you say."

Suddenly he felt like a big brother to Fronda and understood why Never, younger and less experienced, was their leader. In some situations, Theo could not cope, it overwhelmed him. When he was in danger, he didn't care about anything, and he always knew what to do. But when his friends were in danger of something he couldn't beat, he just became helpless, like a child. He was killed by fear of others.

He wasn't the only one worried about Oggy. Gerard and Never also rolled from side to side, unable to sleep. When they finally decided to move on, they all looked like the victims of an earthquake. The proper purpose of their journey suddenly came to the background, and the first was definitely the unborn child of Oggy and the Russian. What will it be like? Will he even be able to live in today's world and how will they be able to protect them from people since they have such crazy difficulties with their incognito? If a child looks like a human, that's okay, but what if he looks like Wookie from "Star Wars"? It wasn't so impossible again.

For now, they had to go further. So they went deeper and deeper into the forest. They knew they were already in truly primeval areas untouched by the white man's foot. The psych location sense of vampires told them, but that didn't mean it was a desert. Sometimes they saw black hunters, so they took the opportunity to feed their blood. At the same time, they made efforts to "stay in the shadows" and not to hurt the natives. There was a chance that primitive hunters would fear them like fire, but it was better not to risk it.

They had no illusions that they remained invisible to them. In a place like this, it would be difficult to hide a group of whites traveling on mules, so they did not hide during the ride - but the hunt celebrated as if they turned into disembodied demons for this occasion. However, they rarely had the opportunity to do so. In this area there were only a few scattered black villages and two settlements of Pygmies. However, the latter did not want to hunt, because they aroused in them invincible disgust, and even some superstitious fear.

They didn't know if they were proper pygmies, but they defined them so because of their exceptionally short height. These inhabitants of the forest were indeed very small, and strikingly ugly, clumsy, wrinkled, with bloodshot white eyes, and very wide nostrils and curled lips. Sometimes they appeared as if they were from under the ground, gave the intruders a malicious look and disappeared without a trace.

After some meeting, friends finally convened.

"What can they want from us?" Never asked the fundamental question.

"They're like ghosts. I hope they don't plot against us," said Gladiator.

"You're a coward, you blonde. After all, these scrubs reach up to your elbow," Oggy grunted. Fronda nodded silently, adding wet twigs to the fire to scare away the mosquitos. It is true that these insects do not bite the vampires, but he was irritated by their buzzing so that he was almost crazy.

"What the hell. I'm not going to fight them, but it's no fun to get hit by a poisoned arrow. Besides, I read a lot about magi grown by freaks like them and I'd rather not have to deal with it."

"Yanek, there's no magic in the world unless we're talking about pulling rabbits out of a hat," Gerard pointed out in a weary voice.

Gladiator contorted his narrow lips contemptuously. Although he was a very young vampire, born and raised in the twentieth century civilization, he believed in magic and nothing could convince him.

"As you sit, you look like Tarzan," Oggy said thoughtfully, looking at the fair-haired highlander.

"I wonder if a monkey can raise a human child." Gerard wondered.

"Natives are sometimes hard to distinguish from monkeys," Theo muttered sourly and made a blow to the side from Oggy. "What now?"

"That was a nasty remark. They are the same people as everyone else, and I assure you, you don't seem too pretty to them either," she said sharply.

Fronda's sad vice was that he still thought in terms of the Middle Ages, also about the issue of equality of people of different races. Nobody and nothing could convince him that he should change his mind.

"He can't raise," Never said authoritatively. "There is not a single documented case of a human baby being raised by primates, and this is because small people do not have the monkey reflex to stick to their parent's fur. Such a child would die quickly. On the other hand, dogs or wolves, of course, sometimes brought up abandoned children, with fatal consequences for them."

"Why?" Gladiator interested.

"If a child is brought up by animals before the speech development period, he will never learn to use articulated language again. For the rest of his life he remains mentally handicapped in the human sense. But we didn't make this break, just to talk about Tarzan. It's about those midgets that clearly watch where we're going."

He looked around carefully. His psych location was silent, but he wasn't sure he could trust it completely. There was something disturbing in this forest. He looked at Oggy, but the girl, having met his eyes, shook her head in the negative. She also felt no danger in the immediate vicinity.

"So what shall we do? Bite them when they appear again?" Gerard asked skeptically. He could not imagine himself as a killer.

"Of course not. Our basic principle has not changed. We don't kill unless absolutely necessary," Never said sharply.

All undead were aware that they must avoid killing so as not to bring misfortune upon themselves and the entire clan. Of course, a psychopath would appear from time to time, and then his kin would try to render him harmless. He was dangerous to everyone, attacked for pleasure. He drew people's attention to the presence of different beings in their lives, and it was deadly.

"What if they attack us?" Gerard asked doubtfully, mechanically breaking the dry twig into small pieces."

"I don't think they'll do it. Certainly not openly. We must be on guard and find Delaney as soon as possible."

"If he's still alive. This lunatic could get place without an exit," Gladiator noted skeptically. He still couldn't understand how one could undertake such a difficult and dangerous trip for a flower there.

Never shrugged. He also considered this possibility, but life taught him that one should not cry on a vampire unless you touched his corpse with your own hands. Their ability to heal and regenerate is so strong that it is hard to destroy them... On the other hand, one of them is still killed by the Hunters or even in the ordinary case. If something or someone shatters the vampire's head and destroys his brain, you can't help anymore.

It is a mistake to think that a vampire is a truly immortal being, but they know it best.

"We must examine this matter with all diligence. Regardless of the outcome of our search, we must not miss anything," he said sternly.

They were already close to the Black Mountain, a wide and relatively low hill, completely overgrown with tropical forest. If it really was a volcano, it probably died out in prehistoric times, because there was no indication that it was ever active.

It was the Dark Blackwood - a place where, if you believe the stories, the white man's foot has not yet stood. It didn't look more amazing than the rest of the forest, it was just quieter. There were no parrots screaming, and less often something was breaking through the bushes. And although Gerard swore that he saw a giant cat high in the branches of the trees, no one else saw any animal larger than a rat.

They had to get to the crater. Black orchids, according to information obtained by friends, grew there. This was likely because they didn't see dark-colored flowers anywhere along the way. Perhaps the crater created a suitable microclimate for this unusual species. However, the road up the hill through the thick bushes, in an atmosphere reminiscent of a Turkish bath, was very tiring for both people and animals. Vampire endurance was put to the test, and although no one complained, it was clear that soon you would have to reach for the iron supply of canned blood.

The little hunters stopped appearing as if they'd given up tracking white travelers, but Oggy still said she could smell them. There was no reason to doubt her words, although friends were not sure if their friend had become hypersensitive due to pregnancy. It was only now that they understood why

Oggy had been so nervous and inclined to extreme moods lately. She could also have olfactory hallucinations, this happens to pregnant women. However, on the third day since crossing the invisible border of the Dark Blackwood, they began to see black dwarfs again, not as they used to, individually, and several at a time.

"In my opinion, it's a sign that we're approaching our destination," Gerard commented.

"I don't know if we are approaching the goal, we are approaching something." Never murmured. "I do not know if black orchids really grow in the crater..."

"Or at least dark purple, as Ernie said," interrupted Gladiator.

"Doesn't matter. Anyway, whatever the orchids, there is something else. And if Del died, it was because of that," finished the Indian.

"Hopefully, we will find it soon. Our mules barely move. Gerard patted his mount on the neck as if he wanted to apologize for any inconvenience. He has liked animals and felt sorry for the patient, gentle creatures forced to wander in such difficult conditions.

Never wanted to go on, but the thick thickets suddenly swept sideways before them. Unexpectedly, the friends found themselves in what looked like a huge sieve - once it was probably larger, but the forest was apparently demanding its territory. A concrete building resembling a hangar occupied almost the entire space of the drain. Its walls were decorated with semi-blurred military signs.

"Military base... but here?" Theo whispered in surprise.

"Probably a godliness after Africa Corps' visit, but maybe... maybe Delaney was here and left a sign? Let's search." Never jumped off his mule and entered through the ajar door.

Inside, the building was almost empty. Everything that could be carried out was long ago plundered by the inhabitants of the surrounding villages. Only what remained was permanently attached to the floor or walls. Friends searched the building, scaling out swarms of scorpions and several harmless snakes, until they came down to the basement underground. Hopeless remnants of military equipment rusted there - machine parts, too technically advanced to use them in the forest, some remains of fabrics and objects that are already difficult to identify. Certainly, there was no one here for a long time, except for vermin and small animals. It was even difficult to say what kind of army was stationed here and what nationality it was. The whole dumpster made an unpleasant impression. It did not fit here into the primeval forest, it was a foreign interruption.

"What do you smell, Oggy?" Gerard asked. "Is anyone here?"

"No," said the girl hesitantly. "Maybe I'm wrong, but I smell the smell that shouldn't be here."

"What do you feel?"

"Hay. Ordinary European meadow hay."

"Here? Impossible..."

Friends looked around, examining the scent of air in disbelief. Oggy was right, as usual - from somewhere came the delicate smell of hay from a European meadow, dried in the summer sun. Suddenly Gladiator shook himself and screamed in an uncomfortable voice:

"Everyone outside! Come on, get the fuck outta here!!!"

Despite his words, they couldn't move. They felt that the air around them had turned into a wall of fire and only Gladiator had enough strength to act. He grabbed Oggy in his arms and rushed with her to the steps. The girl did not resist, she was like a stunned when he laid her on the ground behind the base. Then he returned, grabbed Fronda and Gerard by the neck and dragged them outside, almost unconscious.

"What is going on?" Gerard snapped as Gladiator returned to the building.

"It's phosgene. Combat gas," Theo answered him soundlessly, getting to his feet unsteadily. He was holding his throat and gasping for breath. "This Pole has modern military training, so he got it, and we idiots don't. I'm going to help him, take care of Oggy."

Vampires are less sensitive to chemical weapons than humans, but nevertheless they are dangerous to them. Gladiator, having drawn three friends, as a result of the effort he inhaled more gas than they did, and he could not take Never away. At least it was obvious that he had tried because they were both lying next to the stairs. Theo barely pulled them outside, then closed the hatch and fell down next to his friends, unable to take even a step... He felt that the world was rolling around him and his ribs were clutching iron armor, not allowing him to draw breath. As if through a fog, he saw the small black figures approaching them like a nightmare, and lost contact with the world.

Consciousness returned with a terrible headache and a piercing stinging in his chest, as if someone had stuck several daggers in his chest. He struggled for air that squeezed into his lungs through the larynx squeezed invisible vise and did not dare open his eyes at once. When he finally forced his eyelids open, he saw that he was in a cave, high vaulted, devoid of typical formations, but overgrown with rock vegetation that he had never seen. A hand tilted a mug of rolled-up bark to his mouth, he drank a liquid resin-scented liquid, and sobered up almost immediately. The headache eased, the tightness in chest eased, eyes became sharp as before.

"M'kudu..." he whispered in amazement, seeing the head of the black hunter above him.

"I'm glad you're better," said the African in great French. There was no sign of broken speech. "Others are recovering too. You were lucky that I arrived at the right time."

The almost naked hunter changed beyond recognition. His eyes shone with intelligence, impeccable pronunciation, and the vocabulary pointed to a man of the world.

"Who exactly are you, M'kudu?" Theo whispered, sitting down with some difficulty and looking around distrustfully.

The alleged cave was a kind of tunnel, widening in the opposite direction to the entrance behind which was the valley, covered with tangled vegetation. Theo found himself looking for black orchids and grimaced in disgust as he returned his companions. They also felt clearly better, although their faces indicated complete confusion. They were stunned by this place, how they got here, and above all a dozen small, clumsy armed figures with menacing-looking spears and bows. M'kudu's presence did not calm them down at all.

"I am one of the Black Mountain Guardians," answered the hunter. "You must know that we do not allow travelers or scientists here, nor ordinary adventurers for a very specific reason."

"I think you don't do it for no reason," Never murmured.

He was sitting against the wall, holding his head and trying to control his nausea. In front of him was an open box with a set of antidotes received from Octavio di Mauro. This is where the potion came from, added by M'kudu to the palm wine, with which he drank all five. Fortunately, the Indian did not lose consciousness like others and could advise the hunter what to take from the box.

"You're right. The purpose of my people and the people of Tonga is to protect the Dark Blackwood and its inhabitants. Everything that is growing here is a real treasure and if white people found out about it, they would have wiped out the entire forest to get it. You see, I studied at the University of Cairo and got to know the white man's way of thinking quite well to be afraid of. You are greedy, ruthless and stupid enough not to take into account the consequences of your lust for profit.

"Well, we've already established that," interrupted Gladiator, still gasping for air. "Why didn't you liquidate us when you had the opportunity?"

M'Kudu smiled.

"It was close. Tonga knew that you would not resist the temptation to visit this abandoned base, so at the right moment one of them threw a phosgene container underground, one of many recklessly left behind by the army. Believe me, they are not stupid or primitive, although they live in harmony with nature and do not look special. Unlike white people, they know what is really important in life."

Oggy gathered herself up and stood up, looking around vigilantly.

"This is the Black Mountain crater, right?" She asked. "It's huge."

"Right," M'kudu nodded. "It is surrounded by a network of natural caves made of frozen lava. A real paradise for researchers."

"And there's someone else here," the girl continued, sniffing like a pointer. "I smell the bonfire, many bonfires... and the smell of people, but none of you. Someone live here?"

"Yes," an unknown voice answered.

A white man stepped out of the corridor, dressed in a khaki dress, stiff with dirt and torn here and there. Behind him were a few naked children, whom friends had never seen before. They were fairly stocky, with light, though dark skin, huge black hair and faces reminiscent of drawings from anthropological tables. Prominent eyebrows, low foreheads, deep-set eyes, receding chins, short necks, all made friends feel as if they were traveling in time.

"Are they Neanderthals or early Cro Magnon?" Asked Theo, staring thoughtlessly at the child.

A man like a gorilla, at least two meters high, emerged from the depth of the corridor, girded with the skin of an animal and guttural grunts, and with a few slaps he drove the children back to where they came from.

"Delaney Robbins, I suppose," Never nodded. "And this..."

"Damn, real pre-humans," Oggy squeaked with delight.

M'Kudu nodded.

"That's it," he said. "They are the last representatives of their people. They have lived here for millennia and have not had much trouble so far, but now, in the era of aggressive exploitation of natural resources, they have found themselves in real danger. We guard them, although we don't know how long we will succeed."

"They don't want to make experiments with these men from a stone age in some laborers," Delaney added. "Do you have any idea what would happen if anthropologists found out about their existence?"

"I can imagine that. Probably nothing good. But why are you sitting here?" Never asked in a harassed voice.

Delaney shrugged. He clearly did not want to explain to these strangers that he liked the company of gentle pre-humans, and besides, it was difficult for him to part with the black orchids, which he finally found. He couldn't take them with him - he wouldn't be allowed. The natives knew that too many white people would then like to get them into their collections. It's better that they thought the black orchid was just a legend.

"Your sister and aunt hired us," Gerard said grimly. "They paid a lot of money, forced us to wander through this hell, and you can only keep silent in answering a simple question?"

"My sister is crazy. And I'll be sitting here until you have mercy over me, and until I figure out how to smuggle orchids without revealing to anyone where I got it."

"Just paint them white," Gladiator prompted him stupidly.

"Smuggle the seeds themselves," Gerard suggested another idea.

"I don't know if they'll grow out of this crater. You have no idea what it means to be so close to discovering your life and to go away without nothing," Delaney sighed.

"Octavio warned us he was an avid botanist," Theo remembered.

He drank some more wine and the potion and stood up carefully, holding onto the wall. His ribs still ached every time he inhaled, and he felt like he was breathing only a small part of his lungs, but it was better now.

"How many expeditions have you already fixed here?" He asked grimly.

"None. They all turned back before reaching their goal. We have our ways, as you have noticed," said M'kudu calmly. "Del came as far as the first white man. Well, let's say a man. We know who he is and who you are."

"That's good. I don't like understatement there," Gerard knelt down with some difficulty and raised his eyelids to the eyelids of a Pole lying next to him.

Gladiator moaned and stretched out his hand for the wine, but his hand trembled so much that Gerard had to help him drink medicine, holding a makeshift pot to his lips. Everyone had more or less recovered, but the fair-haired highlander still could not cope with his great body. With oversized lung capacity, he absorbed more poison than his companions and needed more time to fight it.

"If it wasn't for him, it would be bad with us," Oggy said, kneeling on the other side of the highlander.

He smiled slightly at her and touched her stomach with his hand.

"May it not harm the baby," he said softly.

"I don't think it hurts him. I feel good, it probably too," the girl calmed him and carefully wiped his face with a handkerchief moistened with water from a wooden kit.

"How do you communicate with these pre-humans?" In the meantime, Theo asked Delaney. He came closer so that he could easily hear his whisper.

"I don't communicate with them at all. They don't speak in our sense, they just grunt and grunt in different tones. However, in their own way they are nice to me and I don't think they associate me with the fact that sometimes one of them has a bite mark on his neck. You know, I have to eat something, and M'Kudu doesn't want to let his people lead me out of here. They are afraid of that I would say about what I saw. There is nothing to talk about with Tonga."

"I think I understand them. It is good that they live here undiscovered. It would only happen..."

Theo sighed and rubbed his neck with his hand.

His head still ached, though less so, and his clarity of thinking was slowly returning. His shortness of breath still bothered him the most. These little guards were effective, he had to admit it. They did not try any of their "spells" on them - they used white people's weapons against white people.

"M'kudu, are they?" He pointed at the dwarf Tonga. "Really know magic?"

The black warrior looked at him pityingly and tapped his forehead.

"And you call me a savage?" He asked rhetorically (although Theo never vividly addressed him as such). "This is no magic, only a brilliant use of the gifts of nature. They can make an herbal mixture that will cause you to fall into temporary insanity. After other, you will even forget your name. I will not mention hallucinogens. You whites like to exalt themselves, and you are superstitious like any first-best original tribe."

"What about you? You graduate university and fly naked in the wilderness with a spear? I guess you are crazy." Never snarled unfriendly.

"On the contrary. I returned to my people of my own free will, because living in civilization I understood what is really important in life," the hunter replied with dignity.

Raja grunted something that it became better that no one heard him. His thoughts now dealt with something completely different. He looked around again.

"Is this Smenkharei also a legend?" He asked.

At the sound of these words, little Tonga gave an incomprehensible shout and fell to the ground.

"Don't say this name if you like your life," M'kudu furiously warned Never.

"He's serious," Delaney interjected, seeing that the Indian was preparing some sharp retort. "The natives are afraid of this creature, although they do not even know what it looks like. They say that when He is close, a modulated whistle is heard. Then you have to face the ground, because whoever looks directly at Smenkharei will die or lose his mind."

Do you expect any of us to believe in such damn bullshit?"

"I do not know. They are people who live in harmony with nature, and you can be sure such people are not afraid of what is not there. So something is definitely here, but what is that, I don't know and, to tell you the truth, I don't want to know."

Never looked at Delaney. He had no intention of confiding in him to what he had experienced or to the experience of the whole group, because he was not sure that, having learned about their proper occupation, Del would not order them to track Smenkharei. And they were fed up with paranormal phenomena.

Meanwhile, Gerard, who out of curiosity plunged into the corridor, came back with a rather serious face.

"There are more of them there," he reported. "It's probably the missing link in the evolutionary chain."

"Even if it is like you say, it is not our business," Never said firmly. "We came here for a specific purpose. M'kudu, be so good and explain to those little shit that we don't say a word to anyone, because it is not in our interest either. We will not reveal the existence of these cavemen to anyone."

M'kudu shook his head.

"It's not that simple," he said. "See, Tonga don't listen to anyone. I'm just their friend, not their leader. I can't even talk to them because I don't understand their dialect and they don't speak any reasonable language. And they are really very determined that the secret of this crater does not get beyond the boundaries of the Dark Blackwood. I don't think they want to let you go."

"No to klops," said Gladiator, in Polish, but with an intonation understandable for everyone.

"They will kill us," Oggy joined the conversation. "They could keep Del here, but they know they can't control us all."

"They kill, you say? Well, we'll see. Ready to rumble?!" Cried Never.

They have not used this password or this modus operandi for a long time. However, they reacted almost automatically, even Gladiator, who had never been a participant in the implementation of this plan, was theoretically prepared for it. Hearing the command, all four pushed their fingers into their ears, and Never made a terrible, prolonged scream whose secret only he knew. It would seem that the earth trembled, and the air exploded with every particle. Africans fell to the ground, writhing as if in an attack of collective epilepsy.

Never grabbed a dazed Delaney and threw him over his back, Gerard grabbed a backpack with cans, and Gladiator a weapon. Before their persecutors could come to their senses, everyone disappeared into the thick bushes.

Getting out of the crater, friends found themselves in a spot. Their sharp senses gave them an advantage over Africans while it lasted the night, but they knew the area, and they did not. Just because Tonga was stunned and confused by what Never did, it didn't mean they would give up the pursuit. Strangers came to know the secret hidden by countless generations and were now a threat to the small enclave in which people lived prehistorically. Why did they care so much about secrecy? Why did they care so much about this handful of unfit pre-humans?

"No, I'll go crazy," Fronda muttered, sitting down under a tree to even his breath.

Unlike the desert, the forest did not get cooler at night and running in these conditions was a real torment.

"I understand now why the natives go naked," groaned Gerard, sitting down next to him. "What can they want from us, Del? They don't think we'll eat these ape-men for breakfast. Although they may think so..."

Delaney waved a hand.

"That's not the point," he explained. "They are convinced that this tribe is like a guarantee of the existence of all of Africa. They have such a superstition that if they become extinct, all of Africa will perish, and white people will not expect anything good. This is understandable, isn't it? They treat these cavemen like living tribal gods."

"What do we do then?" Oggy asked quietly, pressing her hand unconsciously to her stomach. "When they are awake, they will start chasing us."

Gladiator put his powerful arm around her.

"I won't let them to touch you," he said emphatically. "Not only Fronda likes you here, remember that... and I grew up in Podhale. I am a champion in the fight with picket."

"I doubt you'll find one here... but thank you. You're great," Oggy hugged him gratefully and clearly cheered.

"Let's set up an action plan now," Never said after a moment. "We now have a few minutes after midnight, which means that we have about four hours until dawn. When the sun rises, we must be far away. I don't want to scare you, but I'm afraid that our only chance is to find this Smenkharei. If he, she or it does not stop Tonga, we'd have trouble. Del, are they headhunters?"

"Not at all. They are just cannibals."

"Damn. Cannibals? And you say it so calmly?"

"And how should I speak? We drink blood, they eat the whole man. The difference is not so great."

Theo chuckled silently.

"I wonder if a vampire steak would hurt them," he said thoughtfully.

"You have problems. Let it hurt them, you care so much for their health?" Gerard patted his pockets nervously and suddenly roared. "What pig steal my cigarettes?!"

Gladiator and Fronda exchanged a quick glance, but none of them said a word.

"They probably fell out on your way," Never said impatiently. "Del, tell us something about Smenkharei.

"This creature is hardly just a legend. He's based somewhere here," Delaney said grimly. "You'd have to be guided by hearing and smell. Apparently Smenkharei gives off a scent similar to that of grapefruit, only more bitterly. You can't mistake it with something else."

Oggy shook at these words. She stepped away from Gladiator, concentrated her maximum attention and jumped out of the dress. Then she raised her head, sniffing intensively. The men clustered into a tight group and headed for her as a sign. Although everyone was armed with flashlights and their eyes could penetrate the darkness, such a path was not easy. They were constantly stumbling over something, their hands on spikes, hurting their skin painfully, but they were pushing forward.

They already thought that none of it would be there when everyone felt what Delaney was talking about - the faint smell of grapefruit, with some bitter smell. There was no doubt that Smenkharei was not far away. A few dozen meters and they found themselves in a small valley. The light of the setting moon poured over the tangled creepers, from which large, velvety flowers grew. Even without the flashlights, they could tell that if they were not black, they were very dark. Delaney dropped to his knees and began collecting soil samples in small bags.

"Are you crazy?" Never asked severely.

"Orchids will not grow without tiny mushrooms with which their seedlings live in symbiosis," the naturalist explained excitedly. "I need some ground."

"The ground is power and the power is electric," Gladiator muttered cheerfully.

Delaney quickly picked up a few flowers, then found and cut off some promising branches. His friends watched him with amusement. Nobody paid any attention to Oggy, who was spinning restlessly until she finally bared her fangs and began to growl. Her eyes flashed with evil red light. Only then they looked at her.

"What going on, baby?" Fronda was surprised.

"She wants to drive us away from these flowers, I'm sure of it," Gerard guessed, just in case he took a step back.

It seemed to be right. Oggy did not look like a friendly doggie at this time, but rather resembled a beast that threw herself at poachers and friends in their time, it got strangely unpleasant.

"What are doing, Oggy?" Never reached out for her, but the she-wolf snapped his mouth so angrily that he jumped back.

At exactly the same moment, an arrow whizzed right beside his head. Tonga, as it turned out, must have seen as cats in the dark, because they were following them, and they had just found them.

"They've got us. I know that they poisoned arrows by the venom of the same species as the giant aga. This venom is extremely dangerous to us," Delaney moaned, looking around nervously.

"Now you are afraid?" Gladiator growled at him angrily.

He clearly blamed him for the situation they were in and was quite right.

The sky above the valley brightened - a fast African dawn followed. Now they could clearly see black, clumsy figures of Tonga circling them in the bushes. If Delaney was right, their lives were hung by a thread, and very thin. Vampires are susceptible to hemotoxins and neurotoxins to almost the same extent as humans, and these African hunters certainly used their weapons very skillfully. Anyway, they didn't need special dexterity, because in the case of such poisons, it was enough for the arrow to hit the target, even very shallow.

Suddenly, with the rising sun, a modulated whistle sounded in the orchid creepers hanging from the rock wall. At the same time, the grapefruit scent intensified. Tonga trembled, dropped the blowers and fell face down on the ground, pleading. They were so terrified that their small bodies were trembling as if they were jelly.

"We're out," Never said firmly.

Friends ran between the trees and ran until they had enough strength. When they finally stopped, there wasn't a single Tonga around, only huge trees and tangled liana curtains.

"They left us?" Asked Gerard in an undertone, wiping sweat from his face.

"They thought Smenkharei had put in a word for us," Delaney explained. "They are very afraid of him. Who saw what he looks like? I saw nothing."

He clearly regretted it.

"Oggy, why did you snarl at us?" Theo asked friend, who is now transforming into a human.

Oggy waited for her voice organs to take on a human shape, then said angrily:

"I sensed a threat, okay? And it's closely related to these damn flowers, though I don't know exactly what kind. Delaney should throw them out, that's my opinion."

"No way! I risk my life for that. Once we're in Shani's lab, I'll put some of these flowers in a test tube and try to find out what scared you."

"Are we coming back to her? Oh, Shani..." the girl sighed lyrically, catching the dress in the air thrown by Fronda.

"You are completely crazy," Gerard muttered in shock.

Delaney laughed heartily.

"Give her a break. Shani experiments with pheromones. There must have been a bit of it left on her skin and your friend sensed it. It will pass in time."

"Well, we must finally rest a bit, and we don't have a tent anymore," Never changed the subject. "However, just lie down under the tree, and the sun will do nothing to you."

"I have something better: a decayed trunk. There is enough room here for us to all fit in," said Oggy, who was completely human and was just dressing her dress on her slightly rounded tummy.

The decayed tree inside was very large indeed, so large that they could easily fit inside. It was true that they had to throw out two large snakes and scare away a dozen spiders, but then they could comfortably sit inside the trunk. They agreed that Never would be on guard in the event of a Tonga or Teke attack as the least in need of sleep, and the rest would finally get some sleep. They postponed the discussion on how they would get to civilization. And this was not a trivial problem - they were in an area they practically did not know, in a very dangerous natural environment for the white man, and they had no idea in which direction they should go. The presence of a werewolf among them made things a little easier, but even the dog's sense of smell couldn't be very helpful here. In this tropical forest you could wander for months and find no way out.

In the afternoon, when the sun shone on the treetops sideways, and thus no longer penetrated through the densely intertwined branches, friends opened two of the half-liter cans received from Lilias and ate. The blood preserved by this method had a strong, metallic aftertaste and was thick enough for everyone to feel full. Even Oggy took a few sips because she didn't want to move away from her friends to hunt.

"What now? Gerard finally asked the inevitable question.

"Fronda, you never get lost. Tell me what your intuition tells you?" Never turned to his friend.

Theo closed his eyes and concentrated, but after a while he shook his head helplessly.

"I know which way we should go," he said. "But I have no idea what to do so that we do not lose direction."

"All right, gentlemen. Set out what's in your pockets," Oggy demanded vigorously.

Under her urgent gaze, the men emptied their pockets, placing penknives, small coins, some unspecified talismans on the ground, two lighters, a notebook, a pack of matches, and a few handkerchiefs. In addition, Gladiator added a fountain pen and artificial rubber hose and pulled out the walkie-talkie from the side pockets of the backpack.

Oggy immediately went to work, not paying attention to friends looking at her in astonishment. From a pile of small items, she picked up a large, round ID from some scientific conference, owned by Del, then took possession of one of the penknives and walkie-talkie. Dismantling the microphone, she took out the magnet hidden in it and thoroughly rubbed it with a large needle, from her own "toolbox". Then, with a penknife and a piece of rubber from an artificial hose, she attached the needle to the badge so that it could rotate freely. Finally, with an eternal pen, she drew reference points on top of the identifier."

"All right," she said, rising from her lap. "Here's the compass. Thanks to it we will not be out of the way. All you need to do now is specify azimuth, what I will do as soon as Theo shows me which way to go."

"I... yes, of course..." Fronda muttered, looking at her with rounded eyes.

He had never suspected her of such talents before. He always thought of this girl as a younger, somewhat helpless sister who had to be looked after so that she would not get in trouble, and suddenly it turned out that she did not need such care at all. It was true that Oggy could cope with any situation, but Fronda's overprotectiveness gave her such pleasure that she didn't cheat on it.

"Don't stare like that, just speak," she muttered, feeling uncomfortable under his surprised look.

Theo concentrated his attention once more and after a moment showed with his hand where they should go. Oggy drew several lines and symbols in her notebook, then tucked the torn paper into her pocket.

"Collect your belongings and we can go," she said.

"You are full of surprises," Gerard said appreciatively.

"First of all, our Oggy is unique. Truly unique. And we should never forget it," Theo looked at the girl with full brotherly pride.

Everyone has become accustomed to the fact that he is now whispering, and that is why, when he began to speak, they looked at him so that they could read his words from his lips. Now everyone looked at him and worried. He looked like boiling water burned him. Traveling in Africa clearly did not serve him and even in this dark forest the sun managed to hurt him. Gladiator also had several burns on his skin, but he suffered much less.

Never cursed silently, then searched the backpack and to his relief found a make-up bag with the sign of a red cross. Among other things, there was a priceless thing at the moment - a tube of sunburn ointment.

"Smear it," he commanded. "We should leave you at the Hardygran base, you're too sensitive. The sun can even kill you, remember."

"Chit-chat," Theo muttered dismissively, but he obediently rubbed his ointment. Gladiator also used it. As a "moth" he was a definitely vampire at night, and only the dark interior of the tropical forest could make him move during the day.

Now you had to go, regardless of anything. They no longer had the mules that the natives had appropriated, so they had to rely on their own legs. And hope that a scant supply of blood in backpacks is enough for all of them.

*****

"You had a lot of luck, you know?" Shani said grumpily, dressing her guests.

When they finally found themselves in a safe place, it turned out that all had suffered more or less in this mad trip. Theo and Gladiator suffered severe sunburn. Never had bruises. Gerard was still complaining about the short breath, bloody abrasions on his right arm and torso, though he had no idea when or how it had happened. Oggy's hands and feet were hurt by spikes, even Delaney, the most experienced, had not avoided a few scratches.

He didn't care, however. He immediately disappeared in the laboratory, where he began to study his prey. Shani didn't mind, just warned him not to touch her notes. She was a biologist and, as friends learned from her chatter, she was not afraid of vampires or any other paranormal matter. She didn't want to be preserved.

"I don't need to be one of you," she explained. "I don't get excited about the prospect of living on the margins of the world. I want fame and I have all the views on it if the research confirms my theories."

"Pheromones, right?" Gladiator asked, looking significantly at embarrassed Oggy.

"Yes. If I can synthesize artificial pheromones that cause specific feelings, then there will be a revolution in biology, psychiatry and even customs."

In other words, it'll be a good mess," Theo muttered sarcastically, who didn't approve of such experiments.

"One thing I wonder," Gerard said, puffing on another cigarette with pleasure. "If your pheromone worked on Oggy like that, why didn't it impress us? No offense, but we're far from falling in love with you. Fronda would probably eat you up, but he likes every woman, more or less similar to people."

"You don't know it," Theo muttered, exceptionally unimpressed by the female representative. Luckily, she didn't hear him.

Shani smiled. She knew that she was very pretty and liked the male interest that surrounded her. The man's eyes flattered her, but they didn't surprise her.

"It's probably synthetic pheromones that don't work on vampires," she said. "But the news that it works on werewolves is valuable to me. It means I'm on the right track."

"I don't know if anyone would need pheromones to fall in love with you," Never said, glancing at her flexible figure, clad in something that seemed tighter than her own skin with appreciation. It could not be spandex, because in this heat no one would stand up in the sexy leotard of this material, in addition black with red inserts.

"What material is this?" Asked Oggy, who was obviously thinking the same.

"Virloks," Shani said. "This is a new material, developed at the institute where I conduct research. It is flexible, strong, yet airy like cotton. The world's first synthetic spider thread."

"I don't care what you wear... in truth, if you weren't dressed at all..."

"Rajah, are you starting again?" Theo sighed hopelessly.

Never had affairs less often than he did, but he usually ended up leaving his friends for a while, regardless of whether they needed him or not. In a word, his infatuations were embarrassing. Now that they were a mercenary group and he was its leader that could be all the more undesirable.

Shani looked at the Indian with a clear sympathy and some promise for the future in dark eyes.

"We'll see later. For now, you rest, and I will get some bottles of blood for you in the hospital," she said and left, swinging a shapely butt.

First of all, friends took shower in turn. They really felt they needed it. Tramping in the primeval forest tired them and, above all, heavily soiled them. Return to civilization was a real relief for them, even for Never, who was familiar with wild life in his native India. It seemed that a "return to nature" is not possible for a civilized man, because he will always miss such achievements of civilization as shower or air conditioning.

That was the brutal truth. Civilized people find it difficult to live without plastic pens, watches, ready-made clothes and lots of various small devices. They felt it now, when the refreshed shower sat in a cool room just below the fan.

"This is life," Gerard sighed after a long moment. "This whole M'kudu is probably sick of having voluntarily returned to this green hell. Just think: the guy will graduate from the university, he learned to live like a civilized man, and he flies naked with a spear on the bushes. It's sick, it can't be called anything else."

"Name as you like. I'm glad I won't see him again. Neither his nor those disgusting midgets." Gladiator shook at the thought.

"They are also people."

"Let it be, Fanfan, but they are not the kind of people I would like to meet every day. Especially that they could convert me to meat loaf, and this is not the peak of my dreams."

"I agree with the previous speaker," Fronda said sleepily.

Oggy hugged to him just purred. She was also overcome by insomnia, which was not surprising after so many sleepless nights, especially since Shani fed her generously with raw steaks. The others were also not hungry enough to be able to sleep, so soon everyone fell into a delightful nap.

A scream woke them up. It was coming from the lab, and the woman was screaming apparently. Awakened so abruptly friends broke up from places and for a moment could not figure out where they are and what is actually going on. They sat up and ran to the laboratory. They knew Delaney was working there, but why was the woman screaming then? They came into the studio and saw Shani curling on the floor, held by Delaney. The girl screamed and tried to push him away with a force that aroused admiration.

"Help me, you dolls!" Del called angrily. "What did you come here for the performance? Help her, she's crazy!"

"What happened?" Never asked, hurrying him to overpower the raving girl.

"She smelled my flowers," Del told him. "We have the answer to our question: no Smenkharei exists, but we have a flower whose pollen is an extremely powerful hallucinogenic drug. It is no wonder that the natives added some kind of demon to it. Do you hear what she says?"

Indeed, in Shani's scream you could distinguish the words "monster" and "go away."

"All right, what's this whistle?" Gerard asked after a moment.

"I thought about it. Yes, whistles an extremely rare species of African thrush, which only nests with black orchids. Their smell attracts insects that feed on thrush. What's more interesting, these flowers are really black, because those in the crater were rather dark purple and certainly did not have any intoxicating properties."

"That clears up many things."

Never looked around the laboratory and chose an ether bottle from the reagent cabinet. He poured some spicy liquid on his handkerchief and pressed it against Shani's face. After a while, the girl calmed down and fell asleep.

"I hope when she wakes up she will be sober. It would be dangerous to leave her like that," he said with evident concern.

He was not completely sure of the correctness of the treatment, but it proved effective. After a few hours, Shani woke up completely healthy and did not remember anything that had happened to her. However, after this experience, Delaney decided to move with further research to the Cahville base, where he could not harm anyone.

"Do you have to go?" Shani asked, clearly disappointed when she heard the news. "I thought I would show you the city and everything..."

She seemed embarrassed by what had happened to her, because although she couldn't remember anything, Oggy was happy to inform her of everything.

"We'll take Del to the place and then come back," Fronda promised her. "We are going to have fun before we leave, in the end we have money to do that because we completed the task."

Although the pretty, dark-skinned girl did not impress him, he was too determined a racist, but she was a woman anyway. And Theo liked to please women.

"You will never learn anything. But let it be, some fun did not harm anyone." Never decided, subtly emphasizing who is in charge here.

As usual after completing the task, so now everyone felt a feeling of euphoria. Always in such a situation, they allowed themselves to "go on the bust", which lasted sometimes a week, until they spent almost all the money. It would seem that vampires don't have much to spend on, but it's a false impression. They did not eat, but drank a lot, and the most expensive drinks, they went to dances, parties, where admission was paid the equivalent of the monthly earnings of the worker and renews wardrobe supplies, ensuring that it was in the best grade. They knew how to get fun.

The Cahville base turned out to be completely different from the Hardiygran base. Above all, only men lived here, and besides, it was cleaner and better equipped. Despite this, they did not take advantage of Delaney's invitation to spend a little more time there, after earnest requests they agreed only for a day rest. And they did it because of Oggy, who they did not want to overwork because of her condition. Fortunately, they had car to go, although they left their jeep in Makidu as compensation for lost mules. The base staff put at their disposal one of their cars so that they did not have to use the rental company.

"Clean, nice, but I didn't like it," Gerard said as they set off. "I don't understand it at all, but I felt bad there."

"This place has a bad aura. I felt it myself, although I'm not oversensitive. And you, Yanek?" Theo asked Gladiator.

"Yes, there is something bad, but that's their problem," answered the highlander. "When I noticed to the head of the base that something was wrong in the air, he looked at me like at the crazy man and advised me to mind my own business."

He was very proud that he was a "sensor" and could not be more offended than by disregarding his warning.

"Don't intervene in someone else's case," Never growled. "Maybe they prefer to do it alone? We are strangers here, don't forget."

Theo whistled on his toes to get attention - he had been doing it since he lost his voice and could only speak in a whisper.

"You have gone too far, Rajah," he said. "We should turn where the street is surrounded by yellow tape."

"That tape wasn't there before," Never worried, turning the car around and turning into the right street.

They did have cause for concern. A police car stood in front of the Institute of Biology, where Shani worked, and two dark-skinned policemen were talking about something with the caretaker.

"I don't like it... We have to risk. Who will ask what is going on?" The Indian braked the cart on the side of the road and rolled his eyes at his companions.

"Maybe me, holy memory," Gerard caught his friends' eyes and explained reluctantly. "One of you has always been walking so far. I'm physically weaker, but that doesn't mean I'm worse. Someday I have to be useful."

Theo smiled mockingly.

"Our baby is getting wings," he said to Never, who nodded his head.

"Go but be careful. Don't do something stupid."

Gerard got out of the jeep and approached Shani's house. His friends watched him anxiously, not sure how he would manage, but it seemed that their teachings was good. It was not for nothing that they stuck the rules of survival into his mind and taught him all their tricks.

They waited briefly, because only about ten minutes. When Gerard returned, his green eyes were almost round and full of terror.

"Listen," he said, leaning his hands on the car frame. "Shani is dead. She was found dead in the laboratory this morning. There were no signs of a struggle, so they claim it was an accident."

"An accident? Young girls don't die of this one!" Never shouted angrily. "Anyway, nobody dies like that... Did you find out anything else?"

"The body is in the police morgue, the neighboring district. A quick examination of the corpse showed no signs of violence, the police say it was asphyxiation."

"Are you crazy? In this infernal climate, no one needs to warm up with a coal stove," protested Gladiator.

"Of course not. But activated carbon is needed for filters. Many chemical facilities manufacture it for their own use, because it is cheaper this way. If a certain amount began to smolder, and at the same time the air conditioning failed..." Never rubbed his chin, what he used to do when he thought hard about something.

Theo, sitting in the back seat, was biting his fingers, still unable to understand what had happened. The girl was just alive, helping them dress the wounds, laughing, joking with them... She was so pretty, so full of life. Who would want to kill her? Despite so many centuries of experience, he couldn't get used to such things. He wanted to cry.

"We're going to the morgue," Never suddenly decided. "I have bad feeling, though I don't know why. Such accidents happen, so why do I have so many doubts? Hop in, Fanfan."

After a short ride, the jeep drove up to the building with the inscription "Police morgue". Friends hoped that at this time no one would be there, but they were disappointed: in the middle sat a young man in a white apron and filled out some forms.

"What do you want here?" He asked hostilely.

"We're friends with Shani Batawi," Never told him. "Are you a coroner? Tell us why Shani died?"

The man gave him a suspicious look.

"A simple case of carbon monoxide poisoning, or, if you prefer, overcoming... And I don't have to explain anything to you. Get out of here."

"Did you do an autopsy?" Oggy asked sharply.

"I don't know what you do in your place, but we don't cut anyone here, unless the circumstances of death are unclear. In this case it was not like that."

"If you allow, we'd like to see the body."

"It is impossible. Provisions."

Never leaned forward and whispered something in his ear. The coroner hesitated and a look of uncertainty appeared on his face. After a while he replied:

"Two hundred. And you have five minutes. Drawer 41f."

Friends entered the huge, thrilling cold room. It didn't take them long to find the right drawer, though they themselves felt like it was forever.

"Well, I know one thing at a time," Never said as soon as their eyes appeared to the girl's body resting in a flat container. "This coroner is either bribed or ignorant. I think it's rather the first."

"What do you mean?" Oggy asked not very clearly. The atmosphere of this place meant that she had to use all her will to keep wolf nature in check.

"It couldn't be too overcoming. In this case, the skin coatings are clearly pink, not blue."

Never looked closely at Shani. He touched her head, inspected her arms and legs, lifted her eyelid with his thumb and examined the eye, then pulled her lower lip out.

"I already know everything," he said, straightening up. "We close the drawer and go out politely."

The friends looked at him questioningly, but he only shook his head. It meant that he would explain everything later and now they would only be out of here. There was clearly a reason for this, so they had to restrain their curiosity until the time was right.

And this came soon, as soon as they were back in the jeep.

"It was undoubtedly a murder, well done and well planned," Never said, as he took the wheel again.

"How do you know?" Asked Gladiator skeptically.

"A small detail. There were clear teeth marks on the inside of the lips, and this only occurs in one case. Then when someone is burking someone with a pillow. I examined Shani's wrists and ankles. There were no signs of ties or even bruises, but on her head, under her hair, I felt a small bump. My concept is this: someone stunned Shani with a blow to the head, then smothered her with a pillow and set fire to the coal package to fake an accident."

"But why?" Asked Theo helplessly.

"I am not clairvoyant, I don't know. However, I think we should find out."

"Are we going back to the institute?"

"Bingo, knight. We'll talk to the night janitor. They usually know the most."

Never started the engine and headed for the Institute of Biology. On the spot, it turned out that the policemen had already finished their work, and the janitor stood leaning against the wall and puffing his pipe thoughtfully.

"Good evening. We're friends with Shani Batawi," Never said politely, approaching him. "We'd like to know more about this accident."

The caretaker shrugged and, tapping the pipe from his mouth, tapped it against the wall.

"I told the cops everything, but ultimately... What would you like to know?"

"The coroner told us it was an accident, but we don't like something about it. Did Shani have any enemies?" Never asked a standard question.

"Come on," Oggy snorted scornfully. "We'll hear right away that everyone loved her, and that there is really no one who cares about her death, which is what you usually hear in such cases."

"Oggy!" A friend admonished her sharply.

The caretaker seemed to be amused because all his teeth gleamed in his coal-black face.

"No." He replied. "On the contrary, Mrs. Batawi had a lot of enemies, and many might want to knock her off. Even one of the doctoral students. She was extraordinarily ingenious in the field of appropriating the effects of someone else's work, which they do not like anywhere. In addition, the engagement of the dean's daughter was broken due to her fault, as well as two divorces. There is a lot to choose from."

Theo looked at him with round eyes, not finding words. The rest were silent too. The matter seemed confusing, and they suddenly realized that they knew very little about Shani. The caretaker tapped out the remainder of the pipe ash and added calmly:

"You know what, white man? I like you, so I will tell you something: in this case you will have a lot of suspects, but I personally do not think that one of them was guilty. Many people of both sexes might want to strangle Miss Batawi with their bare hands.... but this crime was committed very intelligently, with knowledge of things and icily. You have a difficult opponent. You can trust me. I am certainly beyond suspicion, because this lady did not chill or heat me."

"Why?" Asked Gladiator.

"Because I didn't care. I can hardly sign myself, I'm old and poor, and I couldn't harm her or help her in any way, so she ignored me. I repaid her the same, because I know women like her well and they don't attract me at all. I have always been faithful to my wife, who was a pretty and uneducated but decent girl. Believe me, that's all that matters. Only a suicide could marry a woman like a deceased Shani."

"It's hard for me to believe she'd steal someone else's work," Never murmured in disgust.

"Someone work, other people's husbands, different. Depends on the whim. I'm not a detective, but I can give you some advice: think about the fact that someone was anxious to hide that it was a murder. That's not what someone who kills in affection does, even I know it."

He mocked them, it was obvious from his eyes, but he was probably telling the truth. He had no reason to lie to them.

"Can we see her private office?" Asked Theo after a while.

"Why not?" Replied the caretaker. "Policemen will not enter it, as long as the coroner has confirmed the onset, they do not like unnecessary work, so you might as well do it."

He led them through the dark corridors to the door bearing Shani's business card and opened it with one of his keys. Friends began to search the office for everything that might have been somehow helpful in their private investigation. They tried not to show it, but somehow felt uncomfortable under the mocking look of an old African. If this caretaker was telling the truth, the pretty and nice girl became the real villain of this adventure, and they didn't like it. In addition, if it was true, the murderer might have a reason for his act, and they thought it was sufficient justification.

"Thank you, that's all," Never said when they looked around the office. "You were very kind. We'll go now."

"No problem," said the caretaker briefly.

Only when they were far from the institute Gladiator, who was still silent, said:

"Enlighten me because I am stupid: what exactly were we looking for and why did we not go to the deceased's apartment with it?"

"Brrr, deceased," Fronda got over. "Sorry to think in this way of this beautiful being."

"See, blonde, whatever was in Shani's apartment, it must have already been found by those who killed her," Never said. "Our only chance was to find something in the office. What do you have?

It turned out that only he and Oggy found something intriguing. The girl peeled off a cardboard envelope attached to the bottom of the desk, and Never took a thick notebook out of her lab coat pocket. The rest had only little things that didn't matter, at least it seemed so at first glance.

The envelope contained black and white photos, the entire bundle, all marked with date and time. Fronda whistled through his teeth briefly watching them.

"It looks like a blackmail attempt... Undoubtedly they were taken with a telephoto lens, and they are not photos from a trip out of town."

Gladiator tapped one of the pictures with his finger.

"I know him from Berlin," he said.

"From Berlin? Place where you had a fight with Nuntia? You aren't wrong?"

"Not at all, certainly not. I just don't know who he is talking to in this photo..."

"He doesn't talk," Gerard objected. "He accepts some money. Maybe it's a bribe? Take a look at hands."

They studied the pictures diligently, discovering something compromising on each one, somehow a small detail that could actually be the basis for initiating blackmail. The very fact of having such photographs was puzzling, but it was impossible to read from them what Shani needed for it. They could have been a murder motive, but they didn't have to.

Oggy started to flip through the notebook she had taken from the study. In addition to telephone numbers, there were mainly chemical formulas and short sentences such as "Pick up the laundry" or "12V - dentist". Suddenly, however, the girl saw something familiar in the jungle of notes.

"Look!" She called out.

On the last page of the notebook, between the various small entries, was the word "Nuntia," which they knew, bearing a question mark. Whatever it meant to Shani, she had to consider it important enough to write in her private notebook.

"What are those dirty people doing in Congo?" Gladiator asked after a moment, scratching worriedly in the forehead.

"I have no idea." Never again began to study the remaining photographs carefully. "I think we can accept the following working hypothesis: Nuntia members have come to Congo for some important purpose. Shani tracked them down while they were doing business dealings with a public figure, then tried blackmail. They killed her, faked her accident, and because they thought she kept her compromising materials at home, they didn't search her office right away. Then it was too late, because the police arrived and in this way the compromising materials came to our hands. What do you think will happen now?"

"I think they won't let it go. Germans is a damn nasty nation," said Gladiator. "But I have an additional remark: how did Shani find out what Nuntia is doing and that it is illegal? Something stinks here."

"Not only to you."

There was silence again. No one had any idea how to investigate in a city they did not know, and in a case in which it was not even known what their enemy looked like.

"Can we just let the police know it was a murder?" Gerard said uncertainly.

Everyone looked at him, surprised by this simple solution.

"That would be the most appropriate. Only here they will believe their own coroner more, who seems to be in it, than some stragglers," replied Theo thoughtfully. "Something tells me that it won't work. The only person we can count on and who certainly is not involved is the caretaker. He certainly was telling the truth, and he wouldn't let us search Shani's things if he was in league with her murderers."

"Not to mention that he would search it himself, and what we found was not well hidden," Never added.

"Maybe we should notify Delaney first?" They were on quite intimate terms," Oggy pointed out, but Never just waved his hand.

"Not worth it. Let him examine his flowers and not find out too soon that his friend is dead."

"Yes. At least we can rule him out, because we were with him when it happened," sighed Fronda.

Just in case, before they returned to the institute, they drove a little on the streets, just to see if anyone was following them.

This was unlikely - but if it turned out that they had misjudged the old caretaker, they would have had a 'tail'. After making sure that no one was following them, they turned back to the Institute. They had to ask this man a few more questions.

The old African looked away from the small TV screen and looked at the uninvited guests in surprise.

"You again?" He asked, putting the half-eaten sandwich on the plate. "Did you forget something or what?"

Never sat across from him across the table.

"That's not the point," he replied. "We want to ask you for a favor. From what you said, you had no reason to wish Shani dead. Will you help us detect who killed her and why?"

"If I can... It's true that I did not like this girl, because no one who knew her closer could like her, but I did not wish her bad. She did nothing to me, she even got a job for me several times... However, I don't know how I could help you."

Theo pulled an envelope of photos from behind a belt of jeans. There was no pocket in his day. Everything important was worn under the bosom or under the belt, and he has not yet got rid of this habit.

"Tell us if you meet someone in these photos," he asked.

The caretaker raised his eyebrows slightly and stared at the pictures, apparently short-sighted eyes. After a moment, he tapped one of the photographs with his finger.

"He was here," he said. "But I don't know who that is. And this... wait, it's our deputy prime minister... Yes, definitely he. But here the same dude talks with Laguardini, the owner of the areas where rare minerals are obtained. This is a terrible sneak and if Miss Batawi got in his way, it's no wonder she had to die. And here again Laguardini and some lady. I don't know her, but apparently Shani knew her. I don't want to scare you, but it seems that our lady was sitting in a nasty swamp. Just move the matter and the swamp will suck in you too."

"We've already heard such threats. They don't impress us. One more question: does the name "Nuntia" tell you something?"

The caretaker didn't answer right away. He stood up, turned the television down and filled the pipe slowly, with measured movements. Then he reached under the flower box and pulled out the folded paper, bearing traces of moisture.

"I once found it in the dustbin of the director of our institute," he said, handing the card to Never.

The Indian laid it on the table. On its surface there were small scraps of several different letters, certainly not delivered by regular mail. They were all written in German, in Gothic letters and only the signature, "Nuntia", could be understood. None of the friends knew German, but they still felt that the cards contain something bad. The angular letters radiated an indefinite threat.

"Why did you decide to keep it?" Gladiator asked, without interrupting his gaze at the carefully stuck shreds of unknown information.

"Professor Nyamara was very nervous at the time, he walked like a hail cloud, and what is more, twice during this period his office was broken into, and he forbade reporting to the police," answered the African. "Maybe I'm childish, but I have a soft spot for detective stories and spy movies. That's probably why I became interested in these scraps. I spent many nights gluing these pieces together so that they matched each other, which was even more difficult because I did not understand anything from this magazine and I still do not understand."

"Nor are we, which is a shame," Never murmured. "But I know who can read it: Ernie. He is German by origin and without a doubt knows his native language."

"Damn it. No wonder I didn't like it right away," Gladiator growled.

"And I think we should pay a visit to Mr. Laguardini first," Theo said. He tried to strain his larynx to speak aloud but waved his hand. He could only whisper.

"You're probably right... Where does he live?" Never asked the janitor. He shrugged.

"Someone brings me a map of Brazaville and I'll show you where."

Oggy ran to the car and returned with a folded tourist map. The caretaker laid it out on the table and marked two places with a pen.

"Here is Laguardini's office," he said, pointing to one of them. "Now of course closed. The boss's office is on the first floor, fourth corridor..."

"How do you know?" Gerard interrupted distrustfully.

"How? That's why..." The caretaker broke off and hit his forehead. "Sure, how could I forget that? A few days ago, Shani sent me to Laguardini with a letter. I don't know what was in it, but judging by the fact that she was murdered, there must have been some unpleasant things."

Never nodded, his eyes not leaving the map.

"This second place is his residence, right?" He asked and, having received confirmation, picked up a map with photos from the table. "Let's go, guys. We have to do this before the guy gets rid of the evidence."

"Do you think Batawi was worth the risk?" the caretaker asked dubiously.

The Indian smiled and patted him on the shoulder.

"It's not about whether she was worth it," he explained. "But that we knew her at all. Thank you, my friend."

They went outside, still leaving an unconvinced African who apparently was beginning to regret that he had told them anything.

"We'll do it," Never said when they were at the car. "Fronda and Oggy will penetrate the president's office and we will pay him a visit to the residence."

"Why do you have a happy row in perspective and we boring rummaging around the empty corners? Have we offended one of your thirty million native gods?" Theo was offended.

"That's because I'm in charge here," Never said coldly. "And besides, you will have to break into the office and there is no such need to the residence. You are our only burglar, and Oggy can disarm alarms. Got it?"

"You're not fair," Theo kicked the jeep's tire and turned his back on the Indian.

Never looked at his back, then sighed in resignation and sat behind the wheel. He knew for a long time that Fronda had his opinion, and worse, he could never explain to himself that he was wrong. Fortunately, he recognized his leadership - in most cases.

Oggy and Fronda got off at the magnificent office building of the company "Laguardini Corp", while Theo still did not speak until the jeep disappeared around the corner of the street. Only then he looked at his friend and cheer up a bit. He had to admit in silence that a safer task was now more appropriate because of Oggy's serious condition, but he couldn't stop sulking earlier than usual.

"Can you can handle the new generation alarm?" He asked.

"Oh, yes," she assured him cheerfully.

They were not empty promises. Soon Theo could calmly manipulate one of his lockpicks in the lock, without fear that a sudden alarm would bring the two of them uninvited company.

The office building was empty except for the security guards who were sleeping in the hall, which they passed easily. However, the office itself did not contain anything interesting. Theo scrupulously searched all desk and cabinet drawers, and Oggy scanned the computer's contents. However, they found nothing. All the materials concerned only company matters that did not interest them, although, as Oggy noted, they could certainly interest the police and the tax office. However, nothing pointed to any links between the company's president and Nuntia.

"That was to be expected," Theo said disappointedly. "No one right-minded keeps compromising materials in his own office. Our friends will soon find something interesting.

"So, what? Do we join them? It is not far." Suggested the girl.

Theo agreed to this idea with enthusiasm, which was not very good at the responsibility he had always boasted.

They left the office building along the road they got to it and followed the dark alleys to the residence institute indicated by the caretaker. Such a walk was only a pleasure for both of them, they were in excellent condition, but they had to hide from police patrols, not wanting to explain to them what they were doing here. Thanks to this, they at some point found a jeep, hidden skilfully in the thickets near the Laguardini residence, on the embankment, from which the road and the entrance gate were visible. Were it not for the fact that they were trying to bypass possible threats, they could have missed it at all.

"The engine is already cold," Oggy said softly, touching the bonnet. "They're gone a long time."

Theo examined the car carefully, wishing he could talk to it, he dreamed of a car with verbal communication.

"Are we going inside?" He asked his friend uncertainly. "They went there and apparently are gone. It can be hot there. Do you have a gun?"

"No, I don't!"

"Neither do I, damn it. Just my slingshot. We can't leave them like that..."

He paused, because a weak rumble of a motorcycle came from the side of the residence. The great gate opened, and a closed truck drove out onto the road below the escarpment.

"They are there," Oggy said suddenly. "In this truck. I hear Never's whistle. He let us know where they are."

"If you are not mistaken, they probably didn't close themselves there."

Never once bought a miniature dog whistle and sewed it into his shirt collar. Thanks to this, he could bend his head properly, even when he was tied up. Oggy, thanks to the nature of the werewolf, heard the ultrasound almost as well as the dog, so he could always give her a signal where he was without alerting people.

Theo reached into his pocket for a spare set of keys. There was no point in making any plans now, it seemed like the situation was out of control. Whatever their friends had discovered brought them a danger they couldn't see. Fronda shoved Oggy into the jeep and directed the vehicle to the road before the truck could disappear from view.

"What you want to do?" The girl asked, vaguely lisping. Increasing tension accelerated the conversion into a dog, and she couldn't control it for too long.

"We will follow them," Fronda replied. "We'll find out where they are taking them and why, and then, well... you will need to make a decision."

Just in case, he turned off the lights. He could have done well without them, but it posed a danger to other road users. Fortunately, this road was hardly used and completely empty at this time.

The truck rolled down the ever-greater wilderness, until it finally reached the edge of a deserted pond - it stopped there. Fronda also stopped the car and reached for military binoculars. Oggy took a second one from the locker. The whole area looked as if no one had ever been there, and probably it was like that, despite the proximity of the city. Three armed muses got out of the cab and opened the box. They pulled out the unconscious Gladiator, and conscious Never and Gerard but battered. Everyone was solidly tied up with barbed wire loops - and so tearless.

"What shall we do?" Oggy asked quietly, trembling like a leaf. "They will kill them and throw them into this pond..."

She couldn't stand it any longer and, growling with obvious anger, emerged from the dress, shaking herself.

"You found the moment," Theo sighed. "Although it may be better. What do we have here...?"

He opened the cache under the dashboard and took out his slingshot, without which he did not move anywhere. It was a miserable weapon at best, but they had nothing better.

"Distract them," he ordered the werewolf. "Only fast. I will distract them, and you try to throw their weapons into the lake. Don't waste time biting them, just take their weapons away, do you understand?"

The dog barked softly and jogged into the dark. Theo picked up a small stone from the ground, put it in his slingshot and, having whirled it over his head, sent this primitive bullet straight into the back of one of the thugs who were lugging prisoners to the edge of the pond. The bandit shouted and snatched his head. As more missiles fell, they started firing around blindly, not understanding what was happening. In this darkness and in this wild area they might think that a demon had attacked them.

Theo, skilled in handling the slingshot, was throwing stones as fast as he could. Trying to spot the mysterious enemy, the gangsters didn't notice the dog crawling to them until he jumped and snatched his automaton from one of them.

"What is going on?!" The thug shouted, but at the same moment another stone hit him on the temple, stunning him on the spot.

Others took no more risk. Having abandoned the prisoners, they got into the truck and in the thrust in the rear run left the banks of the pond on the road.

"What a cowards," Theo chuckled happily, running down to the pond.

"Happy as always. They were close, and they would make us into yellow submarines." Never, freed by a friend from the loop first, looked carefully at bleeding wrists. "Well, if Laguardini does his business this way, it's no wonder he has a bad opinion. What about our highlander?"

"He only has a tumor on his head. Did you even find out anything?" Theo unscrewed the barbed wire from Gladiator's arms and legs, and began sprinkling his face with water from the pond.

Oggy tried to help him by licking the highlander with her pink tongue.

"We learned," growled Gerard, rubbing various injured parts of the body, "that it's better not to stick your nose in someone business. This type has extremely good protection and is certainly not afraid of vampires. Or anything else."

"Well, if you are such a dub..."

"Don't be angry at him, Fronda, he's been hit hard by his neck," Never took the actor in defense. "He may have broken ribs, he would have to be bandaged. Fortunately, we have the information we wanted. Nuntia does business here, so they have the money to finance their fascist campaigns. People who belong to their sponsored organizations don't even know they are being controlled by vampires."

Gladiator moaned, raising his hand to his head. Theo patted him on the back and stood up.

"Shani must have died because she knew Nuntia was doing business with Laguardini, right?" He asked.

"Not only with him when it comes to accuracy. It's an operative, profit-oriented organization. However, that's not why they murdered Shani. It's so damn tortuous, but they killed her because she had an affair with Delaney."

"What?!" He stared at him.

"Nuntia basically condemns vampire affairs with people, and completely does not tolerate... polluting the race. That's why they killed her. Blackmail was of secondary importance here, and from the point of view of interests she could be useful to them alive. Sponsorship of scientific institutes is a great way to launder money, and Shani could be a Laguardini plug."

"Nice," Fronda said disgustedly. "In my life I would not have thought that we would come across such a problem. I don't know about you, but I don't want to go into it anymore."

Never looked at him sternly.

"Who like who, but you should understand them. You are a racist yourself, jackass."

"Maybe, but not to this extent. And I'm not at all, I just don't like..." Theo blushed with embarrassment. Suddenly he saw his beliefs in a whole new light and couldn't find the right words to defend them.

"We could avenge this poor girl," interrupted Gladiator.

He was sitting on the grass and drink greedy cognac from the hip flask given to him by Fronda. He was one of the few vampires who could bear a higher dose of such undiluted alcohol without harm. Usually, even in public places, they added some plasma to their drinks, which served as a buffer. He didn't have to.

Gerard shook his head.

"Stupid idea," he said. "Laguradini is not just a spear carrier. Have you seen how easily his thugs cope with us? Even your gorilla's strength didn't help. Nuntia knew who to take as an accomplice."

"Right," Never said. "Besides, Laguardini is not responsible for Shani's death, but Detlef Vozinsky, his liaison with Nuntia, this guy from the photo. And he's not here anymore."

"So what? Will we just leave here?" The highlander choked his cognac in indignation.

"I don't know if it's just that, but I think we should evacuate from here before we expose others."

They were silent for a moment, involuntarily listening if no one was coming.

"We fooled ourselves this time," Gerard finally sighed.

"What did you think we would only win? Rather, we should thank each of the thirty million native gods of Rajah that none of us died," Fronda said in a cloud of anger, because he did not like to lose, and all his medieval soul demanded revenge for the death of Shani Batawi.

"So, what are we doing? Are we running away?" Asked Oggy, who had already taken the form of a human and even managed to get dressed.

Never nodded slightly, his narrow golden eyes flashed like two daggers. He got up from the trampled grass, drew his torn shirt, and ran a hand through his hair. He straightened his back. He was the leader of his division again, not just a good companion, and it was obvious that he had already made the right decision.

"Now we must retreat," he said. "But that doesn't mean we're letting go. From today we have a new enemy: Nuntia."

PART 2

On Wolf's Trail

Gerard Phil was running through the woods. He was out of breath, stinging painfully under his ribs, but he didn't dare to slow down until he was completely exhausted. When, finally, completely exhausted, he huddled on the ground under a tree, he realized that he probably managed to lose his persecutors. He has not heard them for a long time. He didn't realize it at all, but as a vampire he instinctively chose the best path, so he had the advantage over the people chasing him.

He leaned his head against a tree, panting heavily. These Hunters were well organized, better than the others he dealt with. If they could afford a training center here in the Mexican jungle, it meant that they also knew how much and who to get their hands on... The Van Helsing Institute had to grow and probably found a good source of funding. Gerard stood up and forced himself to go, though he stumbled from fatigue every few steps. He had to get out of here somehow and get to Cancun, where friends were waiting for him. However, he could go there only when he was completely sure that no one was following him.

Somewhere nearby a branch snapped. Gerard jumped up from the stump he had just sat on and grabbed some fat bough, though defense would still be pointless. He had no strength. He was not only exhausted to the limit by this murderous escape. He was tormented by a horrible, inexpressible desire he couldn't bear. He just tried to drink water from a small spring, but immediately vomited. He couldn't understand how Fronda managed to swallow anything but pure blood - he couldn't, despite the burning heat.

The fight was now beyond his means. Gerard thought with fear that his adventures as a vampire would end here and his friends would probably never know what happened to him. However, the boy who appeared among the trees did not look like a Hunter. Pretty typical Indian, in black jeans and a black T-shirt. An elongated face with protruding cheekbones, black hair falling on shoulders, dark skin and completely incompatible with the whole, bright eyes that looked at Gerard questioningly.

"Are you lost, gringo?"

Gerard released a bough and sank to his knees.

"Go away," he croaked. "Go away because I can hurt you..."

He covered his face with his hands, fighting the overwhelming thirst for blood whose presence he felt so close to him. He experienced such a torment only once, right after his preservation, and was afraid of what he would do to this nice boy.

"Are you sick, gringo?" The unimpressed Mexican came closer.

"I'm hungry! I need blood! Now do you understand?! Run away!" Gerard shouted desperately, wishing with all his heart that the Indian would now run away, like any normal man after contact with a vampire. However, he was different.

"Do you need a lot?" He asked calmly, sitting down on a stump protruding from a felled tree.

"No... Half a glass is enough..." Gerard looked up in surprise.

The boy rolled up his sleeve, took a long knife from his belt and cut the skin below his elbow. The vampire groaned and stuck his lips into the fresh wound, drinking the life-giving fluid with hunger. The heat in the esophagus eased, the heart breaking against the ribs slowed down, the thoughts regained their former clarity. With some regret, he licked the wounded area to speed up the scarring and let go of the man's hand. It was only now that he noticed that the Mexican kept the knife ready, right at his neck.

"Just in case," the boy explained. "I like to live, my Dear."

He smiled faintly, wiping his mouth with his sleeve.

"Thank you, you saved my life," he said. "Relax, I'm not really dangerous. Anyway, not anymore. But how is it that you are not afraid of me? Who are you by the way?"

"My name is Sylvestro Bastardi, but they call me Silver," the Mexican smiled at him. He put the knife behind his belt. "And I'm hardly afraid. I grew up in such a district that I saw almost everything before I was five. Vampires don't scare me, it's rather people. Where did you come from, gringo? I thought you didn't go to such forbidden places."

He spoke English much better than Gerard, though he did put Spanish words in, and the way he spoke showed good upbringing and education.

"I ran away from hunters." The actor shuddered at the mere memory. "They have their training base somewhere. They captured me, but instead of killing them on the spot, they hunted me for training purposes. They are scary people. They would not let you go if they saw you in such a meeting with me."

Silver nodded. He seemed to understand him - it was hard to believe it, knowing most people's attitude towards vampires. Unless he deliberately misled him, but that in turn was denied the honest, honest look of those very bright eyes in the swarthy face.

"Come on," he said, rising from his stump. "I'm here near abrigo, you can hide there and rest a bit. You wouldn't go far in this state. They probably chased you out healthy."

"Abrigo"[1] turned out to be a kind of dugout, with a bed made of old boxes and a sort of table - the same material. The roof was made up of evenly planks, covered with soil, and the door with the door frame, fitted into the entrance, probably once belonged to some wealthy house. They were solid and in spite of considerable destruction they kept some elegant decorations. Gerard looked around the dread with horror, for he understood that it was a real palace for his savior. During their stay in Mexico, they saw many people living worse than animals, and undoubtedly this Indian belonged to such unfortunates. Still, he managed to keep his noble heart and serenity. It was hard to believe it.

---

[1] Shelter (Spanish).

"You can wait here until it's dark. I don't know much about vampires, but you probably feel better after dark, right?" Silver said, lighting the old-fashioned kerosene lamp.

Gerard sat on the improvised bed. He felt much better now, and with the improvement of his well-being a deaf rage came to his mind. If any of the Hunters stood before him now, it would end badly. The former lover of French cinema has not even suspected himself of the capacity for such murderous feelings. However, when someone tries to kill a person, even the mildest pacifist can turn into a madman. Besides, Gerard was no longer the man he once was. He already knew how to hide from Hunters, how to pretend to be a man among people, what to do to survive. He learned to fight with different types of weapons, including what was at hand: a stone torn from a cobblestone, a board, a chair, some branch as a last resort... Fronda was a good teacher.

"If I could repay those bastards somehow..." he hissed through his teeth.

The Mexican sat down next to him and began to bite a pear removed from his jacket pocket. After a while he said:

"If you know where they live, you can repay them."

"How? I am alone here, and you must know that most vampire stories are bullshit. I can't fly or penetrate through the keyhole, and when it comes to strength, that's lie."

Silver smiled slightly.

"You don't need physical strength to kick someone out. If I help you... will you smuggle me somehow abroad? I have no future here and I could arrange it there somehow. Unfortunately, I have no money to pay for the smuggler, and traveling through the desert, where nobody is guarding, is almost certain death. I was in the United States, I can manage it. I can work and I don't need much to be happy."

Gerard looked at him thoughtfully.

"I can't smuggle you because I'm not going there," he said after a moment. "But I can give you false documents and some money. You can even get to the Pentagon with these papers. They were forged by the best professional in the industry. The only thing missing is a photo, but you can paste it yourself, and your description agrees with mine, so nobody will question it.

"Ok," Silver patted him with a flourish on the back. "So, listen to me."

He pushed away the "table" or chest after some large household appliances and pulled out a blue bag from under it. He opened it, showing neatly arranged plastic bags with white powder.

"Coca," he said. "I found it once and hid it here. Oh, they were looking for this dirty thing, the brawl broke out, even the shooting took place, but here somehow nobody came to me. Initially, I wanted to sell it, it's worth a lot, but I don't want to have anyone on my conscience. It's death, my dear, instant death. Just drop the bag on the base and call the police. They will go the jail for a long time, they will not want to buck."

"I doubt if they will not want to... they are really haunted. But the idea is good," a devil's fire flickered in Gerard's eyes.

The idea of setting Mexican drug hunters up was extremely tempting. Let them feel what it means to be a game. This young Indian, or rather mestizo, although undoubtedly from the margins of society, had not only a head on his neck, but also some primal morality in his heart. Since he voluntarily gave up money that would set him up for the rest of his life, it was really worth helping him.

He looked at him with sympathy and with a sharp jerk, ripped off the lining of his jacket. He retrieved the spare documents and switches of US dollar bills, hidden "just in case". All of his companions were so stocked, and sometimes it was useful. He gave Silver both.

"We will do it."

"Oh boy, it's a *maldito mucho dinero*[2]! Is this really all for me? For nothing?"

"What for nothing? Dude, you saved my life. These few pennies are really a small price. I still don't understand why you did it. Rarely would anyone do that."

Silver lowered his hand with the banknotes he counted a second ago with incredulous greed.

"See, gringo," he said hesitantly. "It's not the first time I've seen you. When I was less than ten years old, I was abducted from an orphanage by two perverts. No, they didn't manage to do anything to me, don't look so scared. One of you saved me."

"For sure?"

"I saw him drinking they life from them. Until I peered in fear, I thought I would be next. But he then just took my hand and walked me to the orphanage. He told me to never trust anyone, I would live longer. Believe me, I took it to heart."

Gerard sighed indignantly at the thought of how his savior's adventure might end.

---

[2] Damn lots of money (Spanish).

"Terrible. But in that case, it's no wonder that you knew who you were dealing with. If a man once sees a vampire and recognizes him, he will always know it."

"Besides, you seemed like a decent man to me right away," Silver added cheerfully. "You chased me away instead of throwing me down my throat. This is not the way the beast does."

He took a bottle of tequila from under the camp bed.

"You probably don't drink this?"

"I can do it if it's warm. Only on the bottom of the glass."

Silver poured the drink into plastic cups.

"Where did you come from in this god damn jungle?" He asked, falling into a shabby chair, undoubtedly captured in a garbage can. "This is not your fishery, is it?"

Gerard leaned comfortably on the board imitating the wall of the dugout.

"You're right," he admitted. He carefully drunk a few drops of tequila. It tasted like red-hot iron. "This is not my place."

"So why?"

"You see, sometimes not everything can be predicted," he drank more, the liquid stopped burning. "I'm looking for my friend."

"Oh, it's a vampire too, like you?"

"No. That's why I'm worried about her. I had some information that she might be here, but she wasn't there, but I fell into the trap. My friends checked other clues, I hope they did better. I'll find out when I get to the assembly point."

"But first we two will pay Hunters back."

Gerard nodded slightly.

"I can understand that you have some sympathy for me, but why do you want to help?" He asked.

Silver poured himself alcohol.

"*Los cazadores de vampiros*[3] take their toll not only on you but on ordinary people, sometimes they are no better than *narcos*[4]. They terrorize nearby residents wherever they appear. I know that here in Calakmul, they mistakenly killed two boys and a girl who practiced in disguise before *Dia de Muertos*[5]. They shirked responsibility, I suppose a bribe. The families of those killed wanted to seek legal justice but intimidated them."

His words were not a surprise to Gerard. Hunters have always behaved like a paramilitary organization, above the law. They chased people away from their places and unscrupulously terrorized those who came across their real activity. They thought that since they hunt "monsters" they are allowed everything.

"And what do you do in the reservation?" He asked. "You are not a jake, it can be seen at first glance."

Silver smiled sadly.

"You already know that I grew up in an orphanage. I was found on the doorstep when I was about two days old. What can I say, Nuns looked after us. They were not as good and holy as they were in soap operas, but at least they tried. You know, *las monjas*[6] are old ladies, so they don't know how to deal with children. They usually don't have, as you say... *instinto*

---

[3] Vampire hunters (Spanish).
[4] Generally, people living on drug production and trading.
[5] The equivalent of Halloween in Spain and Mexico.
[6] Nuns (Spanish).

maternal[7]. But they treated us decently. We were full, well dressed, we went to school. I even got to college, but then it went wrong. I lacked money even though I was making extra money at night as a bartender. I was still looking for a source of income that would allow me to graduate. When I was offered a place in a courier company, I thought that fate smiled at me."

"And he rather finagled you," Gerard muttered sympathetically.

"You aren't stupid. One of the packages contained a club weapon. I was set up."

"Is that why you live here?"

"I found this dugout when I was a teenager. I used it to hide from the police. And that's all."

"Now I understand why you care about leaving the country. Are you not afraid to help me?"

He laughed.

"Not at all. I'm screwed anyway."

So, we just had to wait until dark, and then... We had to get to their base, which would probably not be a problem. They did not watch it very carefully, rather busy patrolling the area. And Gerard has long ceased to be a naive pacifist. His friends taught him melee combat, stalking and breaking into well-guarded places. And also have no qualms.

Later he was surprised that everything went so smoothly. Vanhelsingans simply did not expect such a hit and were not prepared for it. The police raid was a complete surprise for them, and the drug bags hidden in various places of the base were even bigger. Silver, who made a treacherous phone call

---

[7] Maternal instinct (Spanish).

from a nearby gas station, twisted with joy, watching the hunters massacre from behind. His casual companion was also pleased. To do the more dangerous part of the task - tossing cocaine to the base - he had to train all his skills, but he managed to bypass all detectors. He could be proud of himself.

All he had to do now was get to Cancun, where Jyan Wa lived with a few friends and where the rest of the group was waiting for him. He wondered if any of them had found Oggy. This girl could not dissolve in the air! And yet they had been looking for her for almost a year and without the slightest result. They involved all the familiar vampires all over America, and nothing. The Mexican trail seemed plausible, but instead of Oggy, they got into the Hunters squad and barely escaped them. They had to separate to mislead them, and they were still not sure if their assembly point had been exposed. It was also close to Gerard, who accidentally fell into their hands, to end up as an anatomical preparation. Fortunately, thanks to Silver's help, he managed not only to survive, but to pay back the Hunters for everything more than once. He didn't get to Cancun until the morning.

"We can't leave you alone for a moment," Never said after hearing his narrative. "In addition, you gave this Indian a spare document, so you must have reason in your heel. But never mind. We're going to Europe. Everything seems to indicate that Oggy has left America. Velvet called me. The Los Angeles airport cashier recognized Oggy in the picture."

"That's good."

"Yes, but I'm afraid that we will hit the blind track again. For now, we need to ensure better communication."

Theo handed Gerard a strange object, reminiscent of an enlarged telephone handset with an antenna.

"What is this rubbish again?" The actor grunted belligerently.

He did not like modern gadgets more than Fronda, who, however, forced himself to use them, even when he did not quite understand what they were to serve. This sometimes led to funny misunderstandings - for example, the credit card was initially considered a kind of fancy business card and demanded that a few more be printed.

"It's a cell phone," he explained. "Don't grimace, I don't like it either, but it's supposed to be very useful. Jyan Wa persuaded Rajah to give us this, and he thought it was a good idea. Maybe he is right, who knows?"

There was doubt in his voice. He used to say that "modern facilities" only complicate people's lives and you should throw them all away quickly. Gerard shrugged and put the bulky item in his pocket.

"Let it be," he said. "And you know where exactly Oggy flew?"

"Yes, we know. She bought a ticket to Sevilla, so she probably flies to Octavio. As soon as Gladiator returns from shopping, we go to the airport."

"No way," Theo interjected belligerently. "Today is Halloween, and in Mexico Dia de Muertos, the fun will start in the evening, I will not miss such an opportunity."

Gerard looked at him with big eyes. His friend's voice sounded almost normal, instead of being limited to a soundless whisper, as in recent months. Only now did it reach him.

"Fronda, you have regained your speech!"

"I think it's cool, huh? And if you force me to leave today, I will start cursing so that your ears will fade."

Never waved a hand hopelessly. He knew from experience that nothing would convince him when Theo insisted on something. He wanted to say something, but a knock on the door interrupted him. It couldn't be Gladiator, because he always came in like a bomb and never knocked. Just in case, Never unlocked the small pistol in his pocket and only then called out:

"Please come in!"

Jyan Wa, called Velvet, and Jackie Liar, a former commando, entered the room. They had been together for some time and joined the Mexican vampire commune together, led by a rather mysterious Enbomb. This short, muscular man never showed up without a black hood with holes for his eyes, covering his face, and a black suit of military cut. He shied away from people and his countryman. Never, and his companions, did not even see him, despite quite a long stay in Mexico.

"Are you already gathering?" Velvet asked regretfully. "We were hoping that you would help us solve the riddle of *La novia del dia de los muetos*[8].

"What the devil?" Asked Gladiator, who had just walked in, laden with purchase items. Friends suspected that the word "booty" would have been more suited to his gains, but for the sake of peace, they did not raise the subject.

"*La novia del dia de los muetos*, ho, ho," Jackie the Liar began grimly, settling himself in one of the armchairs in front of a TV mumbling in Spanish. "This is one of the unsolvable matters entrusted to us two. Velvet and I are like a branch of the agents of the local group, but we are not doing well. Mexico

---

[8] Bride of the day of the dead (Spanish).

is swarming with secrets and those that are better not to be looked at closely."

"Talk to the point! Tripe is ripped out of man..."

"Every year, exactly on Halloween here, there are mysterious murders. Both men and vampires are victims. The police then find their bodies, dried to the bone. They look like very old mummies turned into plastic. In order not to cause panic among the locals, the police keep it secret and look for some solution. Velvet and I are also looking for it, but to no avail. All we know is that the woman is responsible for these murders. Two years ago, we saw her killing a tourist, which is why we gave the case the code name *La novia del dia de los muetos.*"

"Good one," Never murmured. "What does she look like?"

"We don't know," Jyan Wa said. "We only saw the dark outline of her body. She is black and wears a kind of black sari, but her hair is flaming red. We know so much."

"Well, that's a lot, don't be so modest again. How she kills?"

"This is the scariest thing, simply by touch. From what we have seen, it would appear that the victim is not even trying to defend himself or flee. Last year, Diego, one of ours who was warned by us like others, was killed, and he was certainly careful. Nothing helped him. This lady is neither human nor vampire, it is something much worse."

Theo whistled softly. He liked it. A dangerous woman who only appears in one night... The case smelled of the row he liked.

"So, will you help?" Jackie Liar asked hopefully.

"All right," Never agreed reluctantly. "We'll sleep the day to have clarity and strength. Come for us at dusk, we will look for this killer. Do not imagine, however, that we have some supernatural abilities. We solved the issues we have solved so far mainly with the help of ordinary human logic and a little bit of luck. Maybe we will come across something, and maybe not."

"Okay," Jyan Wa pleased, and fell out of the room with his friend as if he was afraid that Never would change his mind.

*****

They left early dusk. According to Jackie the Liar's revelation, the Halloween Bride prowled along the seashore, and she never ventured deep into the city. It wasn't strict - after all, no one knew where she was, but her victims were indeed found on the beach. Amused people in bizarre masks had to be unaware of the threat, just like the ubiquitous children dressed up as various ghosts. Everywhere laughter and children's voices shouted:

„*La dulce o la truco*[9]!" which was a nod to American tradition.

The streets were lit by colorful lanterns made of thin tissue paper, here and there mariachi bands in traditional Mexican costumes played, grills and ovens were cooking in the alleys, on which tortillas were fried. Both rich and poor had fun, singing and dancing straight on the street. Observing this exuberant, unrestrained gaiety, it was easy to forget that Mexico is in fact a country of tragic social contrast - on the one hand, rich, dabbled in luxury entrepreneurs, on the other a bunch of poor people living on the street and fighting with each other for every occupation, which can bring at least a few pesos.

---

[9] Trick or treat (Spanish).

The former owners of these lands, the Indians, are often in the worst situation, often deprived of even the necessary minimum living and vegetating day by day. On a day like this, however, everyone had fun, even the poorest - anyway, they are amazingly cheerful people, catching every opportunity to laugh and have fun.

Friends easily tuned into the general tone. Dressed up as musketeers (Fronda's idea), they patrolled the beaches, looking for anything that might prove suspicious. Sometimes they separated for a moment to take part in dances or races, which are a popular form of fun here, but they immediately gathered together in a group. They had a specific task to do and tried not to forget about it for a moment. The weakening of vigilance could prove tragic, and how easy it was for such a night...

It was three in the morning when they wandered to a distant part of the beach. They had not noticed anything suspicious so far and were tired of it all. Had it not been for Velvet and Jackie, they would have returned to the hotel a long time ago, but they assured them that *La novia del dia de los muetos* would definitely show up, you just have to wait. They were looking at various nooks, because they knew that this terrifying figure did not appear in the crowd, that she rather hunted loners who separated from others. So far, nothing indicated that anything would disturb the course of the play, but it was decided not to weaken vigilance until dawn.

"Although it is not excluded that this year this lady will change the modus operandi," Never said, suppressing a yawn.

And just at that moment they saw her, not far from them. She stood on the breakwater, looking at them through the eyes, in which a deep red overflowed, like inside a carbuncle. They didn't make the slightest move. There was an amazing split in their minds, because on the one hand something was screaming in their brains that they would run away as soon as possible... on the other hand they would not want it. Aware of the danger, they waited with orgiastic trembling in every fiber of the body.

They watched, entranced as she descended on the sand and slowly approached them, and the ocean, like a tide, escaped deep into its pool, leaving jellyfish, starfish and seaweed on the sand. She certainly wasn't human. Her skin looked like a perfectly black body - it did not reflect the slightest quantum of light, absorbing every ray falling on it. The fiery hair looked like real, vivid flames. They writhed and twisted around a still face in which those amazing eyes shone, glowing with uniform red, devoid of pupils and proteins. Despite the awareness of the danger that threatened them, they couldn't move, fascinated like birds, hypnotized in fairy tales by the eyes of a hungry snake.

She walked toward them, and the sand glazed into a bluish glaze when touched by her narrow, bare feet. Delicate fabric cut from the side to the hip of the dress fluttered in a light breeze. Her hem touched the legs of Jyan Wa, who stood closest. The Chinese immediately shrunk like a dried mummy and fell lifelessly on the sand, at the foot of *La novia del dia de los muetos.* She stopped halfway and looked at him, for what they thought, with regret. It was enough for the rest to regain their ability to move and disperse in panic fear in all directions.

Only Fronda remained in place, not taking his eyes off the strange creature, like enchanted. He seemed not to know the danger and not hear the desperate calls of his friends, just looking at the inhuman, beautiful and scary face so far away from him. *La novia del dia de los muetos* raised her head and looked him in the eye. Then something happened that no one understood: Theo threw himself abruptly, covered the girl's mouth with a bandana from his neck and kissed her through this cover.

Friends blindfolded their eyes, expecting that Fronda would immediately turn into a dried mummy, like Velvet, but... nothing like that happened. *La novia del dia de los muetos* stepped back with a low, prolonged hiss, sounding like some incredible whisper, and then, without taking her eyes from Fronda, she walked back towards the water, walking backwards. After a moment, her figure dispersed in a cloud of fog that came from the depths of the ocean, like steam from a giant kettle.

"You are crazy, you know?!" Never shouted angrily at Fronda. "It's a miracle you're still here!"

"I don't understand... I don't understand what happened..." moaned Jackie the Liar, kneeling over what was left of his friend.

Fronda touched his lips with his hand. He was still standing, looking at the now hazy ocean shore, as if he wanted to read some secrets from it.

"I know her," he said dumbly. "I've met her before."

And despite asking friends he didn't want to say anything more.

The matter had to be considered unsolved and more mysterious than anything they had dealt with so far. They knew only one thing - this is not a phenomenon from this world and that, although deadly dangerous, it harms people unknowingly. Never, smarter and more experienced than others, said directly that judging from what everyone saw, no fight with this being was possible. He did not think that she could be hurt by any means known to humanity.

"If there is any Hell, she comes from within. This is beyond doubt," he said grimly at the end of his argument.

Everyone was upset by this strange, unspeakably scary and fascinating meeting. They knew that they would never forget *La novia del dia de los muetos* and what they felt when she approached them - some hideously promiscuous, sadomasochistic, painful pleasure that penetrated their bone.

"If there is a devil, then she is," said Jackie the Liar, formulating Never's thought in his own way. Jyan Wa's death shook him deeply, but he seemed more shocked by his own reaction. After all, Jyan Wa could have been in place and, what's worse, he desperately wanted it when she approached them, black, with fiery eyes and waving fire around the elongated head. He had to go back to the commune and tell them what he saw, although he felt that he would gladly keep this experience only for himself. He knew he would never be the same man as before.

It wasn't until many years later that Never and his company learned that since then *La novia del dia de los muetos* had stopped visiting Cancun.

*****

"Is this Segovia reliable?" Gerard asked uncertainly.

Something in Never's voice disturbed him as if he were receiving a telepathic warning. Until now, the former big screen lover did not show any talents in this direction, but for some time he felt some extension of his intuitive abilities. Undoubtedly, he began to mature as a vampire - a little late, but within the time norm.

Never looked at him thoughtfully. Although the decision to "preserve" this man rather spontaneously, without thinking, he never regretted it. Gerard Phil, the green-eyed elf, turned out to be a great companion, a friend you can count on in every situation. A life that had already broken many who were stronger and tougher than he was, could not harm him.

"He's insane," he replied. "But he knows more than anyone. If anyone can help us find Oggy, it's him. If I hadn't been so afraid of her, I'd have gone into hell rather than his home."

"Interesting. When you lost me, you didn't ask him for his opinion."

"Don't be too smart, because your stomach will hurt. I didn't know where he was hiding then, I know now. Unfortunately."

Theo, leaning over the road map, straightened up and brushed his hair from his forehead.

"Rajah, you have seen a lot in your life," he asked. "Tell me why you hate Segovia so much? Why are you so afraid of him?"

"Because this monster is my father," Never shortly replied.

There was silence in the car. Everyone knew that Never never loved his father, but it was widely believed that he neither knew where he was nor was interested in it. Arthur Neville contributed to his birth, but otherwise they did not have anything in common. They didn't even think that the mysterious Segovia and Never's father were the same person.

Initially, they did not intend to contact him. You entered Segovia's headquarters at your own risk, because you never knew if the guest would leave the place. However, many vampires benefited from the encyclopedic knowledge of an old madman who seemed to know everything about everything. He made himself pay dearly for the service, and at the same time drew some perverse pleasure from the fact that everyone loses courage before his face.

"You don't like your daddy?" Gladiator asked sarcastically, simultaneously turning on the windscreen wipers, as small rain droplets began to tap on the roof of the car. "It happens. We do not choose parents. My old man is sitting in a big house, because he hit his neighbor with an ax, and in addition a head of the village who wanted to defend him. It is ordinary in our region in Podhale."

"Watch out for the road," Never advised him. "When you start to groan, you forget where you are going."

He was angry and gloomy. Ever since Oggy disappeared, without even leaving the letter on the table, he couldn't recover. He kept telling himself that they didn't care about her enough, though it was obviously absurd - Oggy didn't need a nanny. However, there was something disturbing about her sudden disappearance. She left all her handy little things, even a laptop, with which they did not know what to do. At first, they waited, then they started looking for her using all their contacts. So far, to no avail.

The trail obtained in Mexico led to Spain, where they were awaiting an unpleasant surprise. The perfectly organized Octavio di Mauro's research station stood empty, dark and quiet. The entire apparatus was dismantled and carried out, it is not known where, the few furniture left overgrown with cobwebs. No sign of residents. Despite a very thorough search, they did not find anyone who had any connections with the station or its creator. It would seem that everything that was associated with this place was only dreaming for them, were it not for the detectors and other small items that they had received from Octavio. So the institute was actually moved. In telephone conversations, Octavio ignored the topic, so that they thought that despite everything he decided to stay with his people where he was. Meanwhile, no. And what is worse, the trail stopped here.

That's when Never came up with the idea to get information from Segovia. Perhaps this thought was given to him by the name of the city they came to and from which Segovia took his nickname. Apparently during the inquisition he was Torquemada's assistant there, or rather his opponent, no one knew exactly how it was. One of the other friends he met knew his current address in Belgium, and Never decided to take a chance. And here they were on the road again. They ran in turn, day and night, not wanting to waste time.

"How far?" He asked impatiently.

"Tisze jedziesz, dalsze budziesz,[10]" Gladiator answered calmly.

"Remember, we're looking for the town of Lissans," Theo reminded him sternly.

"And where is it?"

"Yanek, has anyone ever told you that you have beautiful azure eyes?" Fronda asked with apparent calm as he folded the map.

"It happened, especially at the party."

"Then why the hell don't you look at the signposts with those beautiful azure eyes?! If you're savvy, you'll find the way!"

For the first time since his unpleasant adventure with the airplane, Theo could scream as he used to, and he used it with

---

[10] You go slower, you will be further (Russian).

pleasure. His voice problems suddenly stopped, just as it began, probably due to the shock of his friend's disappearance.

"I preferred it when you spoke in a whisper," Gerard shuddered as he managed to get away from the noisy way of Fronda being.

"Maybe you will be so kind and drive the car?" Suggested Gladiator. "It's wet, it's raining, when I step in the gas, I can put us in a ditch."

He was still hurting words when he spoke French and when he used English. As Never said, his ears hurt when someone talked to him for a long time, but friends did not lose hope that they would slowly educate him. Unfortunately, it had some difficulties. The fair-haired Pole was not stupid, but he hated science, so there could be no question of him learning something of his own free will. Only learning by the conversational method had some hope, but it was arduous and fraught with difficulties.

"There is no way," Theo protested vigorously. "I was driving all last night, now it's your turn."

"It's a pity, because Gladiator leads like a monkey," Never murmured, and asked aloud. "Where are we?"

"If it's Tuesday, we're in Belgium," Gerard quoted the title of the popular film, unable to resist the opportunity.

Theo leaned out of the car at an angle of an accident and scanned the area carefully.

"Turn left, Yanek," he commanded, returning to his seat. "There is a signpost and I think I know what Don Refugio meant by describing Segovia's headquarters.

"Everyone rushed to the windows. Somewhere behind the crossroads, above which a dilapidated signpost waved, a small castle stood. It looked like a miniature of a real medieval castle. It wasn't much bigger than a regular villa, but the details of the fortifications were meticulously impressive. Especially on the road they had behind them and over two days of wandering around the Ardennes, along roads from which, with a little carelessness, it was easy to go straight into the abyss.

The surroundings where don Refugio sent them were sparsely populated - just a dozen or so farms scattered far from each other. From time to time they passed a town or settlement, but in general the trail they followed was quite lonely. Still, they came across Hunters once when they had to go to a gas station. They were not looking for them, it was visible, but they recognized them immediately and there was a regular battle. Luck, however, was conducive to the "bloodsuckers' band." The station owner called the police, who arrested the hunters as an offensive side, and four friends, after being IDed, set off on a further journey. They could peacefully carry out their search, now successful.

"A monument?" Gladiator asked doubtfully. After an adventure in a haunted house, he suffered an injury to the monuments.

"No, it's too small for the original. Maybe a museum?" Gerard gave up.

"Who would put a museum right here in the middle of nowhere? Something seems to me that our Segovia is financially well positioned," Theo remarked as he got out of the car.

Others followed his example, relieved to straighten their legs after sitting for hours in the car. The rain had stopped now, but the swirling clouds were still obscuring the stars and the moon, and there was unpleasant humidity.

Up close, the castle made an even stranger impression, mainly because the windows set in the lead shutters were of thick, dark purple glass. Somewhere inside the light was on, judging by the faint glares in almost black windows. This compounded a ghostly impression, even though for a vampire castle this building was too clean, not damaged at all. It gave the impression of being freshly erected, and certainly has been painted recently. In the light of the car's headlights, it was clear that the paint had not darkened, and the metal parts glowed like polished glass.

"Hmm, something is wrong here..." murmured Gladiator, who felt good only when he was surrounded by a terrible mess. Even a military drill failed to change this feature of his character.

It was not given them to contemplate the building for a long time, because the arched door opened silently, explicitly inviting them inside.

"Well, we can only keep going," Never sighed and stepped forward with obvious reluctance.

"Come on in, softs! What is with you?" An imperious, unpleasant, female voice came from it.

"Oh, fair lady, probably in trouble," Theo was pleased.

A slim girl in black pants and the same tight sweater stood in the brightly lit corridor. Her short-cut hair was dark copper, which in combination with the sharp features and sharpness of her gaze irresistibly reminded Valkyrie. She was full of firmness and strength of character. She looked at friends with repulsive superiority, which at first glance betrayed a militant feminist.

"What have you been hanging around for so long?" She asked. "We've been waiting for you since yesterday."

"We're lost," Never said cautiously. "And we ran into hunters..."

"Typically male. Come now. Just wipe your legs first so you don't carry mud! And you, coquet, don't stare at me like that. Nothing will come of it."

Fronda, to whom this last remark was addressed, snorted a bit, but rather for show. He wasn't used to offending women, which was a rudimentary remnant of his knighthood.

"Forgive me, honey, I haven't heard your name..." he said after a while, carefully wiping shoes on the doormat, as instructed.

"Because I didn't mention it. And say "honey" to me again and you will end up on the street."

"Oh, kitty, I like that," Theo whispered to Gerard with obvious delight.

Women who pushed him away were a double fascinating object of desire. It is true that there were few of them. He usually won the lady with a preliminary fight.

The miniature castle was as clean inside as outside, and even more so. Stylized furniture and candelabra were vacuumed with museum diligence, and the floors shone like mirrors. Passing through the rooms, friends looked at their feet, not to destroy anything, and Gladiator muttered some Polish curses to himself. At one point he could not even stand and said loudly that he would prefer public flogging than one day in this "hotel for retired surgeons". Where this comparison came from, he did not explain.

"Nobody invited you here," the girl said bitterly. "Talk to Segovia and get out, if you can't appreciate order."

"But we appreciate, appreciate... Do not pay attention to Gladiator, he has a mess in his head and always say something stupid." Theo calmed her, assuming the sweetest possible tone.

"Let me not hit you," the highlander growled belligerently.

"Grammar also sucks. Silence this gorilla, or into the cage with him," the girl opened the door at the end of the corridor behind the rooms. "We're going down, watch the heads. Quite a low ceiling here."

A narrow staircase led to the underground, which amazed everyone. It looked like a natural cave - perhaps it was - its walls were inlaid with mica tiles, and the bottom was covered with sand. The light of the lamps, obscured by shades of translucent minerals, fell on the few furniture of bizarre shapes and unclear purpose. All this was in tones from blood red to dark purple.

"My God, it's hell..." muttered Fronda, appalled.

Indeed, one could have such an impression. What they saw was still less frightening than some indefinite horror that seemed to fill this place to the last corner.

"What have you grown into the earth?" A dry, ironic voice was heard suddenly, until they jumped.

Segovia grew up next to them. He was obviously amused by such theatrical effects, because he was smiling with satisfaction, measuring the newcomers with cool eyes.

He did not look particularly threatening, he made a rather pleasant impression. Theo even thought that he had never seen such a typical Englishman. A little more than average height, very slim and elegant, with light blond hair, carefully combed back and gray-blue eyes in a long, angular face, looked a bit like David Bowie.

"Dea, my dear, leave us alone," he asked with exquisite kindness.

Valkyrie, bearing the divine nickname, disappeared in the corridor, and Segovia walked slowly toward something resembling an abstract armchair and sat back comfortably.

"I knew that one day you would want my help," he said.

"We don't want help, just information," Never corrected. "It's about our friend who disappeared in mysterious circumstances. We have to find her."

Segovia looked at him with cold, endless irony in his eyes. In no case could you guess that they were bound by blood, they were so different. It seemed, however, that it did not matter for one or the other.

"Your friend is a werewolf," he said. "I also know that she hasn't disappeared just like that. It's a fatter thing and maybe it would be better if you didn't find her."

"She was in despair after losing a child, maybe she didn't know what she was doing?" Gerard interjected. Segovia didn't seem moved.

"That she got pregnant and gave birth was already a miracle... Only male werewolves can reproduce, female are sterile. What happened was probably the result of planned action, someone really wanted this child to be born. I admit it is an interesting experiment. It is a pity that it was not capable of life, although it probably was also planned."

"But how? Why?" Never asked in a daze.

"Dea would better explain it to you. She is a xeno-medic. She specializes in diseases affecting vampires, werewolves and the like, and in diseases that cause contact with the above-mentioned people."

"Who could hurt our Oggy this way?" Theo clenched his fists involuntarily.

"The one who could profit from it," Segovia replied mysteriously. "All werewolves have subconscious telepathic contact with each other. Besides, nobody really wanted to hurt her. She's too valuable. Lycanthropes are very rare today."

He clearly enjoyed teasing guests and making them aware that they know as much as nothing, and it depends on him whether they will know a little more. Never restrained his desire to leap into his throat. Instead, he stuffed his hands in his pockets.

"And when we find her, what then? Octavio could probably help her, but where to look for him now? Do you know where the research station was moved from Spain?"

"No. Even I don't know that and I'm curious. I can only tell you that, although it is physically impossible, the station equipment and its employees have dissolved in the air."

He seemed truly intrigued and Never could finally afford a smile.

"We'll look for them as soon as we find Oggy. Can you at least show us the direction of the search, is that too much for you?" He asked. Segovia shrugged.

"It's always worth looking where you haven't looked yet. And in this case especially... Who would care about casting your wolf and who would have enough strength for it? I will tell you, because in essence I like you: Hunters have at their disposal the strangest individuals."

Friends looked at each other without a word. Some vague suspicion began to drift through their heads, still difficult to grasp, but still quite clear. Only Gladiator was unhappy and expressed it bluntly.

"Damn you, you know what you want to tell us... Any Pythia under gas would say the same thing," he said contemptuously and bluntly.

Segovia smirked. Slowly, he got up from his seat and walked over to Gladiator, who was backing away without taking his eyes off him until he hit the wall with his back. He couldn't tell what later frightened him, but he shook like a leaf in the wind before Segovia took pity on him and left him alone. He now believed that it was impossible to look this strange individual straight in the eye. What he saw there scared him to death, though he could not put it into words.

"Go now, you bore me," said their demonic host. "And you'd better forget the road to this house."

"There's no fear," Never murmured, turning away from him with relief.

They left the underground with dizziness and a strange disgust in their mouths. All four felt terribly weak, as if after prolonged physical exertion, and terribly hungry. Upstairs, in the living room, where there was as exemplary order as everywhere in this strange house, an unexpected refreshment was waiting for them - a battery of canned blood bottles, cognac and orange juice.

"Thank you, Dea," Never said, starting to mix drinks quickly. "That's very kind of you."

"I don't care about courtesy." She said reluctantly.

Now, in the light of the candelabra, they saw that she was not as young as they previously thought, rather she looked like a middle-aged woman, not a teenager. It was the slim figure and elastic movements that rejuvenated her.

"Everybody went out barely alive from Segovia," she said. "He's an energy vampire. He drains energy by air osmosis from anyone in his cave, and can do so thanks to the microsphere formed by the mineral crystals around him."

"What kind of... sphere?" Fronda asked in astonishment, having greed sip first. He poured pure cognac into the empty glass.

"Urgh. I won't give you a lecture. In any case, the air in the cave is thick with electric charges. That's why I don't go there."

Never drank and came over to her with a glass in his hand.

"Segovia said you were a xeno-medic. Have you worked on Marfan syndrome with vampires?" He asked.

"No, why?" Dea looked at him in surprise.

"See, I..." Never didn't finish the sentence, but Dea understood him half a word.

"Undress," she said.

"What?"

"Urgh. Well, drop the rags," the girl was supported by Fronda, amused. "Are you waiting for the background music or would you prefer pole dancing?"

Slightly lingering, the Indian took off a dark blue silk shirt and narrow pants. He always dressed in a similar way and what looked funny and pretentious to others, suited him perfectly.

Dea examined his slender, but muscular, olive body from head to toe and checked the elasticity of her muscles with her touch.

"Some strange Marfan," she murmured.

She listened with a stethoscope, knocked, checked neurological reflexes and muscle tension. Finally, she calmly announced.

"It is not it. Or rather, not exactly. I have already encountered such cases among vampires. This is the so-called Doyle syndrome. There are some physical similarities to Marfan in its pure form, but the patient has normal musculature, as in your case. However, there are almost always other anomalies, for example, facial deformities to a much greater extent than anyone would have liked. You are not in any danger because it would have been shown long ago. You have a different feature, however peculiar, but less visible: everything indicates that you have a doubled heart."

"What?!" Fronda choked on his cognac and began to cough.

"You heard. I clearly picked up tones of two hearts instead of one. However, this is not dangerous. Such his beauty. Well, get dressed, don't stand like Lot's wife."

"Something similar... And I bet that our Raja has no heart at all," Theo uncapped a bottle of whole blood and relished it with an impressed expression, drinking cognac.

Never slowly began to put on clothes.

"I was afraid for centuries that my Marfan syndrome would become active," he said. "My mother suffered from this. I was still looking for signs and it seemed to me..."

"You thought wrong," Dea interrupted. "People with Marfan syndrome are physically weak, almost imperfect, and you're a big man. The worst are patients who read about a disease and have all the symptoms. You are okay and don't fall into hypochondria a second time."

"I'm a doctor too, though without a diploma," said Never. "I studied in England."

She looked him up and down.

"Yes... And it's even worse. So, you should know that if you actually suffered from this disease, you would look like a gut. There is no reason to adjudicate on the disease only on the basis of physiognomy, understand? And don't absorb knowledge that overwhelms you."

"Hallelujah," said Gladiator, though he did not understand much of this lecture. He was probably drunk now.

"Are you a doctor then?" Fronda gave the girl a seductive look and moved closer. "Why are there so many medics among vampires? You, Stasiek, doctor Kralova, Lidka, even Rajah, although he never practiced..."

Dea winced slightly and began to mix her drink.

"I think it's powerlessness. We are still facing deaths that we cannot overcome, we are still counting on the next years to discover another method of therapy, new drugs... For us, the temptation to preserve is really huge. But in my case, it was different. I just thought that aging and dying are idiocy if you can prevent it. And I could, thanks to my mentor."

"Nice. Did he call you Dea? A nice name."

"Rather idiotic," she said emphatically. "Just moron. Tantor, however, thought differently, and then somehow it stayed. I didn't protest, it's a waste of energy. In the end, it doesn't matter what the name is."

There was silence. Friends sipped their cocktails, feeling blissful laziness. They did not want to leave this peculiar place, even though the demonic Segovia was lurking underground. Something told them that it was difficult to find a safer shelter than this miniature castle. However, they could not, even if they really wanted to, prolong their visit indefinitely.

"So, we didn't get more information and we must find Oggy" Gerard sighed after a moment. „Where is she? How does she manage all alone?"

„I'd rather worry about those who would tease her on the go. And about what form it will be when we find it. I don't know if there's anything worse than a furious werewolf" Fronda said grimly.

„We have vaccinated her against rabies, remember? Then what she bites the vet's ankle."

Never chuckled at the memory while buttoning his shirt. He quickly finished his drink and rushed friends to the door, not wanting to abuse Dei's hospitality. After all, he did not trust her, if only because she lived with Segovia. In addition, he felt somehow uncertain in her company, though he couldn't explain why.

"You just don't like strong women" Fronda said when her friend confessed everything in the car.

"Maybe" the Indian answered. „I'm exhausted anyway. Let's go back to the lowlands because it's going to be storm."

The fear of storms common among vampires is logically justified, as Gusto Vanderbelt proved this: people "fixed" ionize the air within a radius of five centimeters from the surface of the body, which makes them much more likely to be struck by lightning than others. Not all vampires, especially the older ones, accepted this without hesitation. When Theo heard about this, he demanded strongly to show him these "ions" because, as he said, he would not believe in such nonsense. However, whether Gusto was right or not, the problem remained. During the storm, no vampire dared to stick his nose out of the hiding place.

Fiends drove maybe ten miles when their car suddenly gnawed and fall with all four wheels into the ground. Despite repeated attempts several times, the engine did not want to work, although the tank was full and the employee of the rental office swore that it was "almost a new one".

"Well, so we've arrived," said Gladiator, coming to the side of the road.

„That damn trash…!" Never bellowed, kicking the tire, then threw a steak of amazingly colorful words.

It was more than he could handle. The disappearance of Oggy, the skirmish with the Hunters, meeting with Segovia, and now a car breakdown, all this caused that he lost his usual self-control. Friends waited patiently for him to get tired, because in this condition, no persuasion could reached him. Only when he was so exhausted and leaned helplessly on the car, Theo put his hand on his shoulder and said:

„We have no choice man. We need to go on foot and pray that we won't meet hunters. Next time, we may have less luck,"

As if in response to these words they heard the steady sound of horse hooves. Although it was hardly possible for the Hunters to hunt them on horseback, they hurriedly armed themselves with whatever anyone could. Never and Theo took their revolvers from the car, Gerard grabbed the tire bucket, and Gladiator the fireman's hatchet, which they carried in the trunk. The tent came closer, and soon a large perscheron and a rider, a tall and quite fat man in a leather dress and wide-brimmed hat, appeared around the bend of the road.

„Something's wrong about the car?" he asked, stopping the horse with four friends.

„He broke down, bastard" Never briefly informed him. He felt as if he knew the low velvet voice from somewhere, but he had no strength to think about it.

"A storm is about to start" said the rider. „My farm is not far from here. You wait out the storm there and then we think what to do next."

„Do you think so?"

Never looked at friends. The invitation was suspicious, because who in their right mind invites four strange men to the house, in addition at night? But since the Hunters were hanging around, it was better to take the risk. The only alternative was to stay where they would be exposed to rain and storm. The rain was not so bad, but the lightning strike, for normal people was fatal in only thirty percent of cases, for vampires it was fatal in almost a hundred.

Straggle a little, they marched after the horse. Just in case, they inspected the area, trying to spot possible detectors, but nothing somehow alarmed their super-sensitive eyesight or hearing. As they entered the yard of a large farmhouse, the first thunder rolled over their heads. They hid quickly on the porch and waited for their guide to lead the horse to the stable. After a long moment he appeared, opened the door and led them into a cozy, though a bit petty-bourgeois interior, decorated in the nineteenth-century style. All the furniture was antique, and very valuable, according to Gerard, who was an expert in these matters. Fluffy Turkish rugs lay on the floors, carved paneling covered the walls.

There was no Hunters, only two large mutts greeted unexpected guests with barking and snarling, and the sleeping cat on the closet mewed lazily and stretched.

„Lie down!" shouted the host, taking off his hat and hanging it on a hook from deer antlers

„You like animals" Theo beamed, scratching the cat's back with one hand and stroking the head of the bolder dog with the other.

„Yes, I do" replied the mysterious savior. "I have horses, two donkeys, these rascals here, and some small livestock. With animals life is easier, but things are not so good with people.

He took off his riding boots and jacket, then invited friends to the salon in a beige tone. He kindly lit a fire in the old-fashioned fireplace and turned to his guests with a pleasant smile. Only now could they take a good look at him. He was not so young, maybe fifty, maybe older man, with a square face surrounded by graying beard and short-cut, gray hair. Despite his considerable overweight, he was a handsome chap and moved with amazing dexterity. There was something familiar about him, though at first none could specify what. They could have sworn they had never seen him, but they knew that smile and the black eyes under wide eyebrows from somewhere.

Theo recognized him first. He sat on the plush-lined sofa with a flourish and stared wildly at the man standing by the fireplace.

„Oh, Mother of God…" he groaned and in this groaning was everything he could say.

Never, who also recognized him, nodded melancholy.

"You've aged badly, Jean Claude" he said.

„Rajah, it... is it mean that I could look the same?" Fronda said, shocked, still unable to regain his balance.

„You? Certainly not! With your lifestyle, you wouldn't live till thirty, even without the battle of Limoges. Something else is important now. How did you know where we are, and that we are here?"

The actor did not respond immediately. He took a pipe from a decorative drawer, studded it on, and lit. Only then replied:

„It wasn't difficult. Hunters are looking for you and most of all they came to me. You know, it's ridiculous, but they still think I had something in common with you... Anyway, I knew from them that you are hanging around. I've been traveling and looking for you for three nights. I could afford it because I'm alone here. My family went on vacation. I had to stay because of my pets.

„Who is it?" Gladiator nudged Gerard.

"An old friend" Gerard answered him quietly and asked aloud. „Why were you looking for us?"

"What are you so distrustful, Fanfan?" I have my reasons.

The host took a few bottles of wine and glasses from the bar. The friends exchanged glances, then Never asked carefully:

„You know we can drink wine?"

"Sure, I know" Jean Claude said with undisturbed calm. „To avoid further investigation, I will tell you that I know Segovia well, and we are on first name terms with Dea"

„And what, are you not afraid of them?" Theo asked ironically. He remembered well that in the sixties, it was easy to him scarred young actor, and he smiled at the memory.

Jean-Claude raised his glass to his lips and smiled back. He smiled the same way he used to, but it was hard to believe that he was the same man. The impression he made was painful.

"I'm not afraid" he said calmly. „You know, it's weird, but after all that I went through because of you, I changed. I was never afraid of anything. I also ceased to care about what was important to me before. Of the things I couldn't live without, my family and this farm remained. The rest... it is unnecessary ballast. This attitude was useful to me because the offers of new roles did not come in through doors and windows, and if so, they were well-worn or hopeless ideas that were not worth accepting.

"Condolence" Fronda drank some wine and found it excellent. He hasn't drank better for a long time.

„To survive, I went to the theater. They wouldn't accept me anywhere, it was only after a year that one of the directors took pity on me. He gave me a job, but he provided blind obedience. When he tells me to play a coat hanger, he said, I should do it without murmuring. At the beginning it was the way it was. After some time, I got the first episode and had the opportunity to prove how much I am worth. I met Segovia when I was playing supporting roles. He came to me one day after the performance and said some nice words. He was very surprised when I met a vampire in him and I didn't start running immediately with a terrifying scream. He was so impressed that he offered me friendship."

"You're lucky that this friendship hasn't end badly" Never murmured.

Gerard took the gold signet ring from Gladiator and placed it on the dresser.

„Is it yours? Sorry, Yanek is a kleptomaniac" he said. „He can steal anything and everywhere. Last week, he took a bikini suit from the Armani collection and two bracelets from Harrods, and some days are much better. Wait, that thing is more important. Are you saying that you are friends with Segovia? You have indeed taken courage. I wouldn't have entered into any alliances with this weirdo even though I was the loneliest vampire on earth.

Jean-Claude casually put the ring into the drawer. It didn't seem like anything would surprise or surprise him.

"This arrangement suits us both" he explained. "Segovia doesn't attack my family and makes sure none of the local vampires dare to do it. And I help him with administrative matters and confuse Hunters."

"No wonder they don't love you" Theo chuckled.

„Where's your companion?" the actor changed the subject.

„I wish I'd know... We're looking for her. Can I have more wine? It is delicious."

„In minibar, you can handle. Drink as much as you want."

„No way" Never said vigorously. "If Fronda floods his stupid head, he'll always do some trick to us. And you, Yanek? You've sucked to the glass like a calf to milk? Leave it or you'll get stuck."

„No worries. We Poles have strong heads, and we never get drunk on wine. We need vodka for this, and in large quantities..." said Gladiator boastfully, pouring another portion of the drink. Unsuccessful theft, as we can see, did not spoil his humor.

„We are chit-chatting, and we miss the point: why did you invite us here? I won't believe that for our beautiful eyes."

Never returned to the right topic, seeing that there is nothing to argue with colleagues who will not listen anyway.

Jean-Claude looked at the window that was pouring heavy rain.

"I'd like to ask you a favor" he said after a moment. „I know that you travel around the world and still deal with this sphere of life in which most people don't even believe. I have a problem. Segovia would probably help me, but he would have to have some foothold, and there is none, and by the way, you know him.

„Finally, tell me what happened" Rajah urged him.

„Ten years ago my daughter got married and got her first child. They didn't want to show us the newborn. The doctors said it was a boy and he died soon after labor. They told us to buy a casket and made sure that nobody looked inside. The obstetrician explained that the child was so terribly distorted that it was better that no one in the family saw him. I didn't believe it. I bribed the gravediggers. After the funeral, at night, we dug up the grave and opened the casket. It was empty...

There was a silence in which only the downpour and the murmur of thunder were heard.

„What do you suspect?" Theo asked finally.

Jean-Claude looked up and looked him straight in the eye.

"There were werewolves in my family" he said slowly. „I knew it, but I hid this knowledge from everyone. The child... could have been different in some way."

„Haven't you tried to find out something?"

„I tried! However, I could not find any clue. Sandrine gave birth my two another grandchildren, completely normal, but I am haunted by the thought of that child. What could happen to him?"

Never rubbed his chin with his hand.

„We'll try to find out. I promise nothing, but we'll have eyes and ears open. I don't really understand why Segovia didn't help you... but ultimately his abilities are not limitless."

"I know why he didn't say something to him" said Gladiator, mutilating his syntax in his own way „He didn't want the guy to get into a swamp. I think he likes him."

„Yanek is a „sensor" so he may be right" Theo said thoughtfully. "If this child is alive, it's probably in the hands of either scientists or the army, or some dangerous organization." No offense, Jean Claude, but you're a comedian, not a soldier. If you tried to find out the truth on your own, you could die. Segovia might not want to help you, not because he likes you, but you are useful to him, that's all.

He stood up and, with a full glass in his hand, walked to the window behind which the storm was still raging. Looking how the sky is cutting with lightning, he thought with regret that this old, ruined man could still enjoy his youth and full strength, if only he had made the right decision some time ago. He felt like a doctor who could save a patient, but he refused to receive treatment.

„Why didn't you want me to fix you?" He asked abruptly, turning away from the window. „You preferred to grow old, lose your beauty, health and die finally as old man?!"

Jean-Claude laughed and filled his pipe again. He did not look like ‚old man' at all, he rather resembled a life-satisfied sybarite, who enjoys what he has.

„My dear, if you must know, I don't regret a single moment" he said emphatically. „I wouldn't like to be in your place. Unlike many people, I don't want to live forever, all I need is what is given to me as a human. And I received a really beautiful piece of cake called the World, you can believe me. I don't need more."

„Not the rich who has a lot, but the one who has what he has" muttered Gerard approvingly.

He picked up the framed picture that was on the TV and looked at it closely. It represented a stout, fair-haired woman and four teenagers of both sexes. The woman, although she looked very nice, but not so beauty, neither the youth.

„You didn't give your children a beauty legacy" he said.

„Neither do you" answered the host calmly. „Your daughter is not pretty at all, and son looks like your caricature. He is now a TV presenter and I often watch programs with his participation. In the end this is probably not the most important thing. Claire probably didn't have many admirers. For me, however, she was Miss World and remained so to this day.

Gerard became sad and fell silent, trying to imagine what his children looked like now. Jean Claude's words awakened in him a strong sense of loss that nothing could make up for.

Never nodded slowly, and his golden eyes started glowing.

„You are right that beauty is not the most important thing. But it's nice when you have it."

„No. I used to think so, but I found it's not true. Have you read the stories of Alberto Moravia? In one he wrote: ‚In this world only things are beautiful, not people. And if people are beautiful, they also become things. They are bought and sold.'

He was right, I learned it myself. Beauty became my curse and almost destroyed my acting career. And I love what I do and I wouldn't like to do anything else, even if I were to be king tomorrow."

„Beauty is a gift from the gods. However, people cannot properly use it, which also applies to other divine gifts…" Never stopped and looked at Fronda when he heard his warning whistle. Theo got used to getting his friends' attention this way when he was suffering from aphonia, and until now he couldn't get rid of this habit.

„Hunters are outside. I saw them in the lightning. Turn off the lamp."

„Damn, your dogs are useless" Gladiator grunted at the host, grabbing his hatchet again.

„A lot of them, Fronda?" Never asked.

„I counted five."

„No worries."

Jean Claude opened the masked flap on the wall, revealing a modern control panel. He pressed a few buttons, and suddenly strong lights flashed around the house, and the stentor voice roared from the speaker where it was located:

„Give up, you are surrounded!"

„What a fun!" Gladiator squealed with delight as he saw the hunters dressed in military colors, running away.

„Great effect! I haven't heard of such alarm. You figured it out yourself?" Never asked, looking at Jean-Claude friendly and respectful.

„The actor, my dear, is an artist, and artists have good ideas, although they are often unable to implement them themselves" he replied. „The idea was mine and the implementation of a colleague, a specialist in special effects. Even if the attacker has the strongest nerves, he is scared away, especially since the 'electric shepherd' automatically turns on around the house. Only a family knows how to bypass wires and not get kicked by electricity."

„Clever" admitted Theo. „But tell us how we shall leave now?"

„The easiest way in the world. I'll just turn it off and take you to town. From there, a roadside assistance team will be sent to your car and the matter will be settled. There is nothing to panic. The storm has already died down."

Indeed, the thunder was no longer heard, and the last, late rain drops were tapping on the windows. The clouds parted, and a pale moon looked into the window. There was silence all around, which is only possible in sparsely populated, mountainous surroundings.

„You have a car?" Gladiator asked the host.

„Sure, one off-road car and one normal. Do you think I get on the film set on a donkey?"

„Certainly not, because a poor animal would fall under your weight to the ground. You don't deny yourself calories."

„I like to eat, and I can't hide it. There are worse preferences."

„Yanek, put the watch away" Never said. „Damn, nothing is safe with you. There should be possible to find a psychiatrist for vampires who would take care of this freak... I'm sorry, man, he doesn't control it."

„It doesn't matter" the actor replied politely.

It seemed that he was enjoying this unusual situation perfectly and regretfully thinking about leaving his guests. However, there was no time to lose. The hunters could return in greater numbers, bring technicians with them and deal with the security of the house. It was too much to risk knowing their stubbornness and unscrupulous.

Driving on precarious roads, wet after a recent storm, was not quite safe, but it seemed that Jean-Claude didn't care about that. He ran with a steady hand, whistling quietly, and choosing rather the side trails. Friends thought he was doing this because of Hunters, but it soon turned out that it is not true. The actor unexpectedly stopped his car in some wild place, took a large bag from the seat next to him, got out without a word of explanation and went to what looked like the entrance to an underground karst cave. He whistled a soft tune. He repeated it twice more, and then something loomed in the opening of the cave.

„Watch out!" screamed Fronda, jumping out of the pickup truck.

A grayish mass came from the ground, forming slowly into a kind of tentacle, or rather an elephant's trunk. Jean-Claude reached into the bag, took some clumpy substance out of it, and handed it to the trumpet that sucked it in with a deafening sound.

„What's this?" Theo was clearly shocked. The analogy with what had attacked him in Stonehenge was obvious and superstitious. However, it seemed that the elderly actor did not think to be afraid of this creature.

„I don't know what it is" he replied, returning to the car in the most peaceful way in the world. „Segovia and I call it 'IT', and it probably fits best. From an anatomical point of view it's a brain endowed with the ability to absorb food directly. Dea called it a neuro-colloid. But how and why it came here, don't ask, I don't know."

„What did you give him?" Never asked curiously.

„It's a cluster of dog food. He likes Royal Canin for seniors the most."

„Do you even know what you are doing?" Theo still couldn't stand the impression. „It can be devilishly dangerous. The Stonehenge Beast had a similar build... and I wouldn't wish the enemy to meet her. I miraculously survived."

Jean-Claude led the pickup truck back onto the road.

„I don't know if it's dangerous," he said after a moment „It ate one tourist, several local hunters and two cows that have strayed here. They were considered as missing due to the activities of the smugglers group, but they confessed nothing. Now I know why. He has to eat, but he can't leave his cave because he would already do it. When I came across them, it was so starving that I felt it, although I'm not a telepath. Amazing impression, as if someone forced my feelings under my skull. I had meat for my dogs with me, I gave him half. It burned quickly, and I immediately sensed a change, a note of relief and satisfaction. Then I understood what happened to this missing tourist, hunters and cows."

„And you feed this neuro-jelly, even though you know how dangerous it is?" Gladiator asked, looking at him like he was crazy.

„Yeah... Sometimes Segovia does it to me, but usually I do it. You know, I just couldn't bear the thought that IT was starving here. Then it turned out that it is very useful for Segovia, it plays the role of a psychotronic amplifier. In other words, Segovia connects to him telepathically when he wants to know something, and He acts like a radar that searches for information in the air."

„Oh god" Gerard muttered. Somehow, he didn't like the image of living, all-eating jelly.

Theo probably had similar feelings, because after a while he said:

„I saw such a horror movie, ‚Blob killer'. There was also something similar there. I slept in the light for a week and woke up every now and then to see if it was going to jump on me from the ceiling."

Jean-Claude denied.

„Blob was a mindless being, a plasma, and He thinks and feels, though not quite like me or you. Since I feed them, no one else has died in these areas, so he does not kill for pleasure or to eat more than he needs. This is the quality of a rational being. If he's from an alien world and got here by accident, the situation is scary enough for him. I don't want scientists to be interested in it, so I cooperate with Segovia to keep its place secret. It's funny, but I feel responsible for IT as if it were my child. Maybe because of this, he sometimes makes empathic contact with me? I feel his trust and gratitude, just as I felt fear and paralyzing hunger the first time."

„End of the world. The last normal one went crazy" Never said loudly and closed the topic.

Arriving in the city, friends said goodbye to the actor and headed for the hotel. They were already very tired, and soon it was about to dawn. They had to hide in their rented room and sleep off this crazy night. They took the key from the receptionist behind the counter and went upstairs, yawning with fatigue. Now that they were safe, and their nervous excitement left them, they could barely stand on their feet and dreamed of finding themselves finally in bed. Never opened the door and turned on the light, then froze in surprise at the threshold.

„Finally. Where have you been hanging out so much time?" a sharp voice came from deep in the room

„Dea!" Gerard exclaimed in amazement.

„What are you doing here, girl?" Theo repeated to him, entering last and closing the door carefully behind him

„I have reasons" she said. „Immediately after your departure, I talked to Segovia. Your friend is probably in Australia."

„Where?" Never stared at her in amazement.

„For sure?" Gladiator wanted to know.

Dea gave him a look full of cold irony.

„And surely the Gypsy would know that, because she has cards" she said. „I'm telling you what Segovia didn't tell you."

„Everyone who believes in antipodes should be cursed. That's what Saint Augustine wrote."

After this declaration, Theo took a plasma container frozen in the form of snow from the hotel fridge. He put on a full cup and waited for the snow to become liquid while filling cups for others.

„It's kind of you, young lady that you came to us with this message" said Gerard, taking his cup and licking the snow with satisfaction. He liked this vampire ice cream very much.

„No fucking courtesy," Dea growled. „I'm just coming with you. This she-wolf may need medical attention once you find her. In addition, I am writing a monograph on the physiology of werewolves and I will need field research."

"Hope we'll find her." Gladiator sighed. „We've never been in Australia, I think she neither. What is she looking there for? It's a terrible continent: heat, drought, snakes, spiders and other abominations."

„It's quite big, too." Never said soberly „We need to know where to look for her, otherwise we can spend several hundred years of walking on a desert and catching kangaroos by the tails. I know what I'm saying because I was there."

Indeed, ten years earlier, he had allowed himself to leave his companions for two months to respond to the call of Australian brethren. He never wanted to say what he was doing then.

- You have a sensor with you, let it be useful for something! Dea became impatient.

She was looking at them so that now everyone, not just Never, felt uncomfortable. The radical worldview was nothing new among female vampires, but with Dei, all the feminists she met so far seemed suddenly docile to domestic friends. She really gave the impression of a Valkyrie, although as a vampire she was probably quite young, so her history did not go back to the Viking times. Undoubtedly, she had the soul of a leader and Never thought with some concern that if Dea joined them, he would not want to take the subordinate place.

„Honey let's get it straight out" he said firmly „I'm in charge here. If you want to come with us, please, but don't try to undermine my authority."

„Do you have any? It's interesting" Dea snorted with amusement. „Well, go to sleep now. I will bring mechanics to your car and get tickets."

„Are you a marten?"

„Yes. You don't mind it?"

„Not at all. Only when buying tickets remember that Theo and Gladiator hate the sun. That must be night flight" Never said resignedly, finding that he was too tired to discuss about the principles now. He hadn't slept in nearly two months, which even for him was a murderous marathon.

„Without You, I would guess that. You can sleep peacefully, I did it many times in my life. And, for God's sake, take a shower before going to bed! You are as dirty as a herd of piglets."

„Can you respect someone else's lifestyle?" Gladiator was offended.

„As long as you are in my company, you have to be clean. Then do what you like" Dea snapped and left.

„Perfect... we have a real tough women. Probably she will check us behind the ears..." Gerard sighed, obediently taking off his shirt. He was so tired that when he went to the bathroom he tripped over his own legs, but he preferred not to oppose the order of his new friend. Whatever you say about her, she was awe-inspiring.

*****

"What do you think it is?" Dea asked, showing her companions two short and narrow bags of rigid foil connected by an oval ring.

Friends sat on chairs arranged in a row, like pupils in a school class. Dea did not stop at forcing them to pay more attention to hygiene. Until now, only Fronda was a freak of chastity in this group. Others are rarely mistaken, taking advantage of the fact that, apart from extreme situations, they were not in danger of sweating their clothes and did not care about their caravan at all.

First of all, Dea told them to wash it thoroughly inside and outside ("You don't think I will get into a garbage truck!"), clean the stained upholstery and shake the rugs. Then she sent all their clothes to the hotel laundry and demanded a promise of daily hygiene, including cleaning their nails.

Also a lecture on the art of camouflage was her idea. Until now, friends didn't even think of branding food with people, no! They shuddered at the thought of taking something other than a liquid in their mouths. The vampire's esophagus is so narrowed that he can only feed on liquids, and in addition his body basically digests nothing but blood. The idea of confusing Hunters with a tongue overlay was really good - no Hunter would be interested in someone who is eating a cake or ham in front of his eyes.

"It's like a condom for a guy with two..." Theo said, examining the unknown object with surprise.

"Apparently, snakes have a double copulatory organ," Gerard joined Fronda, recalling a very old conversation with his stepson, passionate about natural sciences.

"For you, French, only one thing is meant. Although, I admit, the look is misleading. This is the so-called tongue element. The ring is put on the tongue. In vampires, tonsils along with part of the mucous membrane disappears in the first period after preservation. The empty spaces that remain are priceless for our plan. When you are at an official banquet, you are expected to eat like all other guests. You take a bite of food, chew and, by manipulating the tongue, push chewed food into bags. Then you go to the bathroom, empty the overlay, wash under water and put on again. Of course, it has a small capacity, and the process itself requires some practice, but such an action will fool the Hunters who could watch you. From today you start exercising."

With these words, Dea gave the men several sets of connected pouches.

"Nice things," Never murmured, looking at his cover with some reluctance. "Well, but the idea is not bad. Until now, only Theo was so kamikaze that he allowed himself, for example, ice cream, now he will be able to pretend that he also eats a waffle."

"Do you eat ordinary ice cream?" Dea was surprised, looking at Fronda with involuntary respect. She has not met such a thing yet.

"Yeah. And when white chocolate went on sale, he began to try it so eagerly that he licked the whole bar. You have no idea how he got sick later..."

"Not so much at all," Theo interrupted him, dissatisfied.

"Keep doing this and you'll ever tow away," the girl warned him. "It's not why someone is a vampire to devour things made for people. Noblesse obliges."

"How can you have a refined conversation with something like that in your mouth?" Gerard wanted to know.

"Adaptation issue. As a side note: pieces of food must be small! Otherwise you risk choking because you won't be able to control them. Avoid biscuits and shortbread, because it's easy to choke on."

Gladiator, who had already put on his cover, was pleased to note that it does not restrain the tongue as he thought and chuckled.

"Now the hunters will not recognize us from the crowd."

"You still have to learn how to use it so that nobody notices anything," Dea poured cold water on him. "You already have to be able to do it on the plane. In any case, it would be advisable."

Theo flinched miserably at the mere mention of the plane but said nothing. He preferred not to oppose this woman - she frightened him. She had nothing of the gentle Erzika or even of the dry and calculating Lenor. She did not resemble the women he had dealt with at all, and still the only term he found for her was "Valkyrie." The ease with which, according to Gladiator, "took them by the head" did not bode well for the future.

Dea was obviously not one of those who listened to anyone if they were convinced of the correctness of her opinion - she was rather made to be listened to. Even Never, slow to make concessions, put his ears down in a few days and did not try to oppose his new friend. Admittedly, Dea did not use her advantage. The main decisions were still made by Never, but she "kept order" and the boss himself did not dare to oppose her. Why? Nobody knew. Dea didn't scream, didn't throw herself at anyone with her fists or force anything by traditional means. She just had something in her that it was impossible not to listen to her when she gave the order. Even Gladiator, the horned Polish soul, listened to her, although he often grunted under his breath:

"Devil gave us this cow..."

They consoled themselves with the thought that after finding Oggy Dea would return to Segovia. For now, however, she governed in their company, as at home, which was not bad at all. It was she who arranged the repair of the rented pickup truck and personally returned it to the rental company, at the same time getting a big discount in the fee ("You pasted them a trash that broke down and you still have the audacity to say something about fixed tax!"). She quickly arranged visas, took care of plane tickets and luggage, as well as renting an all-terrain car on the spot (in the end they decided that they would not carry the camper with them to the other hemisphere, the fees alone would exceed their capabilities). When she learned that Fronda hates flying, she gave him a special drug without undue discussion, after which Theo slept all the way like an angel.

"I gave him a little too much," she commented with dissatisfaction. "But in fact, it's all the better, at least he won't cause us any trouble along the way, and het won't be smart aleck. The tripe falls over as he begins to talk."

They barely woke Fronda when it had to get off. Even on his way to the customs chamber he yawned and had to be poked so that he would not fall asleep standing up.

Australia welcomed travelers with unbearable heat. The air was dry and to hot, even now, at night, there was no slight breeze.

"Damn," groaned Gerard. "I can't stand it here."

"Pack in the trailer and turn on the ventilation," Dea advised him calmly.

The car she rented was waiting at Sidney airport. It was a solid roadster, equipped with a large caravan. The fan installed in it was activated by an additional battery, thankfully freshly charged. They crowded beneath him, delightedly putting their faces under a stream of cool air. Because it would be dawn soon and everyone was tired after the trip, they decided to postpone the search until dusk. They found a parking lot, paid for a parking space, closed the trailer from the inside and fell asleep with relief, not switching off the fan.

When they woke up, it was getting dark. They were hungry because they cautiously did not take blood supplies with them. If someone searched the luggage, they might have a hard time explaining why they could have canned blood, so they decided to stock up on the spot. The trouble was that they didn't know the local infrastructure at all and had no idea who to turn to. Even Never during his stay in Australia did not take care of establishing appropriate contacts.

"Urgh," decided the Indian after a brief deliberation. "We have to find a blood donation station and simply rob it. It's a bit risky, but I won't look for anyone there with an empty stomach."

"Neither do I," agreed Gladiator, who had a great appetite.

Dea unfolded the map of Sidney and soon they knew where to go. In the city itself there were four stations, including one near the airport, in addition connected to the blood bank. At this time it was closed for good, but Fronda's lockpick set coped with better locks than these. Fortunately, no one had the idea that someone could rob a blood bank, so the locks were pretty bad.

"Take only the oldest bottles," Dea whispered. "We don't care, and they would be destroyed after the expiry date. We won't harm anyone this way."

Theo and Gerard disappeared inside the building and after a while they left, laden with mesh full of plastic bottles. Dea took them from them and carefully put them in the tourist refrigerators. She wisely ordered three, because she was aware that feeding five vampires in the heart of the Australian interior can be difficult. This supply was to be an iron reserve. Now they hunted in the back of several pubs and only when everyone was sufficiently satisfied did they set off. If Oggy was here somewhere, then definitely not in the capital. That was what Segovia's informant knew about which the girl did not want to say anything.

Far beyond Sidney, Dea ordered the car to be stopped and turned to Gladiator:

"It's your turn now. Try to sense the direction in which to look."

In the case of werewolves, psych location is powerless, but the "sensor" can still catch the lead. And the fair-haired highlander was a good "sensor", although he had never used his abilities on such a scale.

"How can I do that?" He asked aggressively and gloomily.

"Above all, sit down." Dea forcibly set him down and laid out a map of Australia in front of him. "Here we are. You sit facing west. Hold the pen and try to plan a route."

Gladiator, shuddering a little, took his pen and froze in anticipation. He had to "tune" his senses to this place, just as the radio was tuned to a specific wave. The sense of the "sensor" had a limited range, not exceeding the area of one average large country, but there was hope that Oggy was within the range radius. Gladiator slowly began to enter a trance, cutting off his mind from everything that was unrelated to Oggy. He did not like this - to catch what is needed, the "sensor" must fall into a kind of very unpleasant lethargy, combined with apnea. In this state, all the functions of his brain are unbelievably intensified, so strong that it almost burns it from the inside. That is why the "sensors" use their abilities as rarely as possible.

The friends surrounding the highlander also sat motionless, not wanting to disturb him and waited with suspense what this supernatural scanning would bring. They thought they were sitting all night, when suddenly Gladiator's arm dropped and marked something on the map with the speed of lightning. At the same time, what held the highlander frozen in one pose disappeared and Gladiator sank to the ground, gasping for air with his mouth open. His body was wet with sweat, tears flowed from his eyes. He couldn't control his muscle twitching, until Dea, conscious as always, handed him a bottle of blood, cautiously hidden for this eventuality. Then she took the map and looked at it carefully.

"You marked place around Brisbane," she said. "It's in Queensland. We're going there now."

She jumped up from the ground and headed briskly to the cart. Tired to death, Gladiator got into the trailer with the help of his friends. He felt as if he had thrown a few tons of stones and would have gone to bed. His own body was unbearably heavy, but he knew from experience that this unpleasant fatigue would soon pass without a trace. Vampires regenerate very quickly.

"Lie down for a bit," Never told him, spreading the blanket on the floor of the trailer. "It's good that you are so strong because you could strain yourself."

"As if you didn't know what the trance threatens," said Gladiator, relieving his powerful body on the blanket with relief.

Never went to the cab, where Dea studied the road map diligently. They had already agreed that the two of them will drive, because Theo had a tendency to fall asleep above the steering wheel for some time, Gladiator was driving with great gusto, and Gerard had problems with orientation and Dea immediately announced that "she is not curious where to he could drove them if he took the steering wheel". She did not have the rare gift of orientation in every area that Theo boasted, but thanks to innate accuracy and knowledge, she always got where she wanted to go.

In general, she was full of surprises and something new was constantly being discovered. In spite of her love of order, she disgusted something undeniably gypsy. Perhaps that is why travel in all conditions was not a problem for her and she was ready to arrange herself in any place where fate throws her. Once, even as she confessed to Never, she took on a rather unusual form. As a human, she was a cloister in Majorca for several years - of her own free will. However, and in some cell in the area of the abandoned factory, where she lived then, she brought an exemplary order. If she hadn't met Tantor, she would probably still be living there. Tantor, a deadly handsome Greek, as she described him, took her to Capri and preserved her there, introducing her into the world of vampires.

Being in the state of Queensland, friends primarily stopped in the nearest city for the night to hunt. It was only when they were full that they moved on. Gladiator showed them the way without falling into a trance, for Oggy was getting closer and could feel her without resorting to the tiring ceremony.

"We have to find our poor little girl," he said. "I'm sure we'll make it."

Meanwhile, the road he showed led not through wide highways or plains, but to areas heavily overgrown with scrubs, as if he were specifically trying to tease his traveling companions.

"Let the kangaroo kick you," Never sulked. "Where are you going to tell us to go, for one hundred Tasmanian devils?"

"Well, look for the way yourself, if you are so smart," Gladiator was offended and it took a long time to apologize him.

Despite the terrible heat, friends were able to enjoy this journey. So far, the animals they encountered have only been seen at the Zoo, and here they were running freely and looking at them exploring from a safe distance, ready to escape at any moment. Fronda, the lover of all possible animals, enjoyed it the most. Unfortunately, being too eager, he fell out of the open trailer twice, and once he was severely bitten by a koala whom he insisted on petting. The fluffy pet turned out to be quite toothy enough to give him proper clearance. Dea grunted a little, examining Fronda's hand, but she laughed even more.

"You are such a big child, you know?" She said.

Fronda taught nothing from unpleasant adventure. He was still looking for creatures he could pet or hug, but luckily few of them could catch. Even the snakes aroused his admiration and he had to be carefully guarded so that he would not take any with him "as a souvenir". Apart from the fact that with their lifestyle a snake would be at least an embarrassing pet, Australia is the homeland of oxyuranus scutellatus, an extremely venomous and aggressive snake, and a mulga. The venom of the latter does not know why it causes a strong allergic reaction in vampires. As a result, Quinki's edema and long-lasting, extremely painful disease often occur.

"We should tie this wally," Never growled angrily. "He'll make a trouble for us if we don't bring him to order..."

"You'd better watch where you're going," Dea advised him, because at that moment their car fell into the hole with its right front wheel.

"Damn," Never cursed, getting out onto the wet ground. "We blew the tire. We have to patch it somehow, because the spare wheel has already come out. Let's wait until morning, huh?"

"There's a river nearby," Theo said, looking around alertly. "Or rather a swamp, and a big one. Strange, it's not cooler here than on dry ground, and even somehow nastier."

"Because stuffy. Like a steam room. Let's go take a bath, because Dea will sneeze again that we're dirty," Gerard offered him, whose sharp eyes also saw the river glittering in the moonlight.

"Sure. Don't count on me traveling with a bunch of dirty baboons. Go, I will unfold the vulcanization kit and look at the wheel," Dea, as it turned out, had great hearing and did not fail to put in her opinion.

The men went down over the overgrown bank to the water. They had some doubts about whether it would be clean, but after a long ride in the blistering heat everyone felt dirty and sweaty, as rarely had happen. Vampires sweat much less than humans do, but at higher temperatures, the thermoregulation of their bodies is very similar in work to humans. The friends took off their clothes and immersed themselves in cool water.

"Huge relief," Gladiator sighed. "I didn't think it could be that hot anywhere outside of Hell."

"Have you been in Hell?" Theo asked him ironically, emerging from the river a few steps away.

"No, but I probably won't miss it..."

Gerard's shout interrupted the further conversation:

"Boys! Something rubbed against me!"

Immediately afterwards something with incredible force pulled Gladiator under the water. The highlander didn't even shout. In the water it anchored like in a sea during a storm, then Gladiator managed to free himself from what was holding him and jumped on the muddy shore. His friends followed his example and saw what attacked him. It was a huge, at least six-meter crocodile with impressive teeth, which did not like the fact that the victim managed to escape.

A giant reptile jumped out of the water and grabbed Gladiator by the thigh. Theo and Gerard rushed in solidarity to help a colleague, Never, conscious, jumped to the clothes hung on a branch for a revolver.

"Don't get on my shot line now!" He shouted warningly, aiming the weapon at the huge animal.

Something shook his arm so that the bullet went over the trees, and then a young man in khaki shorts and a khaki shirt jumped onto the crocodile's back. The surprised animal released Gladiator, whose friends dragged away to safety. Despite the horror of the situation, they couldn't take their eyes off the amazing scene: in the moonlight, man and antediluvian reptile struggled with each other, until the crocodile broke free and swung into the water. Apparently, he has enough for that night.

All this happened so quickly that only now Dea came with a flashlight, alerted by a scream and illuminated a group of muddled men with halogen light...

"What's got into you to get into the territory of a crocodile, and a dominant male?" Stranger cried angrily.

A beam of strong flashlight hovered from the darkness his tall, massively built figure, a young face with thick features and a distorted pale hair.

"I swear I will never enter the territory of any male again," groaned Gerard desperately. "Even if Dea were to kill me, I won't take bath until we will leave."

"Don't make silly things," the girl interrupted roughly. "I'll bring a first aid kit."

"If it weren't for you, I'd have kill this scuzzo," Never murmured grimly at the blond Australian, examining Gladiator's wounds. The wounds on his thigh and left shoulder were deep, but the bones were intact. Also, Gerard, hit by a powerful reptile tail, suffered in this experience. He was still holding his ribs and was gasping for breath.

"Crocodiles must not be killed," their savior said. "They are wonderful animals and necessary for the ecosystem."

"Ecosystem, ecosystem..." Theo snapped. "I don't want to be a balanced meal for any part of your ecosystem there."

"Not mine, but ours," a stranger responded. "When we destroy it, very interesting, where will we buy the second one? In mail order?"

"But humans are probably more important than crocodiles!"

"Let's say yes, but without exaggeration..."

"Enough," Dea interrupted the discussion. "Stand aside, Rajah, I will dress him. You'd better thank your gods that this freak appeared at all. An injured crocodile is dangerous as hell, and with this toy you wouldn't put him dead."

Never looked at the stranger and a peculiar smile appeared on his face. The Australian returned his gaze and frowned at the change.

"Rajah!" He called after a moment cheerfully. "Well, it's a small world."

He embraced the Indian effusively, patting him on the back until it resounded.

"Do you know each other?" Dea asked, without interrupting the bandaging of Gladiator's leg.

"A bit... Let me, those are my friends: Fronda, Gerard, Dea, and this injured person is Yanek Gladiator."

"I am pleased to. My name is Steve." The Australian introduced himself. "Are you all...? I ask stupidly, because probably yes."

"Well, we've already explained that. Where, however, can we wash reasonably safely?" Asked Theo, trying to wipe the mud off a handful of leaves.

"Not far away, where I have a camp. I'm inviting you."

After a moment's hesitation, friends decided to use this offer. Although they had no idea why it was forbidden to swim on one section of the river, and on the other it was completely safe, but they did not ask anymore. This man, who seemed to be an integral part of the wild nature and did not think to be afraid of them, aroused trust. In addition, Never was apparently on good terms with him, and that was a guarantee of safety.

The encampment was very primitive - a tent, a bonfire, a jeep hidden in the bushes and a black dog that greeted the arrivals with a loud bark and stubborn tail wagging.

"Calm down, Sui!" Cried Steve. "Don't be afraid, she won't bite."

"Who's afraid?" Fronda stroked the she's neck, kissed her head between her ears, and finally followed his friends to the river.

It was only when the mud-washed ones sat down with him near the bonfire that Theo asked curiously:

"How do you know Never, Steve? You don't look like a vampire to me."

"Because I'm not," he explained. "And I know Rajah from the old days. I was still a cub, but I already managed myself in the bush, not worse than experienced animal trackers. I tried to capture a crocodile that threatened people in a certain fishery...

One night two people, a boy and a girl, came to my camp. They fell from fatigue, but they seemed to regain strength when I saw them. I was amazed at the ease with which they overpowered me, but when they started drinking my blood, I fainted, more because of shock than pain. They deceived me and, to my surprise, began to apologize. I was stunned because I expected death, as probably anyone who was attacked by vampires. Slowly, however, I realized that they were not going to hurt me, they were just hungry. They only took as much blood as they really needed, and I didn't even feel it. In gratitude, they helped me capture this crocodile and put in a chest. Their strength and dexterity were useful. And just when we were about to split up, unhappiness happened because Hunters attacked my camp.

It happened instantly. I was stunned by a blow to the back of my head as I tried to defend new friends. When I recovered, they were both dead. What shocked me the most was that their hair, even eyelashes and eyebrows, became milky white. I sat next to their bodies and cried like a child. Until the Rajah appeared. He probably realized that I hadn't killed them, because he asked calmly how it happened. Then he helped me bury the two, and he followed the hunters, commanding me to remain silent about what had happened... I don't even know what they were called..."

"Newt and Valentina," Never said sadly. "I knew them from the nineteenth century and I didn't think they would end so badly."

"Did you even get those Hunters?"

Never shook his head. His face was grim and drawn, his eyes fixed on the ground, and he was mechanically winding a strand of his magnificent hair on his finger.

"They are very well organized," he said. "They escaped me. Well, you can't always win."

"I haven't seen them again, and that's good. I would feed crocodiles with them in the reptile park run by my parents. I am not kidding."

His lips were tight, and his eyes were shining with anger, and he was serious.

"Why do you catch crocodiles if you don't kill them?" Gerard asked curiously, though he winced at the same time. "Dea, bandage my chest. I think this crocodile broke a rib."

Dea took an elastic bandage from the first aid kit and went to work without a word.

"I release them where they don't threaten people," Steve explained and added wood to the fire. "Sometimes I take them to the crocodile park. I want people to know as much as possible about them and stop killing them just because they don't like them."

"Good luck," Theo said kindly. "This will be a Sisyphean job."

"And privately how are you doing? You got married?" Never wanted to know.

"Come on. Which woman would stand with me? My calling is to save animals that are endangered by people, not to have a home."

"I think I understand. You see the same endangered and disliked species in vampires as in crocodiles. That's why you want to help us," Dea said implicitly, without interrupting her work.

"I am not in favor of killing just to kill at all. To clean up the territory. And the Nazis did not think otherwise. It's disgusting to me," Steve said emphatically.

"Something occurred to me," Theo said after a moment. "Maybe you could help us. We're looking for our friend who is a werewolf. We know she's located here near Brisbane. Do you have any idea where exactly?"

Steve stiffened. He was silent for a few minutes, as if trying to sort it all out.

"I think so," he said finally. "I think I know a place you could check. I'll draw a map for you. This is the Animal Research Institute near Brisbane. I've tried to send some control over them a few times, because I have some suspicions about these researches... but they can always get away. I do not like this place, because who ever saw a decent research institute, surrounded by live barbed wire and protected by armed guards? Something is going on there, I can bet even on my head."

"Better not, you will need it for some time. We will check this trail," Never stretched and stood up.

He preferred not to stay in this camp of this nice man for too long, so as not to attract the attention of local Hunters. It could have been dangerous for him, since the Hunters also did not spare people helping vampires. For this reason, they have always limited their contacts with locals, even friendly ones - and people like that happens.

"Get to me if you will be in need," Steve said friendly, shaking hands goodbye. "The zoo run by my parents is barely an hour away by bus from Brisbane. You will be in the car in thirty minutes. And don't tease the crocodiles anymore, okay?"

"No worries, we won't even look at any."

Returning to their trailer, friends first drank canned blood, and then began to repair the wheel. Now that they had a specific lead, they wanted to check it as soon as possible. They didn't know how Oggy could get to this institute, but the question "how?" it was the least important now. If she was there, it could mean real complications. It probably meant that the institute was a camouflaged Hunter base.

"Was this Steve honest with us?" Gladiator asked, observing working colleagues from the trailer (due to injury he could not help them).

"I think so. He is one of those crazy ecologs, and we have always lived in harmony with them," Never told him, struggling with the rusty jack.

"Ecologs?"

"Well, ecologists. Whatever."

This was true. Zealous environmentalists have always sided with the vampires and often helped them get out of trouble.

Anyway, with full reciprocity. It is the help of vampires that is due to the fact that during the famous and disgusting operation of sinking the Rainbow Warrior boat by the French special services, there were not many victims. They also led to the detection of the perpetrators, through a sense of solidarity with the Greenpeace movement. Activists repaid them in a similar way and Hunters hated ecologists - for these reasons.

They found the Institute for Animal Research easily and found that Steve had not exaggerated. Although it was to be a scientific institution, it resembled a rather well-armed fortress. The whole area was surrounded by a steel barbed wire mesh with "Attention, high voltage!" signs placed here and there. Along the fence, well-armed guards vigilantly inspecting the surrounding area. The building itself looked quite ordinary, except for the bars in the windows, but the question was how to get to it.

Never scanned the institute's building through military binoculars until he saw the door with the latest type of locks.

"I have no idea how we will get there," he said finally, taking the binoculars from his eyes.

Dea took it away from him and looked at the security herself.

"It's a combination lock, for a magnetic card," she said after a long moment. "Don't be afraid of anything, I can handle it. I have some useful gadgets."

"And how do we get to the area without raising suspicions?" Gerard asked skeptically, who lost his confidence at the sight of armed guards.

"Yes, that's a question, as if Hamlet said. For now, we're coming back before somebody discovers us. I'm afraid they'd make shashlik of us before they asked us what we were doing here."

"You're right," Dea backed Never up. "What a faces, I'd wish on nobody. I wouldn't be surprised if everyone had a few sentences on their backs."

Theo and Gladiator, locked in a trailer, greeted the "scouts" with questioning glances. They alone could not accompany them, because the sun had not set yet, and both were "moths" and could not stand sunlight.

"Well, this is a suspicious place, you can't deny it," Never replied to their looks. "However, we don't even know if Oggy is really there. Yanek, be so kind and concentrate a little. Try to feel something."

Gladiator gave him a troubled look but did not protest. He also wanted to find a friend and he knew that his sixth sense was a valuable tool in this search. So, he closed his eyes and touched his temples with the tips of his fingers, trying to find the right information from the flood of information that was flooding now. At one point he started, and a look of surprise flashed across his face. He focused again on what he was able to catch and clearly checked something that surprised him. Finally, he took a deep breath and shook his head.

"This job will put me in the grave someday," he said. "I'm so damn sure. I feel like I got a grenade in the head. However, Oggy is there but I sensed something else. A similar emanation as Oggy, although not quite the same."

"And what now?" Gerard asked. He turned on the extra fan and put a face under it.

"If we try to get in, they'll chop us into pieces," Dea murmured thoughtfully. "We need the help of someone they won't suspect."

"Steve?"

"You said, mon chevalier. We're going to his zoo."

The men agreed with her without a word. They also thought of the sympathetic crocodile hunter, though they had some doubts about whether he should be dragged into the matter. He was not one of them, he did not even belong to the so-called "compars" - people helping vampires, although not candidates for this state. They knew only him here, and he seemed honest. If they really wanted to save their friend, they had to use every opportunity.

Initially they made a mistake and it was dusk when they found the right place. In the end, however, a large sign appeared with the inscription "Australia ZOO" and a plate under it, informing "Object under development". They left the car and trailer in the parking lot and went looking for Steve, trying not to attract anyone's attention.

The zoo was quite extensive, well-lit and, as they noted right away, kept in an exemplary order. The animals had extensive paddocks, equipped with everything their animal heart could desire, to such an extent that Fronda could not refrain from malicious attention:

"Many a Christian soul lives in worse conditions, right?"

Dea ignored him. She watched the workers closely, uniformly wearing khaki, like an army, until she finally caught on to one of them, a slim man with stringy arms and legs. Sweatshirt with short sleeves and shorts allowed to admire his muscles, not exaggerated, as in the case of bodybuilders, but undoubtedly created as a result of hard physical work.

"Excuse me, sir, where can I find the director of this mess? Or rather the son of the director? His name is Steve."

He looked at her in resentment.

"You are here with an official matter?" He asked coldly.

"No, with private one, but still important. You know it or not, because we are in a hurry."

The man in khaki meditated a moment, finally shrugged and shouted at a nearby building:

"Steve, come here!"

"What's up, Wes?" Steve tilted his disheveled head through the door and his face lit up a joyful smile when he saw his guests. He was immediately next to them and shook hands exuberantly.

"And what? Did you find out anything?" He asked.

"You were right," Never told him cautiously, squinting suspiciously at Wes. "But we can't do it alone."

"All right, you can talk. This is my friend, we have no secrets from us. Wes, I told you about them."

"It's good that you didn't announce it on the radio and television," Gerard said, patting his pockets for cigarettes.

"We're not smoking here," Steve pointed out when he finally found it. "Fire hazard, and so on. It is also a disgusting addiction."

"What? It will kill me?" Gerard shrugged impatiently, but he obediently put the pack of Gauloises back in his pocket.

"Have you heard about passive smoking? Do not poison the environment. Okay, come to my office, nobody will overhear us there."

It didn't seem like Wes thought this as unusual. He apparently had the same world views as his friend, because he followed them to the barrack serving as the office and took part in the discussion lively. After exchanging the first, rather humorous ideas, such as a frontal attack or throwing several gas grenades inside, friends began to discuss seriously. It was known that it was impossible to get an institute by force. It was too well guarded, and, as everyone knew, Hunters would have no qualms about firing a whole group of people to accompany them.

"There is only one solution. They must invite us there," Steve said finally.

"Are you sick?" Gladiator interested, measuring his strong silhouette with his eyes and wondering casually if this man is good in combat. He seemed to consist of nothing but muscle, no gram of unnecessary fat, and his crocodile wrestling that they had the opportunity to see proved extraordinary strength and dexterity.

"Not quite," he answered seriously. "You admit that you can't go there quietly, and no Red Beret action is out of the question, because they are prepared for that. However, there are various ways to achieve the goal. I have some red-bellied mulches in my hand. If they can be admitted unnoticed into the institute, they can call me and Wes to catch them."

"They won't shoot them themselves?" Asked Theo doubtfully.

"They could, but when they see one, they will be afraid if there are more. There may be a dozen or so young in one nest.

They know that we are professionals in catching reptiles, so they will rather want to be sure that the mulgi will disappear on one before they bite one's backside."

"Let's say," Fronda was not convinced at all. "But what next?"

"What's next? You will hide in a jeep, we will mask you and you will get inside. And inside you will get to work."

"And do you know that if they make heads or tails of your role, they'll smash you without blinking?" Never said sternly.

"Let them try. You can't shoot to me like a sitting duck, and Wes was already in a lot of trouble. We'll make it so that you free your little one."

"It might work..." Dea said after a moment. "But they may also not let the vehicle into the area and we would have problem. It will be better to use a combined plan. Listen, Crocodile Hunter: you enter the institute. You are looking for your reptiles. You imperceptibly place C-67 gas containers at various points. Then you take the snakes and drive away. We're firing loads. C-67 gas is unstable, that is, it cause sleepiness only during the first five minutes, then changes its structure and becomes neutral."

"Where will we get it?" Gladiator wanted to know.

"I have it. I said I'm equipped with various gadgets."

Indeed, it has never occurred to anyone to ask what Dea has in her well-stuffed travel bag - it seemed like surprising things.

The highlander shook his head slowly, looking at her now with round eyes.

"Dziwce, ty mos ale łeb" finally moaned in delight and in Polish.

"A zebyśta wiedali, gazdo," Dea answered him in the same spirit, then added, turning to Steve. "You must both be devilishly careful. Remember that Vampire Hunters are people without conscience and fanatics of their ideas. And what fanaticism leads to, you can see even the example of Islamic extremists. Don't count on letting them pass you by, because you are overtaken. If they make heads or tails of you, fight as if a herd of demons has caught you and we will come to you to help."

"We'll make it," the Australians assured her with obvious amusement.

Both were apparently keen on this adventure, either without realizing the real danger or simply not fearing it.

"What more can you expect from a man who fights with crocodile like a teddy bear, and his buddy," Gerard thought, observing Steve slightly.

He impressed him with his strength and courage, but above all with a purity of gaze that he had not yet seen in an adult. It was felt that this powerful young man with a disheveled face is not burdened by any corruption or sin of a civilized man. Despite the undoubted lack of physical beauty, it was beautiful, and it flowed from within. Gerard never has seen a man who would so vividly illustrate an old axiom that one who does good is nice. He was like that. With all his soul devoted to the service of nature, he simply did not have time for everything that most people pursue, and which makes them corrupt libertines.

Steve must have misunderstood his gaze because he said soothingly:

"Don't worry, we really can handle it. We will not cause you any trouble."

"I didn't think so. When do we go?"

"Patience. I'll go toss the snakes to the institute soon, and then we'll wait for the call. Hurry would only impair here."

"How do you drop them there?" Gerard wanted to know. "They'll notice you."

Steve laughed heartily.

"Me? No worries. I did worst things. You know, there is one problem, you will have to work during the day. Can you make it?"

"We must. Don't worry about us, just about yourself. You can't give yourself away, because the Hunters will eliminate you without blinking."

"Ok, ok. And you wait patiently."

Steve was undoubtedly right, but his friends could not resist the impatient desire to immediately set out to rescue. The thought of Oggy being in the hands of the Hunters drove them crazy, but on the other hand they were glad that their friend was still alive.

"Why do they keep her there, what do you think? To do experiment?" Gladiator asked as they watched the wallaby run together.

"Experiments," Never corrected him. "No, I don't think so. I think they rather want to raise her like a hound, to search for vampires. Werewolf is great for this, don't you think? Hey, Fronda, get out of there, but now!"

Theo, busy stroking the sleepy wallaby at his head, did not pay attention to this call and only the second time he left their area, clearly disgusted.

"You always have to spoil the fun..." he said, sulky as a child. And as soon as they let him out of his sight, he passed through the fence onto the dingo dog paddock. At first, the animals hid themselves, but then they left their shelters and began to sniff at an unexpected guest.

He liked this zoo very much, mainly because it was arranged completely differently than most zoologists. The animals inside it looked happy and did not feel their captivity too painfully. Extensive paddocks even invited Fronda to cross the fence, so he disappeared on one of them. He particularly liked the wombats and, although nervous by his caress, the big male bit him twice, it was difficult to get him out.

The cassowary also delighted him, though one attacked. Then he revealed a strong desire to ride a camel... in a word, he behaved worse than a few years old, he was full everywhere and every now and then you had to call him to order. The rest of the friends liked the place too, though they expressed it with far more restraint than Fronda.

A walk around the ZOO and watching its attractions took friends almost all night. It was only in the morning that they went to sleep in the building offered to them by Steve, which was a tool shed, adapted to a hospital for night animals. It was lightproof enough to make them feel good there. Ailing animals in their cages - four pteropuses, large rabbit and two spotted maws - accepted temporary sub-sellers without protest. Weary of the excess of impressions, they slept soundly on temporary beds from jute sacks and were only awakened by solid shaking.

"I just had a call from the institute," Steve said excitedly. "Take black capes and artificial fangs, let's go."

"Black what? What artificial?" Muttered sleepless Never, but soon sobered up. "Ok, ok. Wake up, lazies! To work."

"Have mercy, middle of the day..." moaned Gladiator, trying to bury himself in sacks. Theo pulled him out of this makeshift country vigorously and without mercy.

"By the way, he is a little right," he said. "During the day we work quite badly. The sun does not serve us. We need some clothes, like space suits... Even "martens" don't like the harsh sun, and that's the middle of your damn summer."

"I figured it out myself," Steve said proudly. "I've got neoprene wetsuits for you, like those for sea divers. They will shield you quite well. The hardest part was with goggles, you know, they don't make masks for diving with tinted glasses. But I managed it too."

"Well done, if the Hunters don't get you, you'll be a great man."

"That's what I'm going to do. Come on, let's go."

Hidden in a jeep with the Australian ZOO logo, they arrived at the parking lot, where they switched to their rented roadster. There, they found Steve's black neoprene coveralls and masks with blackout film on the goggles. They pulled it all over themselves and stated grimly that they now looked like a strong ninja squad embarking on a secret mission. Of course, the main task of these costumes was to protect the sensitive skin of vampires from direct sunlight, but they fulfilled an additional function. It would be difficult to recognize any of them now.

"We'll be cooked like steamed lobsters," murmured Gerard dissatisfied.

"Do not whine. But the sun will not burn us. Quid pro quo," Never started. "We have to endure somehow. Fortunately, this outfit does not restrict movement, because probably a battle awaits us."

"I hope so," Theo began to check the weapon, his expression wasn't good.

They waited a little, then followed the jeep and hid their car in the bushes near the institute. From this place they could see a jeep parked at the gate and waited for them. None of them had an idea of how to catch venomous snakes without harming anyone. But they knew it had to take time, especially since Steve and Wes had an extra task to do. If they fail... they wouldn't even think about it.

Just in case, they watched the institute through binoculars for a change. From time to time, they saw familiar figures in khaki clothes, and this calmed them down, but the time still dragged by. It seemed like centuries before Steve and Wes left the guarded area, triumphantly carrying canvas bags with dangerous contents. They put them carefully on the wagon's pitch and drove away as agreed.

"Well, now we start," Dea murmured, taking the radio transmitter from under the dashboard."

"I thought I was in charge," Never pointed out.

"Do I forbid you? This is your charter and we're your backup. Command yourself."

She turned the switch and exactly one minute later the guards circling the institute lay on the ground like in a slow-motion movie.

Friends waited the prescribed five minutes, and just in case three more. Then they put the masks with darkened glasses on their faces and started running to the gate. The guards slept soundly and none of them moved. They took their weapons - semi-automatic Uzi could come in handy, they didn't know how many hunters there were. It was true that they had their guns, model 66, but that might not be enough. Now you had to get to the building itself, and that required opening the door. Carefully, hiding under the walls, they slipped to them.

"I hope no one saw us, and no one saw the sleeping princes," Dea pulled a small device resembling a mini-waffle iron from her haversack over her shoulder. "Otherwise our future will be bad."

She took a kind of wallet from the side pocket and a magnetic card from it. She dragged it through the reader in the lock, then placed under the top flap of the device, and under the bottom - a second card, like the first. Friends stared at her without a word.

"It's a card duplicator," she explained casually. "The first is a collector, it reads the code, and the second is empty. The reduplicator sticks the code obtained by the collector into it, then cleans the collector so that it is ready for reuse. Smart and useful."

"Undoubtedly," Theo agreed with her, though he understood nothing.

The green LED on the reduplicator started flashing, Dea opened the device and pulled the newly programmed card through the reader again. Lights flickered on the lock panel, then the door opened silently. Friends entered the forbidden area, looking around vigilantly. The interior of the institute was nothing like a research facility, but rather barracks and this confirmed their earlier guesses.

They came across the inhabitants of this place almost immediately. Without engaging in conversations, they terrorized them and locked them in the nearest utility room with a latch from the outside. They just hoped to find Oggy before the others, Hunters or investigators, realized the situation.

"There," Gladiator showed the way. Being so close to the search object, he didn't need to get into a trance, and he could sense the right direction.

They ran through the empty corridor, turned into the next and stood in front of an armored door, protected by a similar lock as the entrance. Dea reached for her reduplicator again and repeated the operation of making the card. After a few seconds, the door was open.

First of all, they saw stairs leading somewhere down. As they descended, they came across a lattice closed to a plain lock, one that Fronda's skeleton key could handle easily. The guard slumbering behind them turned lazily at the grinding sound. He did not expect intruders. He managed to open his mouth to scream and reach for his sidearm, but Gladiator's fist knocked him down immediately.

"Won't he recover to fast?" Whispered Never.

"There is no chance," the highlander assured him.

Two other gratings separated the way, and the proper underground was opening behind them. It housed a living room, medical office, and a well-equipped gym. The woman sitting at the microscope turned and froze with her mouth half open.

"Don't even say a word," Theo warned her.

Dea stepped forward and without further ado tied the woman smoothly with a cable torn from the wall. Disregarding her protests, she finished her work, gagging her victim, and only then looked around.

"I don't think anyone else is here. We keep looking."

Behind the laboratory, they found a barred, nicely furnished room. Oggy sat on the rug by the wall, embracing her knees with her frail arms, and she rocked steadily, hitting her back against the wall. The door replacement grille, unlike the others, was equipped with a combination lock, such as in the front door.

"Oggy!" Cried Theo, throwing himself toward the bars.

The girl didn't even look at him. She did not react to anything, indifferently swaying like a child affected by an orphan disease.

"What did they do to her?" Gerard whispered while Dea hurriedly preparing the card to open the lock.

"I have no idea," she replied. "I'd have to examine her. But it will be time later, now we have to act fast. I am not a 'sensor' but I still feel that there is some danger approaching us."

She dragged the crafted card through the sensor. When the grille opened, Theo first burst in and grabbed Oggy in his arms. The girl, as if knocked out of a hypnotic trance, screamed terrifyingly and began to pull herself with a force he did not expect from her... Apparently, she did not recognize him or the others. Meanwhile, Gladiator, who was exploring underground, exclaimed:

"Come here!"

His voice sounded so peculiar that everyone rushed towards him.

There was another room in the back - a child's room in pastel colors. Perhaps an eight-year-old boy was sitting on the bed, staring at them with sleepless eyes. It was a very pretty child, swarthy, with coal-black hair and eyes, but his ears were pointed, and his fingers ended with typical dog's claws.

"Oh," Never murmured, while Dea, cursing under her breath, prepared the next card. Oggy calmed down at the sight of the boy, apparently, she was talking about him in the loud protest.

"Who are you?" Asked the boy curiously.

"Friends. We will free you both from here," Theo answered him. "And who are you?"

"My name is Daren. What does it mean to free?"

"You will see."

Theo cautiously abstained from invasives to Hunters coming to his lips. Dea finally opened the grille and Never took the child in his arms. Although small, the boy weighed surprisingly much, and the grip of his arms was like ticks.

"Why did they keep him here?" Gerard asked quietly, stunned by the whole thing and taken off with terror. Suddenly he was afraid, though he didn't know why.

"They wanted to train him like a dog," Gladiator answered grimly. "Oggy, too. They probably did her brainwashing, that's why she behaves like this. See, she doesn't recognize us at all. Do you know what I want now? Smash all this business out of the damn thing."

"A few C4 servings would be enough," Theo muttered, pressing Oggy to himself.

"There is no way. No such thing," Dea said sharply. "We're getting out of here."

She was the calmest, as if what she saw here did not impress her. It is not without reason that she urged friends to leave this falsified institute as soon as possible - one can never predict who will appear suddenly in such a place. The sooner they disappear from here, the better. As it turned out, her premonitions had a basis.

In the corridor they came across several armed men, lured by Oggy's scream, no doubt colleagues of men who had sleep because of gas. For the benefit of friends, they hesitated for a moment, seeing Oggy in the hands of Fronda and the boy carried by Gladiator. These few seconds gave them time to break through to the exit before the bells rang throughout the building.

They had to reach the car by a tyraliere, not hiding otherwise from the Hunters, so as not to waste valuable time. Speed was important not only because of the shelling. Despite the black coveralls, the sun burned their skin painfully. Even the "martens" felt its rays, penetrating somehow through neoprene, very uncomfortably.

Oggy, who seemed to be recovering some hazy memories, clutched Fronda's neck and didn't want to let him go. She seemed to be deadly afraid of the world she was taken to. The boy who ran with them on his own, looked around with curiosity and joyful amazement, showing no fear of bullets. Apparently, he had never been outside before.

"Don't stare like that, just run to the trailer," Dea told him. "We have to disapp..."

The last syllable blurred into the dangerously close sound of engines. It is not known where the two trucks came from, about fifteen Hunters in military camo got off. They were armed mainly with AR 15 rifles, but not only. One of them carried a bazooka, from which he immediately aimed at the roadster.

There was nothing to wait for. Friends scattered across the ground, first grabbing from the car what was winding up under their arm. Just in time - the car hit the fuel tank exploded with a yellow-orange flame.

"Wow, in a rental shop, they'll rip us off..." Never groaned.

Now there was no time for any ethical consideration, you just had to fight. Theo, although Oggy seriously constrained his movements, moved agile, changing his location again and again to make it harder to hit him. He fired his pistol again and again, stopping only because he was reloading the gun. Never wasn't idle either. The captured Uzi in Gladiator's hands did not stop even for a moment. Dea and Gerard hastily assembled a folding grenade launcher - the cover with it the actor caught at the last minute from the trailer.

After a while, the primitive, but effective weapon was ready, and Gerard loaded it, praying that he would not confuse the ends. He watched quite a movie in which a fired projectile of cities in the right target hit something lying behind the shooter. However, he managed to avoid this tragicomic mistake and the first grenade caused panic among the Hunters. They did not expect that the undead they were chasing would have such firepower.

"Shoot carefully," Dea warned Gerard. "We only have five bullets."

Although the actor tried to be as careful as possible in the hustle and bustle, the second bullet hit one of the Hunters, literally tearing him in half. Gerard paled like a wall, let go of the grenade launcher, folded in half and began to vomit. Even though he saw a lot in his life, such a view was a novelty for him, which he did not want to watch. Dea cursed silently and grabbed a heavy weapon.

"Molly, damn, it's heavy... Get a grip, you cowardly comedian!" Theo, who was next to Gerard, slammed his fist into his neck.

He ran out of bullets a moment ago, so he finally put Oggy on the ground and, unrolling his inherent slingshot, threw stones at the Hunters. They were not as dangerous as pistol bullets, but they turned out to be biting enough to cause confusion. However, the situation was quite bleak. There were far too many hunters and they were a well-trained unit. They had lost two people so far, several were injured, but they still had a numerical advantage, and in addition they were better armed.

"As soon as we run out of bullets, they will come closer and launch the nets," Never said, being next to the others. "Don't stand in a group, scatter. What about you, Fanfan? What's with you? Did they hit you?"

"No, he fainted at the sight of someone's tripe," Dea snorted sarcastically, loading the last shell into the grenade launcher. "Let's pray better and say goodbye, because these are our last jigs."

"I am an atheist, I will certainly not pray," Gerard growled rebelliously, his face beginning to take on a normal hue.

"Jesus, do you have to repeat it at every opportunity?!" Theo got angry.

Gerard could not answer that anymore. The engine whirred from a distance, then a jeep with the Australian ZOO logo came in full swing, braking so close to them that a cloud of dust covered everything for a moment.

"On board, people!" Steve shouted at the top of his lungs, leaning out of the cab.

Theo grabbed Oggy huddled on the ground, Gladiator grabbed the boy (it seemed that all the shooting didn't frighten Daren the least) and everyone jumped into the back of the car. The jeep started off in such a twist that they almost fell and rushed away, chased with rifle series. A few of them scratched the sides of the roadster, but luckily none went on tires.

Indeed, the Hunters had to orientate themselves quickly, because they almost immediately caught their vehicle and chased them. Their protective paint truck soon appeared on the road behind the refugees and soon caught up with them. Another series whistled above the jeep. The rear window splashed sideways.

"They are chasing us," Gerard reported in a shaky voice.

"Don't be afraid," Dea muttered.

She knelt in the backseat, holding a grenade launcher on her shoulder, and aimed carefully through the broken window. She must have hit the first time because she had the last missile, but it didn't seem to depress her. She calmly aimed and squeezed the trigger when the grenade launcher's sight coincided with the target for a split second. The truck hit the engine, jumped and turned to the side of the road.

"Crickey!" Shouted Steve enthusiastically, who saw all this in the rearview mirror.

"You're good, for a woman," said Gladiator graciously.

"She's good even for a samurai!" Fronda protested.

"What can you know about it? In your time, women sat at home and embroidered tapestries."

"Right! You know a lot, huh. Many of women accompanied her husband on a crusade or battlefield, and not at all as an ornament. And the Virgin of Orleans is a dog for you?"

"Uhm, and for that you probably gave her to the English. Pew!" The highlander spat contemptuously "overboard".

Teo said quietly an extremely nasty curse.

"Do not remind me of this shame... Anyway, I will tell you in secret that this lady did not burn at the stake. A vampire named Sixto saved her, apparently madly in love with her. Disguised as an executioner, he abducted her directly from the pile, leaving a young woman who dead to pneumonia in a beggar's shelter tied to a stake."

"What happened next?" Asked Dea curiously, rubbing a hand numb with a heavy grenade launcher.

"I have no idea. Life is not a movie or a novel, you don't always know what is next. You can know the beginning and never know the end, and vice versa."

Everyone fell silent after this philosophical remark. Now that the danger was over, they felt how tired they were, how their sunburned skin hurt, which even black material could not protect sufficiently. Everyone's eyes stung and watered, despite swimming glasses resembling dark glass covers, their eyelids were swollen and painful to the touch. Theo and Gladiator suffered the worst, because as "moths" they shouldn't go out in the sun at all, but everyone got it according to individual sensitivity. They could not wait for the moment when they were safely in a darkened room.

*****

It was only after a few days that Oggy began to speak. Dea worked with her all the time, trying to get her out of the state she was in, and finally began to get the first results. Unfortunately, it turned out that the girl does not know why she went first to Spain, and then to Australia. The impulse that forced her to do so was not registered by her consciousness, but it must have been extremely strong, since it had mastered her will. Interestingly enough, the Hunters were waiting for her at Sidney Airport, who took her to the base. How did they know? One thing seemed certain, the source of what had happened was to be sought in Africa, for it was where Oggy began to feel strange sensations.

"Vaccination!" Cried Never at some point. "Vaccination against rabies! This Egyptian vet immediately seemed suspicious to me when he asked us out of the office. But what could he do to her?"

Dea thought about it for some time, and finally decided to do the examination with a veterinary scanner. It turned out to be a bull's-eye. Oggy had an implant of an unknown type implanted under the scalp, it is not known when it was placed there. Little Daren had a similar implant. Dea removed both and set to examine them in the zoo's laboratory.

"And if she got that thing in Russia?" Never said when she told her friends about everything. "I never trusted the Russians. Are you betting on them or quack from Cairo?"

"I saw Gusto Vanderbelt in Russia..." Theo said slowly.

"Yes, I took it into account. He may be involved, but let's not jump to conclusions. Maybe it wasn't him if the chip was implanted in Africa. How does it work though? Like transmitter or receiver?"

"I think both," Dea said. "This baby emits a special kind of wave, overlapping the brain's theta rhythm. Technology that goes beyond what we know. Perhaps this was how Oggy's normal thinking was disturbed and ovulation was triggered at the right time."

"But why? Phooey!" Gladiator was surprised, to whom these inkhorn terms did not speak at all.

"They needed the child. But where did they get this technology from, don't ask. I have no idea," Dea answered.

There was a short silence, interrupted by a peacock scream and camel roaring from the nearby paddock.

"Don't you think sometimes that Daren is the missing grandson of our friend from Belgium?" Gerard asked, watching the boy playing with Sui through the window.

"Maybe yes, maybe no. We'll probably never know, but the age is correct, and the kid is a bit like Jean Claude... But what are we going to do with him? A child is the last thing we need." Never sighed hopelessly.

Everyone shared his fears, but they have not thought about this problem yet. They were interested in Oggy, still weak and talkative. She was most likely lying on her bed, curled up and sleeping or staring straight ahead. Only Daren could free her from her passive indifference for a moment. It was evident that they are very friendly and feel a strong bond between them. They definitely couldn't be separated now, so friends had a hard nut to crack.

Unexpectedly, Oggy herself found a solution. One day, she just stood up and shyly went outside, squinting against the blinding sun. She spent the whole day visiting the Zoo in the company of Daren, and after returning turned to friends.

"Don't be mad at me. I will stay here for now. Steve said I could help him in the ZOO, and you know that I understand animals well. I can use it. Daren will be able to live here peacefully, without paying anyone's attention. This will be best for me and him. I don't want you to consider me an ingrate, but I am already sick from the constant wandering and the dangers to which we are exposed. I would just like to live peacefully. Is it wrong?"

Friends looked at each other. They did not expect such a thing and these words hurt them. They liked Oggy, they undertook an extremely dangerous trip for her... and she gives up their company. On the other hand, they understood her well again. They decided to talk to Steve, who may not be fully aware of what he got into. He, however, saw no unusual ties in this matter.

"Let them stay," he said. "This zoo will one day be really great..."

"So it's small now?" Theo interrupted him. "On what scale are you measuring?

"...they will hide in it easily. What a problem?" The Australian finished, ignoring him.

"We don't know if you really know what you're doing," Never said emphatically. "You have two werewolves here, first. The hunters saw you help us, second. What will happen when they come here?"

Steve smiled broadly.

"Let them come. The stomachs of our crocodiles are very roomy, I assure you. I will take care of the two without fear. Nobody touches them while I'm alive."

"All right, if you say so," Theo muttered dubiously. "But I will miss our Oggy, oh my. I'm so used to her."

The crocodile hunter patted him on the back with a sheep shoulder blade sized hand until Fronda staggered. His strength was amazing.

"It is so in life," he said cheerfully. "Why wouldn't you stay here?"

"Because it's too hot. Anyway, we need to find out what happened to our other friends," Never answered.

He meant the di Mauro research station. Nobody gave them this task, but everyone thought it natural that they would do it as soon as they returned to Europe. They were guilty of old friends who disappeared inexplicably along with everything that belonged to them.

*****

"And how's our money holding out?" Theo asked, entering the room where Dea was sitting over the bills.

Account statements, invalidated checks, receipts, and VAT invoices appeared on the table. The girl undertook to sort out their financial affairs, which turned out to be overly confusing, and was just striving over this task.

"I think, no good," she said grimly. "This trip has taken a lot of money. We are in the red. We must catch some profitable job as soon as possible."

She spoke in plural and four friends, not without fear, realized that she considered herself a full member of their group. They didn't have enough strength to oppose it. In addition, they had to objectively admit that she was valuable to them - there was probably nothing in the world that she would be afraid of and that she could not do. Still, they felt some resistance to accepting her constant presence among them.

"I wonder how we should do it," Never said from his chair, where he read "Le Monde." Octavio was our contact, without him we are like without an ear."

"Still, something will have to be done," Gerard took Dea's site. "You can't live without money, especially today."

"There was always like that," Fronda muttered and stared out the window at the wonderfully cool Belgian sky.

"Why are you so sad?" Dea asked, rising from the table and stretched until her bones cracked in her joints.

"We have reasons," said Gladiator. "First of all, we lost our Oggy..."

She shrugged.

"You have me," she said, then picked up the papers from the table and left for the other room.

"Uhm," the blond highlander muttered, looking after her. "And this is the second reason..."

PART 3

Secrets of the underground

In memory of Steve Irwin

"Once again, once again, my bird, my dear... dip me a sweet sing...!" a velvet baritone snatched from the bathroom.

"Wow, silence this birdman from Tyrol, because if I get down to it, the guy won't end well," Dea finally got upset, unsuccessfully trying to focus on her bills.

"So, laugh, buffoon, for my hurt love...!" A changed rhythm came from the bathroom.

Dea threw the pen, opened the bathroom door with a sharp jerk and disappeared behind them. After a moment, from a quiet asylum Fronda jumped out in the towel, wrapped up in a hurry, badly offended, wet from head to toe.

"Voyeur! Strumpet!" He screamed. "You don't know that when a man is stripped, he doesn't like such surprises?!"

"Depends on who, it wouldn't bother me at all," Gladiator murmured with amusement."

"What a man," Dea emerged from the bathroom and handed Fronda his clothes with Olympic calm. "Dress up, naked man. We must gather now. I hope this job is serious because we are hopelessly broke. We barely have enough gasoline."

"I said returning to Poland was idiocy," muttered Gerard Phil, not looking up from his letter.

He tried to describe to the Belgian actor what they saw in Australia, but he did not do it well. He did not know what to write about first: whether the institute behind the barbed wire, or about the Crocodile Hunter, or finally about Daren himself, who could be, but did not have to, the grandson of Jean-Claude. It was like the efforts of Ivan the Homeless, who in a psychiatric clinic tried to describe his first meeting with Woland.

"Why is that?" Asked Gladiator, blushing.

Whenever he got excited about something, his pale face usually blushed like an ashamed flapper, which made him very embarrassed.

"The vampire should be chalky white, his damn right, not ruddy like a paradise apple," he said.

"Paint your face with some plaster and you will be just right," Dea once advised him, not without her usual malice.

But now Gladiator was too angry to think about his appearance. He loved his homeland in an insane, even obsessive way, and in his presence, it was better not to criticize either the Polish landscape or Polish realities. The beautiful highlander was not very good at fencing, but his fist had the weight of a hammer and meteor speed.

"Relax, Tatra bear. Fanfan meant that here people do not need our help in solving their problems. They are doing it themselves, and we need to earn," said Theo, seeing that in a while it could be a fight.

"Themselves, you say? And what if they really haunt some hellish legion or the devil himself?" Gerard asked ironically. "I remind you that haunted houses happen here, we were even in them and we barely carried our heads."

"The haunted house is a trifle," Dea waved a hand dismissively. "Nobody cares about them. And as for the devil, if one of them got lost in Poland by accident, then after two days he would pull himself back to Hell. The nation that was occupied by Hitler and liberated by Stalin will not be scared by any jerk on goat's dumplings."

"I believe you." Gerard tossed his pen and picked up the newspapers. "Is there cable TV in this hotel? Because on M6 goes a movie with a promising title 'Lover'."

"There may be moments there," said Gladiator. "Fronda, don't you mind that the movie will be a bit nasty?"

Theo, wiping with passion on a terry towel, looked at him a little unconsciously and replied after a moment:

"Do not mind. A movie can be nasty, a movie just can't be boring."

"Of course," Dea muttered sarcastically and looked at her watch. "Where is the Rajah?"

Her anxiety was justified. Never had been gone for two days, since he went to check the suspicious order received through Stasiek. It was unlikely that a bunker resident at the Palace of Culture would consciously try to trap him - but it could not be ruled out at all. Never trusted anyone completely. And the order itself was at least strange: they were to check what caused the vibration of the city. They were not tectonic shocks, but seismographs in several independent institutes recorded weak vibrations, imperceptible to people, but non-existent. But what could the undead care about? It seemed like they were not saying everything.

"We worry. It looks as if there were a dozen or even dozens of wild subway trains near Warsaw," said Stasiek embarrassed when this question was asked. "The problem is that these vibrations increase slightly. Slightly but constantly, do you understand? Their epicenter is near our base. It would be good to check, because it gets disturbing. We won't soon find another good base if we had to leave the Palace underground. We made a whip-round in hard currency for you. You'll get ten grand plus expenses, okay? We don't have any more."

Polish vampires did not belong to the elite of their species and usually struggled with a constant lack of cash. The threat must have been serious, since they decided to hire them as a "team for special tasks". They offered little, but they certainly did not manage to collect, and in this situation even a small amount was not to be despised. The trip to Australia consumed almost all the savings of their small team, and the rest of what remained on their account was given to Oggy. They did not want her to stay in a foreign country without her own money, even under the care of a man as kind as Steve. And in this way they found themselves back in Europe literally penniless.

Were it not for Gladiator, a clever thief, they would not even have money for travel to Poland, where Stasiek called them. To tell the truth, Dea screamed indignantly that she didn't want stolen money, but Gladiator did not listen to her at all. He went alone into the night and returned with a sum of Australian dollars, decisively refusing to answer the question of where and to whom he had stolen them. However, it was, the amount obtained in this way allowed them to find themselves in Warsaw, where they faced the same problem again. The money collected by Stasiek could be a lifeline for them, but still, Never decided before accepting the task whether the Polish doctor was telling the truth. Just in case. And he was gone two days.

When the front door slammed, everyone jumped in surprise. Never fell inside, windswept, stinking of canal sludge, his hair covered with brick dust. However, even Dea paid no attention to his appearance.

"And what?" She asked frantically.

"The order is authentic, but it will be dirty work," he replied, taking off his dirty clothes in disgust. "A whole network of other canals, much older, terribly neglected and probably forgotten, runs under the city canals. Whatever it is, is hidden there, and I'm not sure if it's worth looking for it."

Dea snorted dismissively.

"Maybe it's not worth it, but judging by your bills, there is no way out. The highest waiting for us then is a bath in the city bath. Of course, we need to visit an adequate store and buy all the equipment: overalls, gloves, high rubber boots, just in case oxygen masks and helmets with flashlights. I'm calling Stasiek to take this matter. Let him give an advance.

*****

The descent to the "canals-under-canals" was a black void. Probably no one has touched it for centuries, no one knew it was there. To reach it, they had to traverse a large section of the city canals network and descend through a long-unused system, from the Middle Ages. Finally, they found a drainage well in the canal, a well that was supposed to drain excess water, but it was a bit too wide for this purpose. When they descended one by one through a tight manhole, they found themselves not in a pipe, but in a fairly wide room, from which only the proper drainage was leaving. They were lucky that it hadn't rained for days.

It was possible to get to the flap mounted at the mouth only when the whole thing was not under water. People who still had some idea about it, have long since passed away without passing on their knowledge to anyone. And yet the rusted flap lay next to the square opening - not open, but pushed out from within. At least, Fronda decided, looking at the dents in the rusted metal.

"It means that whatever was here it got out," Gerard whispered. He scanned the flashlight from the nearest surroundings, but he didn't notice anything.

"Not necessarily. Maybe it didn't want to leave this shelter at all. Either way, we're going down if they're paying us. Check, Yanek, rope hook, downhill ride for at least fifty meters. And there is no ladder here," Never said, with an involuntary, disgusted sigh. He hated the stench of city canals and undergrounds, he loved space, freedom and the smell of flowers. However, it was not the right time for grimaces.

Slowly, one by one, they descended the rope into that stinking darkness, flinching in disgust at the very thought of what they would have to wade there. The bottom of the old, probably still medieval, canals was covered with a thick layer of sludge, but the wide edges were relatively dry, which was a pleasant surprise for all of them. The air, to their surprise, was breathable, though there certainly was less oxygen in it than on the surface. Man wouldn't be able to search these canals without proper equipment, but vampires need much less oxygen.

Friends took off their uncomfortable masks. When they lit the torches placed on their helmets, they scared the darkness a bit and could look around the corridors leading to it. The farther they were, the higher they were. Built in rough stones, the walls were covered with mold and some strange vines they had never seen. They were unpleasant to the eye, white-gray color and gave the impression of ghostly hands, clinging to stones in a silent scream for help. As they went deeper into the corridor, they saw more and more of them, which made them wonder, they couldn't see rats, very numerous in the upper canal network. It was definitely not normal.

Theo saw it first - the vines moved as if trying to escape the light cast by their flashlights. At first he thought there was an illusion caused by the play of light and darkness, but when he looked more closely, he jumped back.

"They are alive!" He called out.

"Yes, of course. Plants are not still life." Never grunted, but after a while he added. "Strange reaction indeed. You don't have to panic. After all, mimosa also folds up when touched. It's probably a similar mechanism."

Just in case, he examined one of the vines carefully. It felt like woody ivy to the touch, although instead of leaves it had hard, leathery insets of unknown purpose. It did not take energy from the sun, so it did not need chlorophyll, so its color was not unusual. However, something about this plant was anxious. Perhaps the strength with which it clung to the stones, or perhaps it was a fragrance, reminiscent of the smell emitted by ladybugs. For a moment he wanted to cut one of the branches and keep it for later examination, but for some reason the thought of it suddenly seemed disgusting to him.

"I am a pretty good botanist, but I have no idea what species to include these lichens. When I pulled the stalk, I felt resistance, not what it feels like tearing something attached to the ground, but... as if it strained the muscles and counteracted," he said finally, leaving the examined climber alone and returning to the group.

"Don't fool around. It's just weed," Gladiator snorted dismissively.

They have just reached the place from which several corridors diverged. The highlander lit them one by one with his flashlight, and then pointed it at the vault.

"E, wy cepry, pozirajcie ino se na powałe," he said after a moment. "Przisam Bogu, te skole nie cłek tu przitargoł, inacy zjim własny kierpec, hej."

"What?" Friends looked at him in amazement.

"He says it's not a man who built these canals," Dea translated. "To tell you the truth, I've had this impression for some time. A short section of the corridor, at the manhole, was built with human hands, probably at the beginning of the Middle Ages. Something was wanted to build here, but work was interrupted and never resumed. Next is the natural network of caves. Unbelievable, the geology of these areas does not mention anything about the caves under the city... Look at this dripstone. This is called drapery."

Something was running down the wall, from the vault in the darkness to the ground. Something that looked like frozen plaster waves, intricately curled.

"At what rate does it grow?" Gerard asked, carefully examining the limestone sculpture like a work of art.

"About one cubic centimeter per year," the girl answered him. "Slightly counting, this drapery began to form... about ten thousand years ago. Not bad, huh?"

"People didn't come here for sightseeing," added Gladiator grimly. "Otherwise they would break it from all sides and everywhere would be idiotic hearts pierced with an arrow, in the company of inscriptions like "Czesiek was here". You should see Tatra grottoes. Horror."

Dea stopped and picked up something that only she saw. It was a carefully worked, flint leaf-shaped arrowhead.

"You're not quite right. People have been here," she muttered. "Only a long time ago, when almost no one could write. And for some reason they stopped being here. Let's move on."

"Stick together. It looks like a real maze to me. If we get lost here, we will have problem," added Never, adjusting slightly too big for him rubber boots.

"Problem, cold water," Theo agreed with him. "Here, even I can get lost. And our girl is gone so that she finds her way with a sense of smell."

He also felt uncomfortable chills at the very thought that he was over fifty meters below the lowest of the city's canals, in a place nobody knew about. Maybe one Stasiek had some idea about them, and it wasn't for sure. He knew the descent, but did he know what was under it. There was no indication. The hatch was rusted, buried in crushed stone, lying on the bottom of the manhole. It was thrown aside only in recent days. Probably not even one of the canals went down to the well, for what for? They thought they had at most a drain collector underneath. Those simple, hard-working people probably did not have a clue, and they walk on.

They hit one of the corridors at random. The same lichen was everywhere, but it grew larger, and their resemblance to monstrous, rheumatized hands was enhanced. The pungent odor that permeated the air slowly became unbearable and forced places to plug their noses. Suddenly walking ahead, Never stopped, giving a slight scream of terror.

Another branching corridor opened before them. And in this place from which the paths radiated into the unknown, lay a man... or rather what was left of him. Mummy-dried body was entwined with ghostly creepers, penetrated into every crevice in clothing, cut through brownish skin with sharp shoots. The leather appendages looked like leeches sucked to a man's skin - an association that was irresistible.

"What is this?" Gerard asked through his throat.

"Mummy," Gladiator risked uncertainly.

"No way," Dea protested authoritatively. "It is too humid here for spontaneous mummification of corpses. First, the body would rot."

Theo, overcoming fear and disgust, walked over to the corpse and turned his left wrist without difficulty, until the broken bone cracked. They flinched at the dry, sharp sound.

"Watch with date," Fronda muttered. "There's a notebook in pocket, I'll try to pull it out. Listen... this guy was still alive two days ago."

"Impossible," Gladiator protested weakly. He was more hardened than the French actor, but he also felt sick at this sight.

Theo continued to flip through the pages, amazingly white and fresh.

"I'm sorry, but it looks like it. Here is a note. The day before yesterday's date and the annotation "Otrzymałem zwrot 1000PLN od Kosińskiego" (I received a refund of PLN 1000 from Kosinski).

He barely spelled out the Polish inscription, understanding nothing. The content of the note was not important to him, only the date. What mattered was that the corpse looking like an Egyptian mummy was until recently a living man, probably at full strength. Now Dea started the inspection. This girl must have had strong nerves. It seemed that finding dried corpses was not unusual for her. She carefully examined the victim's nails and teeth and devoted a lot of attention to clothing.

"Wondering," she finally said, rising from her knees with obvious relief. "Judging by the clothes, he was a well-off man and had nothing to look for through the canals. Anyway, the appearance of his shoes contradicts the theory that he even entered them. You can argue about whether this was not a murder, but the guy has a wallet full of money, and on his body, as far as I could tell, there is no wound. To sum up, if he wasn't here of his own free will and was not thrown in, he had to be dragged. The question remains, which way?"

"A money for us?" Asked Gladiator, animatedly, as always when money was at stake. "He doesn't need it anymore," he added, emptying his leather wallet, and put the Polish banknotes in his pants pocket.

Dea did not pay much attention to this. Something else absorbed her. She touched the nearest shoot with an open hand. It seemed warm to her, as if warmed by the sun, whose smallest ray did not reach here.

"Let's cut off this meanness if you want to examine it," Gerard suggested.

Dea shook her head slowly. She couldn't say why, but she felt a keen reluctance to hurt these vines, the way she felt when she was told to study a rat vivisection. The rat was humanely asleep, but the scalpel still fell out of her hand. Now the impression was the same, although she explained with all her might that it was absurd that she was dealing only with a plant.

"You better not, Gepciu," she said.

From the beginning, she baptized Gerard with "Gepard", in short "Gepciu," and usually called him that way. She thought that the nickname suited him the best, because - as she explained - he had what a gepard (cheetah) had. He was thin, beautiful, and gentle for a predator, he ran fast and was not worth much in a direct power struggle. The actor initially protested, but then got used to the new nickname.

"Let's move on. We won't help this unfortunate anyway."

Friends were silent. Now, as they stood, they clearly felt the vibrations, this disturbing vibration Stasiek had mentioned to them. They also seemed dangerous and, above all, alien, not reminiscent of anything they knew. Slowly, forcing themselves, they tore their feet off the ground and went on. They looked at the lichen around the walls with different eyes. They were beginning to guess what they were eating, and a shiver was coming to their minds. Now it was becoming clear why there were no rats, mice or even cockroaches here.

They didn't know what to do now. There was more and more lichen, around stalagmites hanging here and there, climbing the walls and stalactites, even venturing into the cave vault. It felt as if they were looking at the intruders, though they had no idea how, since they had no eyes. The most tempting thought was to cut down sinister plants as much as possible, but they were not barbarians to destroy what they did not understand. Soon they came across another body, this time a young woman. It was still quite fresh, although it could be seen that the vines have already started their destructive activity.

"If they bring people all the way from the surface, why don't they attack us?" Gerard asked, unsuccessfully trying to calm his trembling teeth.

"I think it's because of the smell, or rather the lack of it," Never answered him. "Vampires don't smell. Even dogs lose our lead. I think this carnivorous ivy has some sense comparable to the smell of mammals and is guided by it in finding victims. Rather, it is not thermo sensitivity, because they would already wrap us... Wait, I want to check something."

He walked to the wall and touched one of the leathery appendages with his fingertip. After a moment, he took his finger away and, without surprise, found that the entire pad was covered with dozens of tiny punctures. The creeper moved slowly, extending one of its branches towards him. Never jumped back quickly and returned to friends.

"Let's go further," he said. "I already know."

"What do you know?" Fronda asked curiously.

"I know what they feed on. Not blood, because they would be red, not so white. They extract water from the dead body with dissolved organic compounds and mineral salts. That is why the body looks like a mummy. It is simply systematically deprived of water."

"Looks like you're right," Dea nodded, shining her flashlight in the corners. "Look over there."

Everywhere small, oblong hills of dark gray ash could be seen, sometimes retaining some resemblance to human shapes.

Never nodded and adjusted his helmet.

"So much remains of man after full dehydration. I have never heard of something similar in my life."

"Zeb to ślak," Gladiator murmured, automatically making cross sign.

"Okay, we already know what will happen to someone who gets here. But in my mind this ivy is too weak to cause shocks," said Fronda, on which the sinister vegetation did not impress.

"Yes... I would, however, give my head that it somehow connects," Dea passed the girl's body and shone her way with her hand light.

"Come here!" She called after a moment.

The further corridor was literally braided with vines, like a garden gazebo with bindweed. However, these did not stand almost completely still, as they have passed so far. They trembled and rustled ceaselessly, rustled one around the other, and started to feel nauseous. Something that looked like a thick wooden footbridge ran through the center of the corridor. After a short hesitation, friends decided to go wherever they could. In the event of any signs of danger, they could retreat - the vines were obviously afraid of the lights of their flashlights, and in any case it caused them some indefinable distress. They were trying to crawl away somehow from where it was strongest. It wasn't strange, since they had spent all their lives deep underground, but how did they "see" this light? They must have had some photosensitive cells, but that would be absurd. Evolution does not create what is not needed, and here, under the ground, in complete darkness, plants probably did not need light sensors.

Suddenly Dea stopped, bent and touched the path they were walking with open hand. She muttered a vague curse.

"Listen... it's just a root," she said. "Fat but still damn root."

"Hmm... It's getting weirder and weird," Fronda muttered, looking around alertly.

"Stranger and strange," Gerard supported him. He felt a sudden fear that their flashlights might go out and leave them in complete darkness. He had no doubt that these vines would then braid them, like other victims. He was beginning to better understand Never's panic, carefully hidden, fear of the dark - a peculiar feature of a vampire.

The Indian who walks ahead doesn't seem to hear them. A beam of light from the flashlight on his helmet lit the road in front of him, a second flashlight held in his hand swept a streak of light all along the way. Unlike others, he grew up in the Indian jungle and saw enough vines not to be afraid of them. Therefore, when the road was blocked by a thick curtain, made of flexible twigs woven together, he simply pushed it aside as if it were a simple curtain. With some difficulty, he ripped off a few legs that immediately wrapped around his wrist, but did so in a calm and indifferent manner, as if he were dealing with ordinary field thistles. However, on the threshold of the huge space that opened behind this curtain, he stopped uncertainly.

"What is there?" Asked Gerard, who was walking last and did not see well.

Dea swallowed hard before answering, because Never could not speak.

"It's a tree... Damn, a tree..."

Now everyone was pushing one another to see what Dea and Never saw first, and just as they were speechless by impression. The term "tree" was perhaps not the strictest. This thing looked more like a huge tree stump after a cut tree, although no cutting plane was visible. Flat as a large, roughly round concrete circle, overgrown with flowing bark, it pulled out thick, thick roots like oaks of age. As far as the eye could see, they saw only the rough, furrowed surface of the bark and the gray coating of the young branches of the vine. Between them rose goblets of flowers, broad, rosette like water lilies, with thick petals shaped like an elongated oval. The smell of forest rot in autumn hung in the air.

"Man, this stump is probably as big as downtown," groaned Gladiator at last. "What kind of tree would it be if it decently grew high, then? Like African baobabs."

"I've never heard of a tree that would grow entirely underground. This is unnatural and I think maybe dangerous," Fronda studied the roots and "trunk" by touch, trying to understand anything.

"Why dangerous?" Dea raised an eyebrow and looked at him questioningly.

"I feel that it is reason of the shocks or something that causes it. Roots the ground and I'd give head to the guillotine that it pulls people into these forbidden caves. It's like a mother to all the vines we've seen."

"A tree under the city..." Gerard whispered. His artistic soul was more delighted with what the eyes saw than scared by the sight of corpses.

"One day this tree will destroy the city," Never said.

"I do not think so. It wants to maintain the status quo. Sudden exposure to sunlight would not be desirable for it. Living in the dark, it probably didn't develop UV protection," Dea said.

"You sound like it thinks..."

She shrugged.

"Well, certainly not in our understanding of the thinking process. But it thinks its own way. It can prepare a trap that draws living creatures to the very bottom of the caves, where climbers can take body fluids from them. Water, as you can see, is not enough for such a tree, it must have the essence of a living organism.

"It means it's deadly," Fronda said. "What do we do?"

"We're doing nothing," Never said emphatically. "It is not for us to judge it, much less to pass sentences. This tree is older than the city itself, even than Poland itself."

He sat on one of the roots. Somehow, he did not feel particularly threatened here, especially since the roots and offshoots did not move and did not think to grab a man like climbers. An ideal place for a meeting before embarking on a further journey.

Dea sat down next to him. The others joined them.

"Do you know where the name Warsaw came from?" She asked in a tone of social chat.

"I know," said Gladiator. "There were two young people, Wars and Sawa…"

Dea gave him a withering look.

"It's a nonsense legend," she said. "There was supposedly the name Wars, or Warsz, though… though opinions on this are divided. But the name Sawa is definitely male and in addition Czech, not Polish. Unless we get the city name from the names of a couple of ancient Pole guys, forget it."

"So?"

"In the oldest records we find the term "Warszewa settlement". It may have originated from the mythical Warsz, but… Relatively recently discovered the German chronicle… or rather a Visigoth… from the period before the baptism of Poland, somewhere from the fifth century AD. The word warschensir was found there and an explanation was given that the Wened people living in parts of today's Poland described ritual ablutions before sacrificing one of the sacred trees. Some ancient trees. To these trees, probably extinct today, were reportedly being sacrificed humans."

Fronda allowed himself a slight whistling.

"That would stick together," he noted. "The Celts also sacrificed to trees. Maybe it wasn't so stupid at all?"

"Could ancient Pole be Gauls from Asterix comics?" Gerard asked.

Dea thought a bit.

"Do I know, Gepard? Some similarities exist. Apparently, they were always at war with other tribes, Germanic, Lithuanian, and others. Except that there were only forests and forests, rarely human settlements… Few messages survived. The etymology of some words gives some idea about how difficult life was then. In most nations, "raising children" is derived from verbs meaning food or social ennoblement. "Wospitanije" in the Russians, because it was the most difficult to get food for the offspring. For Anglo-Saxons, "bringing up", because there it was most difficult for the child to "exalt", that is, to provide it with a higher social position than his parents."

"And here?" The actor asked to forget about the fear that was overwhelming him.

"Here, in today's Poland, there was plenty of food. Forests full of animals, berries, mushrooms, and wild fruit. No one was starving. However, it was difficult to "save" the child from the attackers, kidnapping or killing. Hence the term "upbringing"."

Everyone fell silent. These considerations, although otherwise interesting, led nowhere. In fact, they had to discuss something much more important: what next? Nobody, however, had any idea what to do. The underground tree was certainly not as dangerous as the Stonehenge Beast, but there was some elusive similarity between them. The best, from the point of view of people's good, would be to destroy this tree... but was there an effective and safe way to do it? And indeed, did they have a right?

"I suppose this warsch, so let's call it, is somehow associated to every tree in the city," Never said suddenly, studying diligently pediculation of the legs and roots. "If it wanted to kidnap people, no one would be safe. However, I think that it abducts people for some specific purpose. It needs them only at certain times, otherwise these caves would be full of powder from dehydrated corpses. And I counted four of them along the way, plus these two freshest..."

"In this one corridor, yes," Gladiator interrupted. "And how much goes to lie in others?"

"And if they only lie in this one? Let's think logically," Never continued, not paying attention to his friend's language errors this time. "Warsch is huge, which requires several dozen kilos of meat to be sucked. It has plenty of water in these caves, with all the nutrients dissolved in it. They seep out of the sewage system, and a layer of soil and stones filter out impurities. No, it doesn't kidnap people because of starving."

"It," Gerard repeated thoughtfully, slowly tasting the word. "It is only now that I realized that as individuals, trees are asexual, although we are eager to use articles to describe them..."

"You French people always look at this world from the side," Dea snorted in disgust. "Is that what this is about now? Rajah, as it turns out, knows how to think, and quite logically. I open free conclusions."

"For millennia people have been destroying nature... Probably it is finally retaliating against us," Theo said softly, brushing his hair mechanically.

When you leave your homes at dawn, and look from your homes to the road, what will you see?

It finally happened at the end.

What had to happen.

A great, green procession

The trees moved across the world.

Menacingly skimming in the wind

They are no longer afraid of us.

Trees as huge as towers

They enter cities by force," Gladiator chimed.

"What's he buzzing?" Never didn't understand.

Dea translated the words of the song as best she could, contrary to her customs, without commenting. She felt, like others, that perhaps Gladiator had hit the nail on the head this time.

For a moment friends wandered around the enormous mass, covered with bark and pale leg efflorescence. They felt involuntary respect for something as old as this tree, which saw all the storms, shocking the adventurous country and survived the entire process of forming its statehood. It was the silent witness of the ages that passed and wars that destroyed everything in its path.

"Where are we?" Asked Theo suddenly, pulling out a map of Warsaw from a haversack.

Taken out of thought, they leaned over the plan. They easily found the place where they went underground, and then, using a compass, determined in which direction they were going.

"Well, we're here now. And we were walking this way," Dea took a lipstick from her pocket and marked the way. Then she looked at the streets above them, shining a paper flashlight.

"They have been cutting down trees there for a long time," she said after a moment. "They're widening the street. Environmentalists protest, so it goes reluctantly, but goes on..."

Theo looked up, his eyes gleaming with understanding.

"It kidnaps people as trees are cut down," he said. "Something from the corpse helps him to heal the wounds or initiate regrowth. You would have to check if these disturbing vibrations sometimes appear only when felling is being carried out or also in other circumstances. It seems to be like that. In other situations, it probably has enough, for example... rats. I haven't seen any here, and there are plenty of them upstairs."

"If you want, you can think. Although you rarely want to."

Muttering this scant praise, Dea stood up, yawned and stretched. There must have been very little oxygen in these caves, because everyone was already feeling strange drowsiness. This tree did not bother to see, like all honest plants, the conversion of carbon dioxide into oxygen. Anyway, without light it could not start the process of photosynthesis, and even carbon dioxide could be difficult in the underground, without warm-blooded beings.

"There was a lot to think about..." Fronda sighed self-critically. "You didn't need Sherlock Holmes to get there."

"I knew him," Never said sleepily.

"Really?" Gerard looked at him with moderate interest. "I thought it was literary fiction... Anyway, the author himself maintained it."

"Oh, it was convenient for him and for many other people... But Sherlock Holmes, a brilliant detective, and at the same time a heavy smoker, a bit of a drug addict, a bit of a visionary, a little musician, and a little lively computer, existed in reality. Likewise, his sworn enemy, Professor Moriarty, is not made up, though in reality he was a common criminal, not a Napoleon of crime, and did not die at all when he fell into a waterfall. Watson was of course the author himself. He had the right to immortalize himself in this form, because he played such a role with a great detective, and even a greater one. Doyle looked after him until his death, for he was a guy, with all his talents, quite unfit for life."

"You can even see it in the stories," said the actor.

"One could say that he existed only when he was meditating on some criminal mystery, in other situations he barely vegetated. At the end of his life he was a shred of man. And his name wasn't Sherlock, but Ebenezer... Ebenezer Holmes. This is not the only minor correction of the author, also the alleged misogyny of the great detective is a myth. The thing is, he has been in love all his life with a woman who was out of his reach, moreover, for her great happiness, in my opinion. This did not prevent him from having a son with another. Interestingly, Professor Moriarty, who, thanks to the efforts of Holmes, spent half his life in prison and honestly hated him for it, had a daughter for a change and with the same woman. Dr. Watson, recite Sir Arthur Conan Doyle, did not mention it in his stories, which is a pity. It would be a great twist."

"Was Sherlock Holmes a drug addict? I did not know, and yet I read about his adventures," Theo interjected, who listened to it with great interest...

"Apparently you read it wrong," Never said. "He was, and indeed, though the author mentions it as if in a half-mouth. There is even a never published story in which a great detective is to solve the mystery of the peculiar inheritance of the old crane man from Crane Manor. The thing is that he has to solve the matter without leaving the family headquarters, since a clever mechanism blocked all the doors and the windows are barred. The matter is very difficult, meanwhile Holmes is on a regular hunger and unsuccessfully begs Dr. Watson for a dose of morphine. I read this story at the Museum of English Literature. It is in the back room, probably the curator did not deem it appropriate to boast about it to a wide audience.

"No wonder," said Dea, "I've never given Sherlock Holmes great esteem. Once, I remember, a short radio sketch made me laugh to tears. It went something like this:

Knock, knock.

Holmes, someone to you.

Great, my Watson, you will have a new matter to report to a wide audience. Please wait for my friend to insert a new card into the typewriter, and I will finish playing Schubert's serenade... Good. Now I will just inject morphine and light a pipe, and I'm already listening to you. What is this?

Dear Mr. Holmes, there is no case. I am the caretaker of this house and I just wanted to ask for something. When you leave, take the Baskerville dog with you, because it howls at night and the tenants complain."

Friends laughed. A cheerful anecdote slightly overwhelmed the horror of this place and thanks to it they got a spirit.

"Or maybe that story is simply not written by Doyle, or is this questionable authorship?" Gerard wondered. "But Maurice Leblanc also wrote about him."

"Arsene Lupine versus Sherlock Holmes" Never nodded. "Leblanc mocked Holmes and Watson, who, in any case, damn know why, stubbornly called Wilson. It was a malicious, flat, envious and aggressive lampoon. I must admit that reading this book I lost all sympathy for both the author and Lupine himself. It is beyond dispute that the difference in the literary workshop of both authors is colossal. Leblanc is not up to Doyle, and what is worse, he knew it and was devouring him. That's probably why he got to the hero because he couldn't get the author himself."

"What to do, in this case, even I agree with you, although I should rather oppose a sense of national chauvinism. Wait, what else interests me. So, Moriarty had a daughter?" Asked Theo, whose all fair sex interest, without any exceptions.

"Yes. You even know her, its Lenor."

"What?! And you didn't tell me anything? So, you are such a friend..."

"You could have guessed it yourself. Her husband's name is Pierce. His real name is Eleanor Shelby Moriarty, you must have known that."

"I didn't associate..."

Dea yawned and suddenly came to her senses. She jumped from the root on which she was sitting and rolled her friends with eyes with heavy contempt.

"Is this a fucking literary workshop or a scientific expedition, damn it?! If we sit here and talk about nothing, I can't vouch for our lives. Let's go from here. We won't think of anything for now. Personally, I would be against any attacks on this tree. I don't know why, but I feel that such a thing could end badly for the whole city."

"For sure," Never agreed, also getting up. He looked around and suddenly asked. "Don't any of you know which way we got here?"

Despite his best intentions, he couldn't look down the corridor that had brought them here. A dome of entwined vines surrounded them, and in the light of what they already knew about them, they did not want to search these festivities dangling from everywhere. They had the impression that they were looking at them, waiting only for the right moment to attack.

"Oh my, not good..." said Gladiator with a note of panic in his voice.

"A kingdom for a herbicide, or at least a pruning shears," Gerard repeated after him, moving quickly to his friends. Although he tried to make his words playful, he was clearly terrified.

They looked around uncertainly for a moment.

"There is nothing to meditate, guys," Never decided finally. "Let's go. Flashlights at full power and we are looking for a way out. They are afraid of strong light."

Indeed, the vines, on which the main beam fell, trembled slightly and tried to crawl out of the light. It was only necessary to pray that the batteries would last before they found a way out. Although the thought of clearing the tangled stems with their hands was disgusting to them now, they had to do it. The situation was exacerbated by the fact that it suddenly turned out that there was something else living outside the tree and its branches. In the thickets of vines there were swarms of small, barely a few millimeters insects, almost round, flat and voraciously at everything nearby. They had not noticed them before, because they had the same color as vines. But now it has become clear that the Tree has a powerful ally and one that is not afraid of light.

Theo, known for his crazy courage, freely jumped back with a curse worthy of the worst derelict. Gerard and Gladiator fled with him, and the three of them were now standing a safe distance from the creeper wall, nervously brushing their clothes and looking at their hands in disgust. Even Dea's steel nerves failed, as intrusive insects covered the sleeves of her overalls and the girl threw herself back with an involuntary scream.

"Relax." Never held her gently and brushed off the nagging intruders from her clothes. "After all, they are only insects, although I admit that I have no idea what species to include them in."

"To disgusting!" Dea shouted angrily.

She had grounds for irritation, because small insects gave the impression of something like an ant swarm and were incomparably more repugnant than ants. Only Never remained cool. He grew up in the Indian jungle.

"They seem to be in symbiosis with the Tree," he said. "It's like his defense. I can bet they sting, and it's very painful... of course not us, because we don't release pheromones, so they don't know how to treat us. They are blind, like everything that lives in absolute darkness, so they cannot see the light of our flashlights. Clearly, it doesn't scare them away. However, for your happiness, my fearful friends, your leader is prepared for any eventuality."

He took a small, maybe a quarter-liter bottle with an atomizer from the bag and methodically sprayed each of his friends with some colorless substance.

"What's that?" Asked Gladiator distrustfully.

"Super repellent. I am a good chemist and I once produced a chemical that repels all possible insects. Since then, I carry it with me constantly, because I would not like to experience the second time such an adventure as in Maidstone."

"What adventure again?" Theo sniffed the suit sleeve distrustfully and winced in disgust. Repellent did not smell good.

"I never told you? It was when Fronda was crazy about Lenor and I was studying medicine at Cambridge. One of my friends from the year, Violet Shannon, confided to me that her family residence was haunted. I decided to help her. Because her residence had an underground part, so first of all I went down to see if anyone was freshly buried there. I was unlucky, I covered three prisoners there who beat me and threw me into the deepest dungeon, the existence of which the owners themselves did not know. When I got it together, it turned out that there were a lot of vermin there. I was overwhelmed so that a week later I couldn't control my chills. I got out of there, of course, but that's a completely different story."

"Brrr," Dea shook herself in disgust.

The chemical proved to be really good, because more than a single insect bothered friends climbing through the veil of vines. Even more, because they buried themselves so well that they couldn't see them, although they knew that their entire swarms were lurking somewhere, and it was a depressing consciousness. After a long search, they finally found a corridor that they could follow. They were not sure if it was the one they came here, but they only wanted to get away from the Tree and its allies as far as possible.

After walking a dozen or so meters, it turned out that it is definitely a different corridor. This one was much lower and wider, full of dark diverticula, which they lit with involuntary fear, not knowing what could crawl out of them. However, they were empty, usually rising diagonally up to several dozen centimeters, which they could not explain. The corridor branched into a whole lot of smaller tunnels along the way, having their own legs and leading nowhere. It irresistibly resembled a schematic drawing of a tree - the main trunk and branches moving away from it.

"Hell, this whole Sherlock Holmes would really be useful to us now, maybe he would lead us out of this maze," Gerard said angrily, when one of the examined corridors turned out to be the next blind branch.

"We can do without this damn drug addicted man," Dea snapped and turned to Gladiator. "John, try to feel the right direction."

"We're going in it," Gladiator shrugged his powerful shoulders with a little helplessness.

"For sure?" Asked Never, incredulously, and stopped abruptly, for a shrill moan came from somewhere - definitely human and very close.

Others also heard it. First, they stopped, then, without consulting each other, they ran in all directions, carefully searching all the corners and all branches of the tunnel. Finally, thanks to a lucky chance rather than intentional action, Theo discovered a ground fault obscured by dry vines. There was a curled shape at its bottom, a black hole with ragged edges of peeled boards above.

"There he is!" He called out. "Ow snap! This is Lambdon!"

"What?" Never in the blink of an eye came to him and shone a flashlight.

It was indeed a Tygier. He lay curled up, his pathetic face clutching the ankle of his left foot unnaturally angled. He was stunned and apparently suffering, but he didn't seem to be seriously injured. Theo was with him in one leap, Dea followed his example, always ready to help in emergency situations.

"Hold him tight, Fronda," she commanded, not wasting time. "It's just a sprain."

"Hey, don't move me, bitch!" Shouted Tygier in horror, but the girl ignored the protest.

She grabbed his foot expertly and jerked so that Theo barely managed to keep his friend. Something popped, Tygier howled briefly, threw a few curses, and fell silent.

"Damn you, French, you have a tune for sadists," he said hoarsely after a moment. "Oh my, my eyes darkened. It's good that you found me. I climbed onto some damn boards and broke below me. I've been here for two hours."

"What are you doing here, Lambdon?" Never asked.

"What? I was looking for you! Stasiek told me where you went, so I went after you. I have an interesting proposition for you. And what, you found something interesting in these canals? Stasiek always makes a big deal out of something."

"Well, not this time. What we have found is dangerous, but I do not think that we can eliminate this threat. We will prepare an appropriate report. I hope your suggestion will be more fruitful for us."

"Oh, yes. Very lucrative. But first we have to get out alive, and I don't know if I will be able to step on that damn leg after treating your new friend..."

Supporting Gladiator's strong arm, he stood up. It did not escape the attention of friends that he looks around vigilantly a little too much for a man who thinks that everything is all right. His gray eyes scurried across the dark corridor as if they were looking for something specific, something that Tygier knew and did not want to talk about. The words "get out of here alive" also had their pronunciation. It was clear that this was not the first time Tygier was visiting these canals and that he was well informed about what was going on in them.

"What are you not telling us?" Never said sharply.

"Me?" the Pole surprised innocently, but under the influence of Never's gaze he turned red and looked down. He couldn't lie.

"All right," he said reluctantly. "Tell me first what conclusions you have reached, and I will complete them if possible."

Dea briefly told him what the discovery had made and what they had guessed, but as they all told each other, Tygier knew much more about it. He smiled indulgently and with a slight irony. And when Dea was finally done, he said emphatically:

"You are very childish and very naive people. That's all."

"Why is that?" Fronda asked, offended by such a summary.

"A tree that drills tunnels and pulls people underground in retaliation for cutting down trees on the surface... This is a very tempting prospect, I admit, and what a powerful argument for Green Party! Only, unfortunately, the conclusion is completely wrong. What you have reached implies rational action. It would no longer be the usual, commonly known tropism, by the power of which every living being strives for a source of food, but intelligent planning, which plants are not capable of. You understand?"

"I don't," Gladiator admitted blankly.

Tygier struck him lightly at the back of his head with an open hand.

"What's in there?" He asked.

"Brain... I think."

"I think so. And the plant has no one. So, what's it supposed to think, moron? What?"

"Wait a minute," Dea interrupted him. "So, what is abducting these people?"

"Exactly..." Tygier hung his voice in some sinister way. He tried if he could step on his sprained leg and grunted in pain.

In the silence that now fell, the murmur that had already caught their attention was louder. It sounded as if something rough was rubbing against the excavation walls near the intruders from the surface, or like falling off sand from a stone slope. The friends crossed their eyes, overwhelmed by the homogeneous thought: "Let's get away from here..." Even the usual bravado of Fronda disappeared somewhere when, clutching the flashlight nervously, he looked around the corridors. He couldn't recognize the way. The corridors changed their configuration, looked different, he could not tell which way they came or which way they should come back. And Theo was known for never getting lost anywhere.

They surrounded them unexpectedly, as if they had grown out of the ground. The association with Wells' monstrous Morlocks was all too tempting, but only at first. Immediately afterwards, differences were invisible. First of all, these people were not physically terrible, although they were undoubtedly different from the inhabitants of the sunny area. Body shapes and proportions were slightly elongated, but not in some caricatured way. Very long fingers ended with flat, thick, brown nails, reminiscent of wood. They had white-gray skin, and their elliptical heads were devoid of any hair on both men and women.

They all wore similar outfits, a kind of tight pants and sweatshirts, made of seemingly many rat skins sewn together. On each of their left arms there was a kind of corrugated metal band, looking like some electronic device, completely incompatible with the whole, giving a rather primitive impression. However, this was not all terrible, but rather the view of their faces - elongated jaws, slit lips, flattened nostrils, and especially the complete absence of eyes, even a trace that once, in a distant generation, these people had organs of sight. Their ears, on the other hand, resembled bats' ears and clearly had well-developed muscles because they moved them like desert foxes.

"Relax," Tiger said quietly. "We do not emit any typical smell, so they know that we are not human and therefore do not attack us. They are Druids."

"I thought the druid had a white beard and robe to the ground," Gerard whispered weakly.

"Of course, they are not Celtic druids, but those by the big D. That's what I call them, because they worship the Big Tree. Hell knows who they really are... I only know about them that they have a different genetic structure than we do. In this respect, even chimpanzees are closer to us than these underground beings. However, they are definitely reasonable in our sense. They have their own culture, science, religion and even politics, although of course their religion is the most dangerous. They kidnap people and sacrifice them to the Tree."

"Are they cannibals?" Dea asked, unable to control her cold shiver.

"Not at all. I said they were intelligent beings."

"Primitive Black people were also intelligent beings."

"Come on, woman. I don't want to insult Native Africans, but they are far back from them."

Theo took a step forward and examined the closest being.

"Maybe it's a forgotten branch of homo sapiens...?"

"Maybe," replied Tygier. "You must know that the tunnels in which we are now are by no means the lowest story, although they were also built by them and equipped with a mechanism allowing them to change their layout. Underneath is all a vibrant world: cities, homes, schools, and factories of all goods, workplaces, places of worship and places of entertainment.

"You're lying!" Dea looked at him in surprise.

"No. Do not be fooled by their appearance, they are not well developed in scientific terms. These kinds of armbands, what they wear on the shoulder, is a kind of sonar, thanks to which they compensate for the lack of eyes. A primitive tribe wouldn't construct such a thing."

Druids whispered something among themselves. Their speech sounded like the softened hissing of giant snakes and it did not resemble any of the known languages.

"If we were human, would they sacrifice us?" Dea asked quietly, unable to control her trembling voice despite all efforts.

"Only if the ritual required it," explained the Pole. "They don't murder mindlessly. They kidnap people for sacrifice from specific places and at specific times, with all the necessary calculations being made by their chief priest, fortune teller and scientist in one. However, if we threatened them, they would tear us apart."

"They probably kidnap women to interbreed with them," said Gladiator, his voice full of terror.

Tygier snorted dismissively. In the light of his earlier lecture, this absurdity was so bright that he did not even deign to answer. He tried again to step on his injured leg, but the pain was still too big.

"Silence," Gladiator murmured, keeping his eyes on the Druids. "Listen, guys: the one with the black collar is talking to us. In Polish."

"What?!" Tygier looked at him in amazement, then raised his ear.

"What does he say?" Gerard asked. He, despite the best intentions, could recognize only unpleasant hissing in these sounds.

"Get away from here."

"Tell him with wild pleasure if they tell us which way."

"Also, add that you can't kidnap people and that if they continue to do so, they will eventually ask themselves for trouble," Never added.

Gladiator, proud of his superiority, turned to Druid in the black collar and translated what he heard into Polish. Druid answered him and for a moment they were arguing about something, which Tygier listened attentively and with some amusement.

"He says people are cutting trees on the surface," he finally translated, seeing that the excited highlander was working on translating Druid's words into English. "It hurts Warsch, who needs a human sacrifice to heal the wounds. Warsch is the most important for them. Thanks to him they can breathe, he also provides them with medicines and... A word I did not understand. Something else. They will defend him until the last Druid."

"Well, if it turns carbon into oxygen... though the devils know how, since there is no light needed for photosynthesis," Dea muttered.

Druid spoke again, emphasizing Polish words in a rustling manner proper to his people.

"He says they're not enemies. They just want to live, having nothing to do with Kasaya, that is, like those on the surface," translated Tygier.

"So, advise him to limit the construction of new tunnels or to do it in a less expansive way, because soon everyone on the surface will know about them," Never told him.

He wanted to get out to the open air with all his heart, and although he understood that he could not panic, he had more and more difficulty keeping calm.

Two amused, several-year-old children ran out of the side corridor. Before the adults could stop them, they flashed between them and bumped into Fronda. Theo instinctively held them so that they would not fall. One of the Druids roared violently, throwing himself forward.

"Relax, I won't hurt them," Fronda said in the friendliest voice he could do, and, sitting on his heels, began to tickle the little ones.

The children laughed happily, touching his face, hair and arms with interesting hands. Everything astonished them - and the thick hair on the head of the vampire, and his eyelids, and the cotton shirt that they felt overwhelmed with disbelief. They did not know such clothes. The babble rattled on and on, and although you couldn't understand a word of it, you could see that they were not afraid of anything and nothing.

"They have children, and their children... play with dolls," said Gerard, picking up a clay figurine in a dress clumsily made of a piece of fur. "They are not so different from us, although their eyeless faces make quite an unpleasant impression. Now the question: what should we do?"

"Leave," Tygier replied firmly. "And never mention to what we have seen here."

*****

"Who exactly are you?" Dea asked, conscious as usual.

They went to sleep in a small house near Warsaw, rented for money from Stasiek. It was supposed to be safe there. They believed, although the hostess who gave them the keys did not say a word and looked quite strange. However, they woke up in a completely different place, which they did not know, and everyone felt as if someone had beaten them. They were not given time to orient themselves. Under the arms, they were brought to a nicely furnished office and left there. And then he showed up the gray-haired man in an impeccably tailored suit and very kindly greeted them.

When Dea asked, he gave her a friendly smile.

"Robert V. Dagwood, general in Her Majesty's service," he replied.

"What's going on here? Has my country declared war on England and surrendered in twenty-four hours and I know nothing about it?" Asked Gladiator. The rest were silent, staring at the general with hostile eyes.

They had no reason to be proud. They were surprised like amateurs and if they were surprised, they were still alive. But on the other hand, again, this general did not look like a Hunter. Slim, elegant elderly man with calm movements, giving the impression that talking to vampires was his daily occupation. And it would be hard to suspect that Lambdon Tygier would deliberately trap them.

"What are these nerves for? Poland and England have been cooperating for a long time and no declaration of war was needed," said the general calmly. "This resort is over forty years old and has great achievements. In creating it, my predecessor modeled on the American ORSI, the Office for Research and Scientific Investigations. There are many phenomena and cases that do not undergo standard evaluation. No serious scientist will deal with them, as he would become a laughing stock for his colleagues. And we don't have to consider recognized authorities."

"Okay, but why us?" Gerard wanted to know. He was still dizzy after gauze, which had been put to sleep and yawned incessantly.

"And that's another story. Can any of you read American comics?"

"Fronda. But what does this have to do with it?"

"It has. If any of you read these stories, you probably know who X-Men are."

The general looked at them questioningly.

"Mutants," Theo said with bottomless astonishment. "The radical group is commanded by Magneto, a moderate group by Professor Xavier."

"Exactly," the general nodded. "Although this is officially denied, mutants exist. Of course, none of them shoots lasers from the eyes or fly, but they have different above-average abilities. We have, for example, a girl who can read the print with her fingers, as if she had fiber optics in her fingertips. We have a semi-paralyzed genius whose brain works like a computer and so on. We pay for such highly talented people to study, and then bring them to our agency. Thanks to them, it is easier to solve certain problems that people encounter in various parts of Europe and even the world."

"Oh. And we would also be such an operational group for special tasks?" Fronda asked, his eyes brightening like a light bulb.

"Yes, but slow down a little. Don't expect to save the world or fight super villains and even ordinary terrorists. For this there are others. Your task would be to solve puzzles that official science cannot solve."

"And if we refuse, then what? Is it over for us?" Growled Gladiator unfriendly. He also felt terrible.

The general smiled pityingly.

"Not at all," he replied. "Stories of people who become secret agents under duress are nonsense, cinema fiction. That way you can't recruit a good agent and who the hell can't someone you can't trust? If you disagree, you will leave slowly. However, I hope you will accept my offer. It is not bad."

"Nobody claims it is," Dea relaxed a little. "However, you will admit, general, that this whole situation is for us, well, unexpected. It is not easy to make such a serious decision while you wait."

"I understand. However, I would like you to answer now. I know from experience that vimani have no sense of time and I would not like to stay with anything."

"What did you say, vimani?" Never asked. "Vimana is not a man, he is a type of vehicle of the gods flying, described in the Mahabharata and the Vedas."

"Yes, but we call vampires this way for simplicity and camouflage. V-Men. It's a better name and hardly anyone will guess its true meaning, even when it overhears a conversation not intended for his ears," the interlocutor explained politely without losing his patience.

Never rubbed his forehead with the back of his hand. He felt that this older gentleman was telling the truth, but somehow, he was terrified by the thought that they would be "full-time" in a secret scientific organization, in addition managed by people. No vampire makes his fate dependent on man, it's too risky. However, something appealed to him in the perspective of this work.

"General, we may get along," he said. "But on our terms. We must have maximum freedom and minimum supervision, otherwise nothing from the whole business."

"You don't trust me? It is clear. Maybe someone in your blood will convince you?"

The general pressed a button on the table. The door opened and Lenor entered the office in the company of a man with not quite ordinary exterior. He was almost as tall as Gladiator, and unevenly muscled. His face, wrapped in twisted, pitch-black hair, was dark, brash and wild, with a low forehead and wide jaws. Only blue eyes in which cheerful sparks smoldered softened its expression.

"You already know Lenor," said the general. "And this is Conan, our head of training. I'm leaving, and you can talk from the heart."

"Conan from Cimmeria?" Fronda asked, appreciating the massive muscles of his new friend.

The giant assumed the pose of a circus athlete.

"I'm Conan the Cimmerian, the barbarian and Crom's chosen one," he roared, but then he laughed and added in a normal voice. "My real name is Conan Kandisky and I'm from Ohio. Still, you are right to some extent. I knew Robert E. Howard well and was friends with him until his tragic death, and he immortalized me in his stories. Although, to tell you the truth, I should capture him, even against his will," he added grimly.

"I know how you feel, brother," Theo said sympathetically. "I was in such a situation myself..."

"And you won't say hello to me?" Lenor interrupted him. He looked at her with unfriendly eyes."

"Ultimately, I can, it doesn't hurt me. Hi, witch."

"Oh, not nice, knight. Is that how you address the lady?"

"Lady? Do you think I'm an idiot?! You serve people, but that's not enough. You put us to sleep! You came up with this! Tygier is too straightforward for such a dirty trick..."

"What did you want?" Now Lenor got carried away. "I called you, I wrote! You didn't want to help me. Dagwood saved my life, pulled me from the Hunters paws. I will work for him, whether you like it or not."

"Stop it now," Never cut in disgust. "Nice to see you, Lenor. We were all worried about you, this jester too, he just won't admit anything. Do you work for the general?"

The Englishwoman sat back in her chair and lit a thin cigarette.

"I work for an agency, but in the laboratory, not in the field. I have no inclination for this. You could do more. You won't sit there anyway."

"Does Tygier serve them too? We've got to talk to him, oh we've got," said Gladiator, eloquently folding his hand into a fist.

Lenor shrugged impatiently.

"Get away from him, he did what he should. How else would we convince you to visit this base? At best, it would take a long time, and we're in the middle of an investigation that has stalled. Only you can help here, that's why we had to hurry."

"I'll talk to him anyway," insisted Gladiator, who was not easily convinced to change his mind, even when he was not emotionally involved in the case.

"Talk to me better," Conan suggested. "Here or in the exercise section?"

"Come on, Conan, you can see the guy is crazy," Lenor said scornfully. "There is nothing strange about it, considering who it is with. In the company of Fronda, everyone will fix sooner or later."

The conversation began to deviate dangerously from the usual muzzle, so Never decided it was time to bring it to the merits.

"Tell me, Lenor, why is this general so angry with us?" He asked. "Why does he want an answer already? Is everything falling apart or something?"

"Rather 'or something'," she sighed. "Recently, we had a problem with reports of unusual matters, and one of them was particularly interesting. It concerned the Great Pyramid of Giza. The thing is that the scientific expedition sent by the agency has completely ceased to speak, and the best agent of the general, who was to check what happened on the spot, was lost."

"Oh, nice," Theo was happy.

"The general doesn't want to send more people to Egypt, because it is some kind of dirty matter, so they should be investigated by people like us. So far, however, he only has me, Tygier and Conan. I will definitely not go anywhere, Tygier is organizing a research workshop for us and he is devilishly busy. And Conan is our head of training, he trains agents for melee combat and he should not leave the center either. He is needed here. We have you, and it is good that we have found you, thanks to Tygier. What do you think?"

"That probably the ghost of Ramses the Great scared there," snorted Fronda.

"Terry, this pyramid was built for Pharaoh Hufu. At the time of Ramses the Great, it was already a very old monument. And there can be no ghosts there. The general is not interested in reports that the dead aunt is scaring somewhere."

"He doesn't know what he is losing..."

"Can someone give me a cigarette? It will twist me inside in a moment," groaned Gerard, holding his head.

Conan rummaged in his pocket and offered him a packet of Winston's. Lenor also took one, the others refused with thanks.

"All right, Miss Moriarty," Theo said after a deep reflection. "Let's say we enter this business. Don't say anything, Rajah, this time I will decide, at least for myself... and I advise you. It's always better to have a steady income and a place to hide than live like homeless cats. So let's say we agree... what does this English offer us?"

Lenor put her legs crossed on the desk and put on an official face, which was not disturbed by the cigarette dangling from the left corner of her mouth.

"Security first," she said. "On each request, a false alibi and properly prepared data for computer records, if needed. In addition, supply with a known article, a fixed salary, two thousand greens per capita plus expenses, and a separate bonus for each order. In addition, the right of permanent accommodation in the center, training no worse than in the FBI and the opportunity to participate in the social life of the agency, which is not the latter."

"Let's say," Never murmured, not sure. "Does everyone here know about our unusual diet?"

"Of course not, Mowgli. This would be too much for even paranormal researchers. Only the general is fully oriented."

"All right call him. We can at least try, guys?"

The general had to eavesdrop, because at the same time the door opened, and the older man entered the office. Lenor, shocked, jumped from the desk.

"Have you thought?"

The Indian looked at Dagwood with some hesitation, but answered after a moment:

"Okay. If you so politely ask..."

The general smiled.

"Fine. Tygier said that one of you is a doctor."

"I," said Dea, "a xeno-medic, to be precise."

"Great. We lack a doctor who would know, apart from human problems, the physiology of vimans. If you agree, you will be responsible for all our medical care. Our current general practitioner has retired and the other two have no experience at all. I prefer not to initiate them."

She thought for a moment, then nodded.

"Why not? That sounds pretty reasonable."

"Well, it's been agreed. Lenor will now lead you to the apartment you will occupy and introduce you to the rules of the resort. Here are your stamps with which you can move freely around the entire complex. Your codenames are Tau One to four, since the fifth member of the team as a medic drops out of active service. You don't give your own names to any of your employees or ask about them. Only nicknames are known here. Sleep well, then we'll talk about the action."

Friends got up from their chairs, examining brass stamps with curiosity. They were quite large, in the shape of the horizontally crossed letter V, consisting of stylized feathers. At the point where the quill touched, an equilateral triangle was visible, with a round dark metal object the size of a pinhead.

"There's a microprocessor there," Lenor told them. "The display shows a barcode. Thanks to it, this stamp can be used as a pass to the facility. Learn how to fasten it properly, because it is not so easy. Note that the fastener is connected to the microprocessor. If an unauthorized person would get a stamp, the jerk would be registered, and protection would be immediately caught. Come, I'll show you the quarters."

"Can I call before? It will be quite far, because all the way to the other hemisphere, you don't mind?" Fronda asked the general.

"Of course, call where you want. Just go to the communications department with this. And remember, don't give anyone the location of the resort."

"Sure! I don't even know what city it is..."

"Klewki."

"Nice. Almost like Cleveland. And you can pronounce it without problem," said Never, who was amused by this all.

"This is the name?" Theo grunted angrily. "I don't like it. Where is this communications?"

"I'll take you," Conan offered eagerly, who clearly liked the new recruits.

Communications department was a well-equipped switchboard, full of all kinds of equipment. Fortunately, apart from very modern devices, there were also ordinary telephone booths. Theo entered one of them and carefully tapped a number on the keypad, coded on a tiny notebook he would not part with.

"Hello, Steve?!" He called into the receiver. "This is Fronda, do you remember me? Give me Oggy."

"Fronda! Nice to hear you," came the perky voice of a Crocodile Hunter. "Unfortunately, I can't call her. This girl disappeared a few weeks ago, and despite painstaking research, I haven't been able to find her. She left only a letter with a note in it that she doesn't like this country where spiders crawl into your bed and scorpions in your shoes. I don't understand at all what is bothering her. I don't deny that these things happen, but is that a cause for panic?"

"I have no opinion on this subject, although I must admit that I do not like such filths myself. Not sure where she might have gone?"

"No, but she probably had left Australia, since she left such a note. If only some bad adventure would not befall her. She wrote that she would call but had not yet done so."

"No worries. Our Oggy can handle whatever she intended. I need to contact my fellows all over the world, so they can keep an eye on her. How's Daren going?"

"Great, thank you. He grows and develops brilliantly. He is a very intelligent child, although he has a lack of education. We all look after him and he gives us a lot of joy. He also helps a zoologist as much as possible."

"That's great. Kiss him from us and good luck."

Theo hung up the receiver and scratched his crown anxiously. There could be no doubt that Oggy had left Australia with the intention of finding her friends, which might have turned out to be quite difficult for her. He only hoped that she would not bump into the Hunters along the way, and that some other, equally unpleasant adventure would not meet her, for he could not help her this time. After all, he did not know where she was now, which roads she was traveling, trying to find their trail.

"Bad news?" Conan asked.

He was standing outside the cabin, leaning against the wall, massive arms crossed over his chest. Indeed, even in jeans and a polo shirt, he looked like a warrior from ancient times.

The disheveled black mane and strong jaws intensified this impression. In his dark face, his eyes glowed like blue LEDs, softening the severity of his features a little. In the entire vampire community, he was as unique as Gladiator, as they are generally rather asthenic. This is due to caution in selecting candidates for fixation - the emphasis is on aesthetic and mental qualities rather than muscles. Athletes have never been good candidates for preservation, but there have been occasional exceptions like Conan. It was easy to understand why Robert E. Howard was so impressed that he immortalized him in his saga.

"I do not know." Fronda replied. "Not very successful, but time will tell. Are you supposed to teach us?"

"Yes. I mean, I know very well that you, for example, require little training when it comes to combat. However, it includes not only direct clashes, but most of all ways of avoiding it and all investigative propaedeutic. Our agents must be really good. The general probably warned you that we are not an anti-terrorist organization and we are not in the business of saving the world like in the James Bond movies. Even so, you must all be prepared for any eventuality." Niech to diabli...

Theo himself did not know if he was satisfied with such an unexpected engagement or not. If he had been sure that General Dagwood was honest with them, he probably would have been, but even the words of his kin did not quite convince him. The fact that he agreed so eagerly to his proposal was because he already wanted some kind of stability. Living in constant danger was tiresome even for him. However, he decided to keep his eyes and ears open to everything that was happening here, and that he would not be surprised.

Conan led him through the various sections of the facility to the living area, where they were assigned accommodation in one of the standard apartments. They all had the same floor space and the same layout: the main room, serving as a dining room, a work room and a living room at the same time, two double bedrooms and one duel, intended to be an isolation room in case of illness. Other residents of the center, however, usually converted it into an additional bedroom, as almost every operating team consisted of more than four people. An isolation room was not necessary, as the center had its own medical point, with several beds and well-equipped.

"Here you will live," Conan said, pointing to one of these apartments to Fronda. "Of course, you are not prisoners. You can move freely around the resort and go out to the town. It's just that then you have to enter the book of entries and exits, this is the procedure."

"And do we enter the code name or real name?"

"A code name, of course. I'll take some signature samples from you later, but now make yourself comfortable and wait for the general. He'll probably want to send you to Giza right now."

Theo looked around.

"Maybe... Conan, tell me are there any other vampires besides you and Lenor?"

"Vimani, my dear. Get used to the word, everyone, it is a question of safety."

"Yeah," he agreed with him for the sake of peace. "Most importantly, occupational health and safety. Are there or aren't there?"

"Only Tygier. He tried to persuade some others, but so far to no avail. You know, our clan prefers to stay away from people, even the kindest. Anyway, the vimani don't really like discipline, and they don't like anyone over themselves."

Conan smiled sympathetically, patted Fronda on the shoulder and walked away down the corridor as Theo entered the apartment through the ajar door.

They are quite modestly, but functionally. In the main room there was a table with drawers under the counter, chairs, a long sofa in front of the TV and several wardrobes of various sizes. The walls were painted a pearly color and there were several paintings on various themes. The bedrooms had couches, bedside tables and chests of drawers.

"Not a bad cuddly place, as if someone were asking me," said Gladiator, who sat on the couch and switched the TV channels with the remote. "They also have a video game room, a gym and a library in several languages."

"So, it doesn't matter how many languages. You have nothing to say about any of them," muttered Never.

He did not like closed rooms, although he knew that in their situation a windowless room was better than one with a beautiful panoramic view of the area. Sooner or later someone would be interested in why they cover the windows so carefully on sunny days. The door, locked by the Fronda, opened again.

"One thing's for sure," said Gerard Phil as he entered the apartment. "There is no chemically pure silver in this entire facility. I ran all over with the detector and nothing. It didn't even beep."

"It's really comforting. Have you seen anything interesting during this inspection?" Never looked at him questioningly.

"Four flies and one ladybug. But the field is said to have a Colorado potato beetle."

"Little angel, you are squaring your head again, as the good soldier Švejk would describe it. It is the result of being in the company of Fronda, he is dangerous to the sane."

"The senses know the way to the gates of the paradise," Dea sang innocently, appearing in the doorway behind Gerard. "The medical facility is not the worst, although both will have to be changed. On the other hand, the patient file is useless, a lot of important data is missing. I have to fill them up if it's going to be good."

"And it has to be?" Theo grunted belligerently. Apparently, he had fallen into a quarrelsome mood.

She did not pay attention to him because the general had just appeared.

"One of our detectives has returned from Giza," he said. "They brought him, I should rather say. He's in shock. He does not recognize anyone and cannot say what happened. Delta 5 and Delta 7 found him in this state on a city street, and he was bloody lucky to find him. He could have wandered in that state for God knows how long."

Dea ran out into the corridor. The general lit a cigarette and only then looked at the four not quite ordinary men who were looking at him expectantly.

"Zeta 2 is a great specialist, it would be a pity," he said as if to himself. "Look, you have to go there. The whole pate started with the fact that five out of eleven people died at lightning speed when they opened the sealed chamber in the Great Pyramid. The others were hospitalized with strange symptoms that resembled an unusually severe allergic reaction or poisoning. The folks started talking about the curse, which is absurd, of course, idiotic, but very catchy. Professor Zani Pahwass, who contacted me, did not want to speak clearly, but he made me understand that the chamber was not empty... and that what was in it was gone."

Fronda's black eyes flashed upon hearing this, but Never anticipated his words.

"Let's not draw conclusions now. We do not know anything concrete yet and we will not know until we see everything with our own eyes. When are we flying, General?

"Oh, I like this attitude... You'll fly tomorrow, when the documentation department will prepare everything you need. Relax for now. By the way: this corner cabinet is a freezer / refrigerator, you have a stock of known goods there. Have you found the bar already?"

"Yes, we did!" Gladiator raised his glass, half filled with amber liquid.

Like Fronda, he liked undiluted alcohol, and because he had a high tolerance for alcohol, he could indulge his passions without hindrance. Especially now that he knew he wouldn't have to do anything until the end of the day.

Dea didn't show up for several hours. She returned to the quarter as they were getting ready for sleep. She was very tired.

"Zeta 2 looks like lobotomized," she said. "Fortunately, the brain exam showed no abnormalities, but his condition is even more surprising. This man saw something that shook him deeply..."

"Aliens," Theo said quickly.

"In your stupid head, I guess! But what he saw must have been no less terrifying."

"Did you find something specific?" Never asked impatiently.

"Not much. General physical and nervous exhaustion. Anemia, which is even more surprising since he did not have it a week ago. Depression and strange confusion that cannot be explained. Burns on the right side and thigh as from a strong rule. Clothes in this place also burned through. Anemia, as I said, and thrombocytopenia. Lymph nodes enlarged. The patient's gums are bleeding, the nails are falling off the body, the hair is breaking and coming out in bunches," she finished, quieter. "Does it tell someone something?"

"Bloody hell!" Never, who had already gone to bed, sat up straight on the bed.

"Radiation sickness? But how? After all, they opened a burial chamber, inaccessible for a good few thousand years, not a sealed reactor," Theo looked at his friends with eyes rounded with amazement.

Dea shook her head and ruffled her dark red hair with her fingers. She didn't understand it herself, she could only communicate her findings.

"I know as much as you do. Worse, the guy can't tell what happened to Zeta 4 and Zeta 5. But the hell didn't they evaporate?"

"Drink something," Gladiator offered her kindly. "Everything is possible. No one was surprised when twenty billion evaporated from the State Treasury, and together with the perpetrators of this scam."

"Money is money, but it is about two people... A man and a woman, he is 50, she is half his age, married, two children. The general will give you photos."

"Us? Does that mean you're not going?"

"No. I have duties here as a doctor. There are a few of our blood in this center, not just Tygier and Conan. And they are doing fascinating research here, I will be of use in the laboratory. You can do without a nanny anyway, you're all big boys. I'm right?"

Never listened to her with one ear, biting his fingernails and staring blankly at an undefined point. Something disturbed him, some vague association, but he couldn't pinpoint what. He had a similar feeling before, and trouble was always there.

"Everyone sleeps," he ordered suddenly. "We must be refreshed. Dea, prepare something for Fronda to calm down, so he won't embarrass us on the plane."

"You know, you're cheeky!" Theo said indignantly, and, mortally offended, demonstratively covered himself with the blanket up to the top of his head.

This insult, however, did not prevent him from trembling with fear at the airport, so that Never with real satisfaction stuck the syringe needle into his arm. It wasn't the first time he had had this problem with his friend when he had to fly somewhere - Fronda hated planes and had the worst opinion about them. Whenever he heard of a plane crash, he would exclaim with utterly inappropriate satisfaction under such circumstances:

"What now, didn't I tell you?"

Once he was even arrested after such a cry, because he was mistakenly mistaken for an assassin, and Never had great difficulty getting him out of jail. It was only when the fingerprints were checked, and it became clear that Fronda was not even at the airport on that unlucky day, not mention the plane, and he was released home.

After the injection prepared by Dea, Theo calmed down to the point where he sat quietly until Cairo itself, refusing to open his eyes.

"I keep repeating to myself that I'm on the bus," he explained to Gladiator, who finally asked him why he was closing his eyelids.

"Frenchmen are stupid," snorted the highlander, who was just at the stage of the new Asterix notebook.

Gerard smacked him in the neck angrily, the highlander gave him back and if not for Never, who had separated them, there would have been a scandalous overhead row. These two did not like each other very much, for some reason. They used every opportunity to bite each other or play a prank on one another, as if they were a couple of preschoolers, not adult men, undead at that.

"Are you drunk? Sit politely on your ass, now," Never hissed furiously at them, his golden eyes flashing menacingly. "If not, I'll order to tie both of you, okay? We have a serious task and you have fights in your head."

Offended opponents squeezed into their seats and did not speak to Cairo itself, where they happily forgot about the misunderstanding and in the best agreement got off the plane. Never looked around closely and, noticing the sign that read "Dagwood" had been raised, drew his companions in that direction. The plaque was held by a gray-haired man with dark skin, wearing a gray shirt and gray shorts.

"Rajiv Khenari," Never introduced himself, as he had in his passport. "And this is my team."

"Zani Pahwass," the Egyptian replied. "Come to the car."

He was cloudy and seemed to be rather hostile. This would be quite strange considering that he himself asked the agency for help. The friends were reasonably silent, not wanting to start the conversation first and hoping that it would all be cleared up anyway. It was only in the small hotel where they had rented a common room that Dr. Pahwass began to speak.

"I would not have summoned you if it were not for the fact that I prefer not to get involved in the whole police affair. I have the worst experience with policemen investigating archaeological sites. Never mind that they steal whatever they get. Worse, they are clumsy and inattentive, and in addition they are completely ignorant of archeology. For them, destroying a single hieroglyph is a little accident at work, and for us, you understand, it can be a real tragedy and burying the chances of reading a text correctly. Besides... what am I going to tell them? Here, gentlemen, we opened a chamber sealed seven thousand years ago and five of my colleagues are dead and the other six are fighting for their lives in the hospital? After all, I won't even be able to tell them what was in the chamber, because I don't know it myself!"

"And what was there, even if not exactly?" Never asked. He opened the hotel bar and examined its contents carefully.

"One of those who entered the chamber said before his death that there was a sarcophagus there, but strange because without any paintings, and uniformly gray. The thing is, the survivors didn't see anything with their own eyes, and whatever it was, and it vanished without a trace."

"There were no signs on the walls?"

"Only at the entrance, a drawing of a baboon with two knives. It's a familiar image, although we don't really know what it meant."

"According to Däniken, it could mean what a corpse's head and crossbones mean to us," Theo could not deny himself, knowing how the name Däniken affected every real archaeologist.

"He's a wally, but he might have been right about that," Pahwass muttered reluctantly. "But that obviously doesn't explain what happened to the crate."

"I don't think the sarcophagus rose and did not come out on two legs," Fronda snorted. "Hence the conclusion that there was someone else in the chamber after your colleagues' visit. And do you even know what happen to them?"

"Curse of Tutankhamen," said Gladiator in a grave voice.

"Of course! Tutankhamen walked from the museum to the pyramid and beat the archaeologists with a ritual cane. Come on, there's no curse." Gerard eyed him with immeasurable pity.

"First," Dr. Pahwass rubbed his forehead as if trying to collect his thoughts, "This name is pronounced differently: Tuth-Ankh-amon. Besides, the curse, my dear, was a harsh reality…"

Never, just pouring wine into glasses, looked at him with wide eyes. Even he did not expect that.

"Come on, doctor…?"

Zani took the glass handed to him. It was evident that it was not easy for him to talk about these things to complete strangers, but he had to push himself if they were to help him.

"Of course, the community of serious scientists did everything to cover up this matter. The thing is, of those reported to have been at the opening of the crypt, only two were there. They and some of the natives helping them died. The curse was very prosaic, just bacteria. In the days of Akhenaten, Egypt was a disease caused by bacteria related to the anthrax bacillus, with a high mortality rate. One of the porters may have been a carrier, and an invisible enemy was locked in a crypt with the mummy. Protected from the sun's ultraviolet light, the bacteria survived and, after opening the crypt, attacked humans. Fortunately, it turned out that the usual anthrax vaccine immunized against it, although they were not the same."

"If you stimulate the right immune mechanism, you will produce antibodies..." Never muttered.

"Then check the sick blood!" Theo blurted out, licking his lips a little at the mere thought.

"It was done right away. What the others got infected was not found. No virulent microbes, fungi or viruses have been detected at all, and these people die in the same way. Their blood degenerates, ulcers open on their skin, and there are also severe symptoms of gastroenteritis and swelling, as in the case of nematode infection. However, no trace of the parasites was found. If what causes these symptoms has been picked up by someone, there may be many more victims."

There was silence. Everyone tried to imagine this strange, unusual sarcophagus, the contents of which could be deadly. Even the fantast Theo did not try to guess straight out of Hollywood horror this time - the reality could be much darker than what special effects experts conjure up. Even though friends were used to dealing with a side of the world that most people don't know a bit about, they still didn't know anything about it. And with each assignment they undertook, they had to consider factors that were not entirely ordinary.

"I'm afraid that we will have to look at the crime scene, I mean the excavation or whatever you want to call it," Never said at last, picking at the braid which was tossed over his shoulder. "We promise not to destroy anything and not to steal anything. Do you know the VASP agency has already sent detectives here who have disappeared without a trace?"

"Yes. It means no. This is... I knew they had come, but I thought they returned to the agency without finding anything. They only contacted me once, and then they said that they had picked up a lead and I had never heard of them again. How did they disappear?"

"Just like that. The human eye hasn't seen them since they contacted you."

Zani Pahwass looked gloomy. The case was starting to take on a criminal overtone, and the archaeologist was concerned that they should inform the police. If people die of an inexplicable disease, that's a matter for the medics - but if they disappear, it must be assumed that usually a police investigation will be necessary. Never easily guess what the Egyptian was thinking about and smiled.

"No, Dr. Pahwass, we are not calling the police. This is an internal matter of VASP and we will deal with it on our own. You will only allow us to see that place in the pyramid that you have opened and not a word to anyone."

"Agreed," the archaeologist clearly breathed. "We fenced off this corridor and no one entered it anymore. Are you not afraid of infection?"

"No," the Indian replied shortly. "And don't worry about our precious health. Let's finish the wine and go."

The Egyptian looked at him in surprise.

"Now? It's already dark."

"We usually work at night. This is much handier."

Dr. Pahwass no longer asked why. He was not very inquisitive for an archaeologist, it even seemed he preferred not to know more than necessary. It was better that way, because they didn't have to come up with any far-flung excuses for their actions.

*****

The off-road cross-country vehicle stopped next to a huge structure, black in the moonlight, though, as Gerard noted with some disappointment, no more majestic than a huge pile of rubbish. Zani Pahwass shuddered at the iconoclastic words, and Gladiator and Fronda burst out laughing freely.

"Shut your stupid mouths," Never growled with displeasure and jumped out of the vehicle, looking out of habit for a possible threat.

Since there was no one around except the guards, he urged his friends with a wave of his hand, and they all followed the Egyptian who was leading them. The guards, having met the excavation director, let them pass without checking, and their bored expressions showed that they really didn't care what the night strangers were doing here. Having entered the pyramid, the friends turned on their flashlights. Beams of light brought out the walls from the darkness, surprisingly they were devoid of sophisticated decorations known from publications.

"Why are there no frescoes here?" Fronda asked softly, with obvious disappointment.

"Because this pyramid, contrary to popular belief, is no one's tomb," Dr. Pahwass replied, and added angrily. "If you like Däniken so much, you should know that. There is no evidence that the mummy of a ruler ever rested here. It is assumed that it was supposed to be a tomb, because that is simply the best explanation, but it is only a theory, and not confirmed. I have been researching this pyramid for many years, I have participated in all excavations in the area, and I know the weight and dimensions of each stone that was used here. I tirelessly search for new corridors, cataloged every shard of bone or pottery that I could get my hands on in this area, but so far I have not found an explanation for what this Herculean work was supposed to be for."

"It seems to me that you spoke differently in the press," Never looked at him questioningly.

"In front of the media I put a brave face on things, but I admit to myself that so far I am as stupid as a newborn baby. The only conclusion I have made is that maybe I just don't know what to look for."

"Perhaps," he agreed. "Could that disappeared sarcophagus contain a mummy?"

"I seriously doubt it. It was of an unusual shape, devoid of decorations and made not of wood, but of metal. The ancient Egyptians never used metal for sarcophagi."

"What metal was that?" Theo asked. "Because if gold or even silver, I am not surprised that it has disappeared."

"It is not known what, but not gold, not silver and not platinum. It was weird, I know that much. Maybe an alloy. Those who looked at the sarcophagus and touched it died, and those still alive did not touch it, so they could only judge visually. They know precious metals well and can judge them even from a distance, but not the alloys. They are not metallurgists, they are archaeologists."

"You do not know many things... You know where to go?"

The archaeologist stopped, pointing to a barred corridor.

"It is obvious that I am not going any further, and you, as you wish," he said. "Really, I'm surprised you go to a place like this without your protective suits.

"This is our concern, so to speak. Go back home, doctor. If we find anything, we'll report back to you." Never replied absentmindedly, shining his flashlight down the corridor partially covered with rubble. "Please do not delude yourself, for us the matter of what was lost from here is secondary, first we will look for agents. They were here?"

"What?" Zani, who had already gone a few steps, stopped and looked around. "Yes, they were. I left them in the corridor as you are now."

"Everything is starting to fit together..." Never muttered and boldly crossed the yellow tape with a black warning sign.

The others followed him, intrigued by his remark, for they could not see any logic in what they already knew. The corridor ended at the entrance to the chamber, partially obscured by a large slab of stone with a barely visible drawing of a baboon. The animal stood on its hind legs and held two knives in its front legs: one blade up, the other blade down. It did seem like a warning of a mysterious danger.

The chamber itself was less interesting than this drawing - just a rectangular room, devoid of any objects or decorations, with something smooth, dark gray on the walls. Only in the middle of the floor, the irregular stain brighter than the background marked the place where the lost sarcophagus stood. For the record, they examined both the floor and walls, shining their torches over them. Never carefully scanned the sarcophagus trail with the light, then pointed the flashlight at the entrance and shook his head slightly. Gladiator, who had at least half the IQ but prided himself on highly developed "sensor" abilities, initially stood motionless, as if listening to his inner voice. Then he walked over to one of the walls and began to tap it methodically.

"It is all like..." he said enigmatically at last. "Look here, you bastards."

Under the pressure of his hand, a rectangular, barely perceptible protrusion gave way, and the entire wall shifted without the slightest scratch. Behind her was a wide corridor, much wider than the one they had entered and much cleaner. After a moment's hesitation, they started, shining their torches on the walls, floor and ceiling for fear of traps that might be lurking here. The chamber wall closed behind them so suddenly that they twitched. Despite attempts, they could not open it, you could only do it from the inside. There was nothing for them to do but continue along this corridor wherever it led.

Never, who was going first, bent every now and then and picked something up from the ground or illuminated the walls and watched them closely. He did not deign to answer the questions why he was doing this even once, so in the end they all fell silent and walked in silence, broken only by the rustle of their steps. This is how they reached the wall closing the corridor, which, like the one in the chamber, gave way after finding the appropriate "unlocking button". They found themselves outside the pyramid again and sucked the night air into their lungs with relief.

"Look at the thickness of this wall," Gerard said softly. "It's one block as wide as my body. And from the outside, carved so that it gives the impression of a few stones, arranged like others. It doesn't stand out at all."

"But someone has discovered this passage, and I wonder when," Never muttered.

He did not explain how he came to this conclusion. He swept the light of the flashlight around the sand, then shone it on the Sphinx towering over the landscape, and unexpectedly turned the flashlight on Gladiator.

"Do you feel anything?" He asked.

"I feel a headache," Theo blurted out, though not asked.

"So am I." Gerard joined him. "And I'm kind of nauseous."

"I don't," said Gladiator. "And that's what you told me that I drink too much. As for feeling, I know which way what was taken from the pyramid was trapped. And I don't mean only the sarcophagus. This corridor seemed to serve as a repository for illegal antiques dealers, because walking along it constantly had flashes, that is, half-second visions of what was there. It is very annoying, I assure you. Fortunately, it rarely haunts me..."

"You think those traders took the sarcophagus?" Never interrupted him impatiently.

"And who else, Santa Claus? In my opinion, one of the archaeologists opened the wall and probably blocked it with something to keep it from closing. During the night, the others came, saw that their hiding place had been discovered, they took everything and stole what they found in the chamber. Then archaeologists began to fall ill, and no one dared to check this place anymore."

"It's quite logic," Gerard said after a moment, looking at Never.

The man shrugged slightly, as if he didn't know what to say to that. That Gladiator wasn't the fool he had posed for was no secret to him. So, it did not surprise him that he was capable of quite a wise conclusion. But he was clearly thinking about something else.

"Rajah, what could be in that chest?" Fronda asked him after a while, his eyes poking around the neighborhood as if he expected to spot something in the desert shrouded in darkness.

"Oh, I don't know what was there," Never answered him absently. "I just have no idea how it got there... Five thousand years is a long time. Now the traders have it, which means that they are either dead or in a moribund state... We're back. I need to consult Meres-Ankh."

"Sorry, with whom?" Gerard asked, completely bewildered.

The Indian looked at him with unseeing eyes. He looked now as if he was in a religious trance - as he always did when he tried to solve a mystery with insufficient data.

"Meres-Ankh, oh, she is the head of the local women's commune and the local guru in general," he said after a moment. "Nobody's going to help us if she doesn't agree to it. Fronda, I need you."

"Me, why is that?" Theo was surprised. "I'm not a communist, God forbid."

"And I am," Gerard said belligerently.

"You can even see it," Gladiator chuckled, which finally knocked Never out of his trance.

"But I used the word to mean 'community'," he said impatiently. "Meres-Ankh likes Fronda-type handsome men and he can put her favorably on us. Otherwise, we may have problems."

"Why we need help at all, Mr. Omniscient?" Gladiator wanted to know.

"Because we do not know the most important thing: where is the hiding place of the traders. I can't deduce that anymore, dear Watson."

He started toward the guards' voices, kicking stone fragments along the way. One could get the impression that he was trying in this uncomplicated way to "dig up" the entire ancient history, of which these stones were relics. Suddenly he stopped - so suddenly that Gerard, following him, bumped into him with force. He must have been struck by a thought as he turned back toward the still open passageway, triggering his silver detector.

It was impossible to guess what he meant. The detector only detected chemically pure metal, deadly to vampires, so it certainly wasn't trying to locate any of the ancient ornaments or figurines with it. Was he suspecting the presence of Hunters in the immediate vicinity of the pyramid? They could barely keep up with him as he quickened his pace. Never's long legs carried him effortlessly at a speed that forced the others to exert all their strength, until finally they cursed softly and loudly demanded him slow down, or at least explain what the hell he was looking for.

"Very interesting," the Indian muttered finally, pausing and looking around carefully. "It seems to me that Mr. Sphinx will have to explain this and that to us."

They were standing under the Sphinx. The enormous statue obscured their sky and horizon, looking lofty into the distance, high above their heads.

"And what can this puppet tell you?" Gerard gasped, gasping for breath. "Gosh, I'm barely alive... You couldn't wait for some transport, you just had to run like that?"

"Unfortunately, I had to." Never carefully checked the readings of his detector, wrote down the settings and only then looked at his friends. "We must visit this place again, but we will visit Meres-Ankh first. I wonder if the pyramid guards will lend us a vehicle."

"First we have to go back to them," muttered Gerard sourly.

He didn't like the idea of way back across the desert sands to the Great Pyramid, especially since he really felt a peculiar dizziness and was feeling unwell. But there was no way out. They had to get there if they wanted to get to the city before sunrise.

The guards at the archaeological site lent them a jeep the more willingly that Dr. Pahwass asked them for it when he was departing. Only thanks to this they reached the place called "Luxuria", where they allegedly got help. If they didn't hurry up, the sun rising over Egypt would flood them with its hot rays, which would be a nasty experience even for "martens".

Luxuria was a private club, as the sign at the entrance said, and certainly not everyone could enter. But when Never, leaning into the microphone by the door, whispered a three-part password, they were admitted without further ado. Through a very narrow corridor they came to stairs as narrow as it was. As they guessed, this narrowness was for defense. In the event of an unexpected attack, it would be very difficult for the attackers. The stairs led down to the huge club rooms, decorated with panache and eastern splendor.

They looked around the club curiously. The navy blue, starry vault supported slender columns stylized as date palm trunks. Clusters of dark amber "fruits" hung between their large leaves, each polished from a separate malachite plate. The walls were covered with airy draperies, exuding a faint scent of incense and violets. Somewhere, out of nowhere, soft sounds of eastern music were coming.

All the employees of the club were dressed in fancy cloths, reminiscent of the scenery of "Fairy Tales of 1001 Nights", crossed with the court of Amenhotep III. Fortunately, the guests were not required to adapt to this semi-real décor, so they wore casual clothes and had lively conversations over cups full of cocktails.

"Full blood for everyone plus gin," Never said to the waiter in an ancient Egyptian armlet and a stylish wig that fell over his shoulders. "And repeat this order until we say "enough"."

They swallowed the first portions with a greed that amazed them. They didn't know how hungry they were until they swallowed their first sip, and then a terrible thirst awoke in them. They drank greedily until they could squeeze a drop into each of them, then slumped down on the padded sofas, gasping for air with their half-open mouths.

"What happened to us?" Groaned Fronda, who was the first to conclude that this sudden hunger attack was nothing normal.

"The same what happened the archaeologists. It's just that we are stronger and more resilient, and we have a completely different metabolism," Never called the waiter again, nodding at him. "I need to speak to Meres-Ankh. Tell her that Rajah is here."

"Okay, but don't blame me if our Hanim sends you to hell," the waiter replied without surprise, and left.

"Hanim?" Gladiator looked questioningly at Never.

"In Turkish it is like "my lady"," he explained to him. "The man is a Turk."

After a long moment, a slender female figure appeared between the tables, resembling a typical odalisque drawing. Round hips and tempting breasts at the absurdly thin waist, pearly gray harem pants, eastern slippers, heavy, wide belt embroidered with jewels on the hips. Her bra was adorned with jewels as well, and her exposed navel gleamed with a gorgeous emerald. She had a yashmak on her head, so friends couldn't even tell if she was pretty. All they could see were the eyes, black, almond-shaped, shaded by gorgeous lashes and heavily accentuated with mascara. But the gaze of those eyes was not too friendly.

"Hello, Rajah," she said in a strange screeching voice that did not match the image of a "tempting apparition" as she sat down on the pulled-up pouf. "I see that the devil brought you here again, and also with the company. Probably the same beasts as you."

"You won't get far with flattery, sister," said Gerard coldly.

"Do not interfere, Cheetah." Never poured a little more blood and spiced it with gin. "I have a business with you, Queen of the Pyramids. By your grace, tell me what you know about the secret antiquities dealers and their activities in Giza?"

Meres-Ankh shrugged her slender shoulders adorned with heavy bracelets.

"What do I care about them?"

"Are you not interested in taking your national heritage abroad, to private collections?" Theo couldn't stand it.

"Not at all."

"After all, in this way the ability to read hieroglyphs and supplement knowledge about the history of the Old Kingdom is often lost..." Gerard said indignantly.

"Not my problem. Archeology is the stupidest science," said the Egyptian scornfully. "Nobody benefits from it except for a handful of researchers who pretend to be doing something important. Tell me, what will mankind achieve when you learn that after twenty years of research some fixate deciphered from an old papyrus, that a pharaoh had a diarrhea of dried quince? Who cares today? The same goes for these figurines. For me, it is the same commodity as any other, and since everyone who could claim ownership is extinct, in my opinion the owner should be whoever finds it. What will he do with it, that's his business, right? Found not stolen."

"I won't argue," Never said amicably. "But now you should help us. I know you work with traders sometimes and I'm not going to talk about it but tell us where they are hiding."

"And why is that? They are useful to me."

"Because, Queen, they stole something this time that they shouldn't have stolen. This thing has killed some archaeologists, and it's still as hellishly dangerous. I will not deceive you: your friends in the gang are definitely dead by now, but something must be done so that no one gets hurt again."

For a moment Meres-Ankh drummed her ringed fingers on the table as she considered what she heard. She had known Never for ages and had no reason to question his revelations, however unbelievable they sounded.

"You know what this is?" She asked finally.

"Of course, I know. That's why I'm so worried."

She nodded.

"You must be telling the truth. Jusup didn't come to yesterday's meeting, and he's a very solid man... Okay, I'll give you a map, but... won't it hurt you?"

Never glanced at his companions.

"May be harmful," he said. "But I know what I'm doing. I'm not exposing anyone unnecessarily."

"Maybe this is how you will end these puzzles, because if not, I will kick your ass," Gladiator could not stand it, "Tell me what the hell was in this chamber!"

The Indian looked at Meres-Ankh, then at his friends, and finally decided to speak.

"Okay, but you won't like this. There was some radioactive substance in the sarcophagus. I know scientists are stubbornly saying that the history of radioactivity on Earth began with Marie Curie, but that's not true. Radioactivity is as old as our planet, it wasn't just tamed. Here, I believe, the matter was as follows: the ancient Egyptians acquired a lump of quite pure substance, probably plutonium, because its half-life is just over 26,000 years - no wonder it is dangerous today as well."

"What was they all that dirty for?" Theo interrupted him.

"Initially, they wanted to use it for defense or attack, but they couldn't handle it, and after many fatal accidents, they decided to bury the killer lump so that no one would ever get to it. It would be easiest to bury it in the desert, but it was believed that this item belonged to the gods who could plague the land if their gift had been treated without due respect. But something had to be done to isolate it. It was for this purpose that the Great Pyramid was built - which archaeologists estimate as between four and a half to seven thousand years, which gives us an answer to the question of when it was," added Gerard. He also became more and more interested in this matter.

"These are very uncertain calculations, because dating with known methods will not do anything. The C-14 carbon method is useless when dealing with stones. And the thermo luminescent method has a fundamental disadvantage: it will determine the age of the stone but will not answer the question of when it was processed. And all the stones on our planet are much older than the human race... So, we must believe archaeologists, also people and fallible ones, about the age of the pyramids. But you must know that there are those who say that the age is twelve thousand and have strong arguments against which only one sentence, unsupported by any credible evidence: no, because it is impossible. The thing is, we know very little about the time when the first civilizations arose. Nothing could have survived after them, given the history of our planet and all the changes that have taken place on it."

"Wait a minute," Fronda interrupted, who was a little dizzy with these scientific arguments. "Let's get back to the heart of the matter. As far as I know, there are no spontaneous, pure isotope nuggets on Earth, certainly not of any significant size..."

"Not on Earth, that's right. But there are meteors whose nucleus is entirely made of an isotope. It's a huge rarity, but when something is rare, it doesn't mean it's impossible. Probably one of such weirdos exploded in the Earth's atmosphere, and its pieces scattered across several continents... In the legends of many countries, there are references to "divine stones", which were not allowed to be approached because you were dying. That an unusual gem found by someone caused a strange plague that wiped out the entire city..."

"Wait, a murderous gem? Isn't that an exaggeration?" Gladiator looked at Never in disbelief.

"Radioactive cesium is sometimes found in the form of cute blue crystals. The energy of passage through the atmosphere could be high enough to crystallize the radioactive material. After millennia, some Sumer or Hittite found a miraculous jewel, and that was the beginning of misfortune. From the same parish, it may be what killed our archaeologists and caused us a headache."

"Indeed. I feel better now," Gerard noted in amazement.

"Sure, because you got blood and the radiation in the chamber was only trace left. Our tolerance is several times higher than typically human, but not unlimited, but our way of absorbing blood allows us to reduce the effects of irradiation. Of course, without exaggeration, a dose of about a thousand sieverts to the whole body is lethal for us."

"So, why do you want to go get this... whatever it is?" Theo asked. His eyes showed that he was beginning to think his friend was insane.

"Trust me. Have I ever got you into some problems?" The Indian replied with a smile.

"A whole lot of times. I won't even count how many times."

Meres-Ankh returned with a folded sheet of paper, on which a map of the immediate vicinity had been carefully drawn, along with the route marked.

"Just remember, no police. Promise me that, Rajah," she asked. "In return, you can sleep in the back of the club."

"You bet your life, Queen of the Pyramids," Never solemnly assured her, "I prefer to avoid cops too. Beloved, we end this delight and go to sleep. We will go as soon as the sun goes down."

The friends mistakenly thought that immediately after dusk they would go to the hideout of a gang of traders. Never's plan was completely different. The first thing he did was telephone to Dr. Pahwass that those of the first team of archaeologists who were still alive should be treated for radiation sickness, and he hung up the phone without listening to the invective at his address. He had no claims to a noble scientist. He understood well that it was difficult for him to change his mind about the era he had studied for twenty years, but he had no intention of arguing with him. Immediately after that call, he gathered his squad to an off-road jeep from the local rental shop and drove them straight to the Sphinx.

"Did you lose your brain?" Asked Fronda, seeing his friend get out and start tapping his fingernails at the detector turned on, which - treated so bluntly - responded with short squeaks.

"Shut up, old coot." Never muttered, absorbed in his activity.

"Not old coot!" Theo was offended and demonstratively fell silent, which was what Never meant in this provocation. He did not want to explain to him now that the detectors, which had saved their lives more than once, were coupled to their creator's personal computer and could also serve as a kind of telegraph.

"What he is doing?" Gerard asked Gladiator, the only one who showed no surprise.

"Morse code," replied the highlander quietly and listened to the dripping sounds. As a former soldier, he had completed a radio telegraph course and knew the Morse code as well as any other. "Octavio, open up, I'm at the Sphinx, dot, Rajah."

"Octavio?!"

There was no time for further explanation. Under the left leg of an ancient statue, something like a narrow black well, no more than sixty centimeters in diameter, opened. It was so unexpected that the friends opened their mouths in silent amazement. Only Never acted as if there was nothing extraordinary about it.

"What are you standing like the harem of Lot under Sodom?" He growled. "Follow me, team."

He jumped neatly into the hole, and his companion hesitated for a moment, and they followed suit. The well turned out to be a tunnel-slide, leading down in bends somewhere, so that they felt like in an amusement park. The impression was even stronger that they landed in a pool filled with small, colorful balls made of some soft substance, like for kids.

"Gosh, that's wild..." Fronda groaned, gasping for breath.

"Mom, I want to go home..." Gladiator scrambled out of the pool, laughing to tears.

Mercedes standing nearby, dressed in a flowing white dress, looked at him with a bit of distaste and shook hands with Never. Octavio helped to recover from a bewildered Gerard, who had been unlucky enough to land in a position that would bring honor to the Tibetan yogis.

"We tried different types of landers, but the ball trap proved to be the safest," he explained. "Hello, you crazy people. What brings you here?"

"Us? Tell me better, how you got here?!" Theo yelled happily and hugged him. Then he gripped Mercedes in his arms, but he got such a slap from her that it whistled.

"Not only me, we're all here. We had to flee Spain after the Hunters found us. Better not to delay," Octavio explained.

"Have you built a new shelter here?" Gerard asked, looking around.

"Not us, it was already built. Rajah told me about this place, hence I knew it. It is a whole series of caves, corridors, larger and smaller rooms. The ancient Egyptians were great masons. We only got electricity and connected to the water supply. We had a bang of work with the reconstruction of our institute in this underground, but we finally succeeded.

"How is it that archaeologists did not discover you?" Gladiator tapped the walls as if he expected them to collapse.

"You can't dig under the Sphinx. Once an attempt was made, but luckily no one discovered the descent then, and then excavations under the statue were forbidden to protect it. The Americans used to feel for empty spaces with radars and made noise, but before it started to be checked, we installed anti-radar screens from the inside. Now everything is blamed on measurement error. But what brings you here?"

"Problem," Never said. "Pretty serious. Where can we talk?"

"Sorry, I do keep you on the threshold, like a lout. Come on."

Octavio led the friends down a rocky corridor to an expertly furnished studio, lit by fluorescent lamps in a casing imitating stone. The air conditioner hummed in the corner, keeping the room pleasant and refreshing. There was a small refrigerator beside a white, paper-strewn desk on which a state-of-the-art computer flaunted.

"Would you like a drink?" Octavio reached into the refrigerator and took out a bottle of plasma and a cognac.

"Maybe a little," Never agreed. "We got drunk on blood in Luxuria, but an extra drink will not hurt us. We all need reinforcement, and it is closely related to the purpose of our visit."

He told the red-haired Spaniard everything he knew and what he could guess, and as he spoke, Octavio's eyes grew bigger and bigger.

"Are you saying that the fourth dynasty pharaohs knew about fissile material?" He finally asked in open disbelief.

"Yes and no," he replied, lounging back in the padded chair. "They knew them but had no idea what fell into their hands. The very phenomenon of radioactivity was completely incomprehensible to them. The pharaohs weren't the only ones dealing with cursed gems or the mysterious weapons of the gods, as you like. Look in old texts."

Octavio jumped up from his chair and rummaged in the bookcase. After a while he pulled out a battered copy of the Mahabharata and began flipping through the pages in a hurry.

"If you are right, you have solved the greatest mystery of ancient India," he said finally, his eyes skimming a description. "I never believed that the ancient inhabitants of India knew the atomic bomb, let alone that some aliens dragged their pathetic butts from the other side of the Milky Way in order to destroy some earthly city. It has always been absurd to me, but since I never considered the old chroniclers to be fantastic or crazy, I found it hard to comprehend these passages. You give me the solution I need. I have yet to verify it, but it's quite logic."

"What?" Theo groaned hopelessly. He understood nothing.

"If Rajah is right, Mohenjo Daro's destruction could have been caused by the fall of a large meteor with a nucleus made entirely of uranium or some other radioactive element," Octavio explained to him. "It had to give an effect like dropping an atomic bomb. The existence of such meteors is a hypothesis for now, but very likely and would explain a lot. Listen to:

A single missile carried all the power of the universe. A scorching column of smoke and flames as bright as a thousand suns rose in full splendor. The heat burned the elephants as they ran madly, roaring and trampling everything around. The bodies were burned beyond recognition. Hair and nails fell out, vessels broke for no apparent reason, birds turned white. Villagers, townspeople and soldiers jumped into the river to wash away the poisonous dust. The survivors lost their hair and nails. All food and water were poisoned by dust."

"I know these descriptions. Let us put aside theoretical considerations. Now the point is that this inheritance from the pharaohs should not harm anyone. Will you help us?" Never asked.

"Why do we need his help? We can do it ourselves!" Fronda interrupted belligerently.

Octavio looked at him amused.

"You would go for the "god stone" alone, knight?"

"Yes, of course."

"Oh, what a naivety... In a few minutes you would get such a dose of radiation that you would die for sure. Here you have to take all possible precautions, after all, we do not even know what element we are dealing with. Wait for me here, I will give orders to have what we need ready for us."

It seemed like the whole thing put him in a good mood. Nothing has changed - as always, he greeted with enthusiasm every opportunity to challenge the existing scientific canons. He even had a theory forged on the spot, according to which it was clear that "divine stones" were also hidden in the other two Giza pyramids. When put together, they would create a supercritical volume, with terrible effect. He even wondered if this was not what had happened in Sodom and Gomorrah, because he didn't believe in the sulfur rain from heaven.

Upon his return, he shared his guess with his friends. Fronda stared at him, and Gladiator shrugged. He did not show surprise, only Gerard managed to protest weakly:

"But it would follow that the ancient Egyptians already in the time of Pharaoh Khafre had some idea of the critical masses. Absurd, impossible."

"Theoretically not," Octavio agreed. "But let's try to think like them. Here they have divine stones that no one can touch or even look at. Left stealthily in the enemy army camp, they cause foreign aggressors to develop a mysterious, incurable disease. The priests learn that somewhere these stones were put in one place, and one day, when another one was put on the pile, hell raged on and swallowed two cities. The gods showed their anger. For this reason, they keep them separately, in special multi-layer metal boxes. They were found, right?"

"True," agreed Never. "According to the biblical accounts, this is what Noah's Ark looked like."

"We can safely assume that one of the layers was led, because lead was then commonly used as the core of ritual containers, the Spaniard continued. "It is cheap, easily fusible and easily malleable, yet strong and non-corrosive. The lead casket, clad with a thin gold plate, was heavy, like solid gold, and much cheaper. Of course, the pure profit went to the pockets of the priests, figuratively, because pockets were unknown then. The deeply human urge to snatch something for oneself in this case saved the priests' lives as the dangerous material was isolated. However, after the death of the chief high priests who knew how to handle "god stones", a few mishaps again occurred, so it was decided to hide them in structures that no one, at least assumed, would be able to break into."

"They didn't know archaeologists," said Gladiator.

"No, no. In their time, no one was interested in history and it is difficult for them to imagine a different approach to the subject."

Two lab technicians entered the laboratory with a short report that everything was ready.

"Here we go," Octavio said shortly, not specifying what he had ordered his men to prepare.

It was easy to get to the surface, and it wasn't, as the friends thought, the arduous climb up the slippery walls of the slide they already knew. On the contrary, it was very comfortable - you just walked up the narrow stairs to the stone wall that was sliding on large ball bearings and came out under the right paw of the Sphinx. There was hardly anything to see from the outside. Soon it turned out that the lab technicians had brought a van for them, in which there was a large, square container with lead walls and a few suits that looked hellishly heavy.

At the steering wheel sat Mercedes, dignified and silent as usual, but instead of her "rhapsodic draperies," as Gerard had described her gown, she was wearing a black embossed leather suit. Her golden red hair was tied in a kind of bun and held in place with an old-fashioned comb. Without saying a word, she took Never's plan to reach the traders' hideout and started down the desert road without turning on the lights.

Along the way, Octavio chattered all the time, spewing scientific terms and telling stories like in "1001 Nights". Friends understood only few words, none of them was a scientist, not even Never, who would be the first to indicate this by extraordinary intelligence. Still, they took on Octavio's excitement, and they listened to him with interest, trying to comprehend even a thing.

"First of all, you have to make it clear once and for all that the ancient Egyptians were not primitive farmers," said the red-haired Spaniard at the speed of a machine gun. "They had excellent medicine, they even performed surgeries, giving patients opium anesthesia... yes, and they knew opium and used it for various purposes. In addition, they were excellent architects, although they did not have Roman concrete, but only wood, stone and mud brick. Their works of art delight us to this day, and when it comes to astronomy..."

"They had radar telescopes," Never said, skeptical as ever.

"No kidding, Rajah. They were diligent sky watchers, which may be closely related to our cause. The falling meteors must have fascinated them and seeing their path they could calculate where they would fall. Hence, they knew where to look for 'divine stones'. Many of them were completely harmless, but not all of them. While passing through the atmosphere, they were subjected to extremely high temperatures, so the radioactive element inside the nucleus could crystallize. When falling to the ground, the outer shell cracked, revealing colored crystals stuck in it. They must have made a great impression on those who found them. The beautiful jewels, however, were lethal, so they were hidden in temples, in the boxes I have already mentioned. It really is quite logic."

"Here we are," Mercedes interrupted.

Octavio paused his lecture and began putting on the suit, while instructing the others to do the same. The suits were exactly as heavy as they looked and very uncomfortable. Their weight was increased by oxygen equipment, and friends would prefer to do without the armor, but Octavio made sure everyone put them on and buckled them securely. He also hadn't forgotten to check the tightness of the round helmets and the stiff gloves before letting them follow him.

At first glance, the place looked quite wild. Something like a cluster of several dunes, between which, however, there was a tiny oasis perfectly hidden from the human eye with two low, thorny bushes and a bit of greenery above a small spring. Tucked into the dunes, there were barracks made of planks, one of which probably hid the sought-after object, and between them lay the decaying bodies of several men, covered with open ulcers.

"The Valley of Josaphat," muttered Fronda to the communicator built into the helmet.

Octavio triggered the Geiger counter, which began ticking madly. Following his instructions, the friends opened one of the barracks, ripping a huge padlock from its door. Although they were prepared to see the looted antiques, they stopped.

The barrack was literally filled with smaller and larger figurines, vessels, bronze and copper weapons, and papyrus rolls in wooden casings.

"Any Egyptologist would have a heart attack to see it," Gerard said, waving his eyes over the priceless artifacts.

"We'll give Dr. Pahwass the location of this place, but we'll clean it first." Octavio looked around intently, the counter he was holding growling madly. "I guess it'll be that box."

Indeed, between the shimmering gold and jeweled ritual vessels stood an inconspicuous box with the lid ajar, measuring approximately 50x50x75. Octavio walked over to it. As soon as he opened the lid wider, his friends' eyes almost popped out of their sockets. In the center was a single, irregular melon-sized crystal, iridescent in the torchlight with all the colors of the rainbow. It was even more peculiar as its proper color was difficult to determine, and only under the influence of shafts of light projected onto the crystal's surface, the unusual play of all colors that exist in nature was revealed. The counter squealed from the overvoltage, and instead of a rattling sound it began to emit a single, continuous sound - or so it seemed, since the frequency of the growls no longer distinguished them. Octavio turned it off impatiently and closed the lid of the box.

"I've never seen anything so beautiful," Fronda sighed deeply.

"And if you hadn't been wearing a suit, you probably would never have seen anything again," Never said. "You also found an object of delight. What are we doing now?"

"We're taking it. I'm not sure yet, but I think we're dealing with a breakthrough in inorganic chemistry," replied the red-haired Spaniard. "This element, my dear, is almost certainly not found on Earth. I'm a pretty good chemist and expert geologist, and I can swear to you that I don't know a radioactive element capable of crystallizing into something like that. I don't even know if there is a place for it in the Mendeleev system."

"I don't care," said Gladiator, helping him pick up the box. The beautiful object did not make the slightest impression on him. "Instead of being delighted with your discovery, you'd better secure the damn thing so that it doesn't hurt anyone else."

*****

"Dr. Pahwass, I don't have to explain myself to you!" Never shouted into the telephone receiver. "I gave you a list of medications to be administered to these sick archaeologists, and the fact that you don't understand is your business! You'd better do the cataloging of these oasis finds of yours and leave the medicine to the experts! No, I can't get in touch with the doctors, your colleagues are lying there and that's your business. Goodbye!"

He dropped the receiver and collapsed onto the hotel couch, clearly disgusted.

"He disturbed you, huh?" Gerard chuckled, tidying up his notes. He had been chronicle of their adventures for some time, just for fun.

"Some people are geniuses and idiots at the same time," growled the Indian. "If this Egyptian hadn't been blindfolded, he would have guessed what I was talking about right now. I couldn't make him understand more clearly that these people had been irradiated and were suffering from radiation sickness. Where's Fronda and that Goliath?"

"They went to Luxuria for a farewell drink. After all, we're leaving soon."

Never sat up in bed suddenly, as if he had remembered something.

"We're not leaving. What we found does not explain in any way what happened to Zeta 4 and Zeta 5. And why Zeta 2 was so shocked when he was found. After all, this could not only be the result of the contamination it underwent. There is more to it. I'm leaving, Cheetah, I don't know when I'll be back."

The actor shrugged his shoulders slightly, but without a word he obeyed his commander. He had long ago concluded that although he was an intelligent man himself, he was far from Never, who, if not blinded by emotions, reasoned precisely and quickly like a computer. If he had become a professional detective, his work would have been a success story. On the few occasions when friends conducted something very close to a typical investigation, he revealed brilliance and analytical skills truly worthy of Sherlock Holmes. When necessary, he could extort information, steal it, or obtain it, using his exotic beauty and charm. He knew well that women and men of homosexual orientation liked it, and when it was convenient, he used his charm unscrupulously.

Left on his own, Gerard went down to the hotel library, found one of Arthur Conan Doyle's short stories, and plunged into reading. It was a long time since he had the opportunity to relax so much. A soft armchair, soft light, loneliness and blissful silence had a soothing effect on him, blurring the memory of an oasis full of corpses. Despite the already quite long "career" of the vampire, Gerard was not bloodthirsty at all. He hated violence, and he felt sick to seeing someone's corpse.

"If some fact seemingly contradicts the chain of conclusions drawn, it does not mean that it has to be rejected, or that we were following a false trail..." he read and at the same time wondered what was bothering him. There was some dissonance with the whole thing. Unable to concentrate on reading, the actor finally put down the book and stared at the wall, trying to recall what clearly contradicted the picture of the situation. There was something like that, he was sure, but what was it? It seemed to him that he was trying to break through some black fog and kept coming back to where he started. What could it be? He knew one thing - they had overlooked a small but very important fact right from the start, and if he could now pin down what it was...

"I wonder what Sherlock Holmes would do in such a situation?" he whispered thoughtfully, looking at the cover of the book.

He wished that Never, or at least Dea, was with him now. They both had the intelligence and knowledge without which the puzzle could not be solved... Exactly, Dea! It was she who was saying something important that probably everyone missed. What was that?

Gerard stormed out of the hotel and stopped only at the door of the Luxuria. He did not remember the password, but happily the doorman remembered him and, after a short negotiation, let him in.

"What if Zeta 2 took his injuries not in contact with this lovely crystal, but in completely different circumstances?" He blurted out without preamble, sitting at a table where Theo and Gladiator were drinking with Meres-Ankh.

"Who took offense at whom?" Gladiator did not understand.

"It means?" Theo asked.

"Remember what Dea said? Zeta 2, apart from the symptoms of radiation sickness, also had burns with a strong base," said Gerard feverishly. "Where did you have the base there? And why was he so shocked that he couldn't remember who he was? It doesn't match. The general would certainly not hire people who would become so panicked at the sight of a few bandits. So, the question arises: where can fissile material and a strong base be found simultaneously?"

"At the nuclear power plant," said Meres Ankh. She sat with her elbows on the table and listened carefully. "But there's none here."

"I'll tell you where. In the laboratory of a large oncology hospital! I know what I'm saying!"

There was silence. After a while, Gladiator took his cell phone out of his pocket and dialed Never's number on its keys, then handed it to Fronda.

"You talk to him."

"Rajah, what are you doing?" Fronda asked.

"Checking one lead, why?" Came the answer.

"Mark Twain once wrote that you wouldn't hang a lead in place of the murderer, and he was right. Come to Luxuria, Gerard has an interesting theory. Who knows if he didn't solve the mystery on his own while we sipped, and you chased the wind in the field."

"Don't be so wise, you stupid donkey. Okay, I'll be right there, but if it turns out you're bothering me unnecessarily..."

Shortly thereafter, four friends were driving a rental car to the address Meres-Ankh had given them. Never was convinced by Gerard's conclusions, although he did not yet know how to connect all the facts. As he was driving, he thought hard about it. He had to admit that this actor, the "green-eyed elf" as he sometimes called him, was the only one on the team to track down something that might lead them to their missing agents. If he was found to be right, he should have gotten a detective's badge, though of course there was a lot of confusion about the whole thing. If members of Zeta's group were investigating the pyramid, why would they have come to the oncology hospital? What were they supposed to do there?

It was only when he stopped the car in the hospital parking lot that he struck his forehead with his hand and cursed in Sanskrit.

"That's where four of those archaeologists brought them here!" He exclaimed. "They had symptoms of acute myeloid leukemia, so they were tested for it. Gods, what an idiot I am! And I'm the brain of our squad!"

"That doesn't explain what happened to the Zeta," said Gladiator soberly. "And if they was hit in this place, guys! We could be on a really nasty scandal."

"What kind of scandal could be at the hospital?" Theo was simply surprised.

"You would live a bit in Poland as an ordinary citizen, you would experience such a miracle that you would undoubtedly change your mind," the highlander solemnly assured him.

"Are you done? Then we go. It's nighttime so we have to slip past the security guards somehow, and we'll be safe inside. If Gerard's theory is correct, evidence to support it will be found where radiotherapy is located and the entire diagnostic testing department," said Never.

He didn't say it aloud, but he thought the same thing as the others: that for an ordinary hospital, there are a bit too many security guards. Fully armored, athletes in black uniforms circled the building, looking for the invisible enemy with a vigilance somewhat strange at this point. What could they guard so hard? Cancer patients?

Apart from other abilities, vampires can move noiselessly, and their BMI index is almost half that of people with comparable parameters of height and physical structure. By using these properties, most of them easily develop a circus dexterity. No wonder, then, that after a short consultation, the friends decided to get to the hospital grounds by a route that nobody guarded - through the roof.

For this, it was enough to climb a huge tree that cast part of its spreading crown on the hospital outbuilding, and such climbing was within the limits of each of them. One by one, they slid down the dangerously thin branches, avoiding even the slightest rustle, and landed on softly bent legs, heart pounding hard. They felt - a bit exaggerated - like comic book heroes and had to pull themselves together so that this feeling would not hit their heads too much. Finding the safety hatch on the roof wasn't difficult, but Fronda had to work it out for a good ten minutes with his kit of lockpicks before they could slip in and shut the hatch behind them. The fact that it was locked from the outside, not from the inside, should have made them think immediately, but it wasn't until they smelled the chemicals that they realized where they had entered.

Never turned on the flashlight and the beam of light swept across the room. They were in some kind of laboratory, but it didn't look like a hospital at all. One of the rooms was dominated by containers of various shapes. They contained, as they found out, some powders and solutions that they had not studied for lack of time. The second was filled with jars full of preparations: distorted and discolored organs, monstrous human and animal fetuses, and degenerate insects. The whole collection was nauseous and some vague, vague terror even in the hardened Fronda. The third room contained elaborate apparatus, batteries of reagent bottles and all the usual laboratory equipment, and the fourth, smallest room, a computer and a table piled high with papers.

The small metal stamp was so hidden among the piles of papers that Never noticed it after a long time. It was undoubtedly the badge they were wearing, torn out with a piece of cloth. Never looked at it carefully and put it in his pocket.

"Zetas was here," he said. "Now the question is what happened to them. I don't want to crow, but I suspect it's not good."

"I have no illusions about it either," Fronda said grimly, opening a door they had not noticed before. They were so well disguised that if Theo hadn't accidentally tapped them with his elbow, he wouldn't have even realized they were there.

Behind the door was another room, more spacious than the rest. There was a large container with an unidentified liquid in it, and around it on metal supports - the skeletons of animals and people. Unprepared for the sight, Gerard almost screamed, but this time he was not alone in the urge to run away. The sight was ghastly, like a bad dream, though as they cooled down a bit they realized it was just an anatomical aids lab. Many hospitals in Egypt made extra money by making skeletons for students, museums, and workshops. Everyone knew about it, it was no secret, so why exactly in this hospital was a workshop hidden in a place that could only be accessed through the roof?

Never first checked what liquid the container contained.

"Potassium hydroxide," he said after a moment, turning his shining eyes on his friends. "They're etching it on the bone. Could you... wait."

He looked at human skeletons intently. There weren't so many of them - five sets of "adults" and two small ones, probably for children. The rest belonged to monkeys and small mammals, so he had no interest in them, concentrating all his attention on humans. He spent a lot of time examining their teeth. After a long moment, he reached for the phone and pressed a few keys, carefully dialing the number.

"Dea, be so nice and check the computer for the health records of Agents Zeta 4 and Zeta 5. I wonder if they've had any fractures and what the dental records look like," he asked.

"And this message, Indian damned soul, you need it right now?!" Dea screamed, obviously awake.

"Right now. It is very important."

"May it, because if not, your fate is miserable."

Groaning and cursing softly, Dea wrapped herself in her bathrobe and went to the medical center, and Never, taking advantage of the break in conversation, took a closer look at the bleached skeletons. The three others turned their heads not to look at it - the smell that permeated the room was enough to make it nauseous, and the company of skeletons added to the depressing atmosphere. They couldn't understand how Never could keep his icy calm in a place like this.

They also didn't understand what he wanted to find and weren't even sure if they wanted to know it. And so they slowly began to understand what was happening here, and this aroused the desire to run as far as possible. Even Fronda, accustomed to all horrors, was clearly muted. Finally Dea spoke up and Never pressed the phone tighter to his ear.

"Zeta 4 had a broken left shin in two places last year, and the fibula of his right lower leg during his unfortunate parachute jump," she said. "Zeta 5 has never broken anything, but she has two teeth stuck on: top left six and five. Artificial crown on a titanium screw."

"Okay. Dea, we have a computer here which data can be very interesting and even more important. We have probably found ourselves on the scandal that may threaten many people. How to download or upload the computer content to the control panel?"

"No chance. It's probably password protected anyway. Remove the main drive and bring it back, this is where IT will take care of it."

"Thanks. And I'm sorry I woke you up."

"No problem, I slept for half an hour."

Never put the phone away and looked at his companions.

"Fronda, go to the computer and take it apart," he ordered. "And you guys find me some sacks or bags."

"It is not enough that he rushes us like slaves. Now he wants us to go with the bags," Gladiator used to vent his bad temper with the most bizarre remarks, but he didn't dare to oppose Never, who was their unit's commander after all. His military upbringing did not allow it.

If it were not for this, there could be trouble with him, for he was arbitrary and stubborn like a mountain goat, and he was not too intelligent. His brother knew this well, and on the day he was "put under the command of Rajah" he said sternly:

"Listen, Jasiek, people can be divided into wise and stupid. You're stupid, so listen to the smarter than you if you want to survive. Understand?"

Gladiator was terribly offended, but he followed his advice and listened to Never like his captain's soldier, even when he disagreed with his orders. At best, he muttered some sort of today's comment, but that Never was not a military after all, so he didn't mind.

They found the bags only after a while - linen, quite large, of unknown purpose. Never looked at them carefully, and then, to the great astonishment of his friends, he removed the two skeletons from the metal supports and put them in the sacks, tying them tightly.

"What are you...?" Gerard began, and stopped short, fading in an instant to chalk white.

"Yes, they are most likely their skeletons," Never answered him. "Fronda, what about this computer?"

"In pieces," Theo replied triumphantly from the other room. Not having a clue about modern technology, he was able to disassemble literally every mechanism into screws, using a universal penknife and nothing else.

Never scooped up the hard drive from among the pile of debris and signaled the retreat. Staying in this place for a long time could be dangerous, and the fight here could end badly. Despite a thorough search, they found no other way out than through the hatch in the roof, so blocking it would have been enough to put them in a death trap.

One by one they climbed onto the roof and closed the hatch behind them. Now they had, what was much more difficult, to get down to ground. The tree could not help them, because those of its branches that were within reach were too thin to make the way back with them. They had the option to make trouble: slide down the gutter, which made sure they would run into security guards. Still, they decided to at least try to avoid trouble.

They descended to the ground one at a time, looking for the moment when the guards were invisible and almost succeeded. Unfortunately, they did not foresee that the gutter made of light, galvanized sheet metal would not bear the weight of Gladiator, which was supposed to come down at the end. Although vampires are much lighter compared to humans, an athlete like Gladiator, especially since he was still a very young vampire, weighed too much. This was the cause of the exposition of the entire project, as the gutter at some point broke away from the wall and broke halfway like a cardboard sleeve. Gladiator was fine, but the noise he accidentally made was in the ears of his friends comparable to an artillery shell explosion.

*****

"How did you get away from these thugs?" Meres-Ankh asked admiringly as she listened breathlessly to Never's account.

"There are no strong ones on them," said Octavio.

He was leaning against the wall, sipping a drink. Luxuria was filled by one of the institute's teams, as Octavio used to organize weekly games in this place, each time for a different department. It was, in a way, an antidote to scientists who were tired of hard work. This time the biochemistry department was playing there.

"We'd have problems there if it hadn't been..." Theo muttered.

Once again he recalled what had happened in front of the hospital. The fight was fierce, genuinely brutal, like an action movie, although Fronda's unfailing instincts made it clear immediately what to do. Not succumbing to the urge to start fighting immediately, he threw himself to the side, unrolled his slingshot and, in record time, destroyed the hospital floodlights with it. In the dark they had the advantage, so they quickly got their weapons and managed to fight for themselves. Still, their chance was in retreat as soon as possible. And for a moment it got really dangerous.

Everyone heard the warning scream of Never as the last of the guards, armed with a Kalashnikov rifle, ran their way. Fronda saw him too. He knew that they would not have time to do anything, because the other would only pull the trigger and hit them with a long burst, but instinctively he reached for his pistol. At the same moment the glow of the moon cut through the black shape and the bloodthirsty beast fell with a hollow growl onto the guard's neck. The surprised man dropped the rifle and fell to the ground, trying in utter horror to push away the wolf's head with red-burning eyes and a suit of sharp fangs.

"Oggy!" Theo exclaimed happily.

"But how did she know where to find us?" Gerard asked, pulling the she-wolf away from the guard who had passed out from fear.

"When we were going to leave, I called Steve and said that if she had contacted us, we were in Gizeh, but I don't know how she knew we would be in the hospital..." Fronda began to explain.

"I wish you had announced it on the radio and TV," Never snapped at him angrily. "You're hopelessly stupid sometimes. But never mind. To the car, because we're about to have the local pharaohs on our necks!"

Indeed, the signals of the police cars could be heard from afar. Oggy jumped into the backseat of the car, the others took their seats as quickly as she did, and the black pickup truck Meres-Ankh had borrowed hurried away from outside the hospital.

On the way, Oggy transformed into a human, hugged all her friends one by one, even Gerard the driver, and only then covered herself with Fronda's shirt, almost to her knees.

"How did you know?" Theo asked after everyone had calmed down a bit.

"I got to Octavio, then to Meres Ankh," she said cheerfully, buttoning up the buttons. "Then I scent you down and I think just in time. Isn't it?"

Theo smiled at the memory and put his arm around Oggy.

"Glad you're back with us," he said kindly.

"Of course it's good, but maybe let's talk about something else this way," Never offered sourly. "For example, what is happening in this stinking hospital? I already have a theory, but to be honest it is not very cheerful."

"Speak," Octavio encouraged him.

"First of all, let's consider why Zeta 4 and Zeta 5 died and Zeta 2 became confused," the Indian began, involuntarily assuming the pose of Sherlock Holmes: elbows on the backs of the chair and hands touching with the tips of his fingers. "It's not because of the research lab we discovered. Initially, I considered trading organs for transplantation, but no sane person would take them from people with cancer. It must have been something else entirely. We'll find the confirmation on the hard drive I took, but even without it I'm sure I'm right."

"Sure, because you are quite infallible, normally the Spirit of All Things," Meres Ankh remarked ironically. "Talk without preamble."

"Think about it: if a terrorist organization wanted to build a dirty atomic bomb, where would it do so that would not attract anyone's attention? In a place where radioactive material is commonplace. In the oncology hospital, there are appropriately insulated rooms, for example accelerator cabins, and there are also a lot of equipment that can be used. I also suspect that they conducted more extensive research there, and Zetas discovered this."

Octavio meditated for a moment and asked:

"But how did they come up with it?"

"I don't think that's what they were looking for. If Zeta 2 does not regain clarity of mind, we will have no confirmation, but I believe they wanted to question the archaeologists brought here, and they discovered something suspicious by accident. They started checking it out, with obvious success."

"They've been made into anatomical slides," whispered Gerard, and he felt a shudder.

"A dirty atomic bomb can be of different types," said Octavio thoughtfully. "If the transport problem was solved, it would be enough to spill the isotope or scatter a powder with the addition of fissile material somewhere and get out. In a matter of days, people in the area will get sick and then die, and no one will know why. And if you had to pour this damn thing into the main outlet in the water tower, it would be a brick apocalypse. In fact, this radioactive contamination of the site could be dealt with by any little punk, if it weren't for the fact that before he got the business on the site, he'd gulp down the lethal dose of radiation himself. Apparently not an obstacle, because there are many suicide terrorists. However, even they do not really want to die in the torments of radiation sickness. Fortunately, people fear all radioactivity worse than the devil himself. And the use of conventional shields increases the risk of detection, for example, you will not load an X-ray impervious container into an aircraft. However, it does not stop trying, as you can see in the attached picture."

"What does all this have to do with the Great Pyramid?" Gladiator asked helplessly, trying in vain to grasp the logic of the events taking place.

"Nothing," Never answered him calmly. "It is only ironic that these two things have overlapped. On the other hand, this lovely crystal could do a lot of trouble if it fell into the hands of terrorists... Have you examined it yet?"

Octavio nodded his light red head while making a very indistinct face.

"I was right," he said. "This element is unknown on Earth. I have named it astralon. So far I have calculated that its life is not less than ten thousand years, and its atomic mass is 246.0357. I don't know anything else yet. It's good that it hit us, not the terrorists, or that some kids didn't come across it."

A girl in a Hurissa costume walked over to the table and whispered something to her boss lady. Meres-Ankh got up with obvious regret and, having apologized to the guests, disappeared into the back room. Theo followed her with his eyes.

"Why does she constantly wear this rag on her head and never take off?" He muttered with obvious regret.

"You do not know?" Octavio was surprised. "Meres Ankh has a cat's face,"

"That's nice."

"You do not understand. Not a cat's beauty, but a normal animal face, like the goddess Bastet. So, she wears the yashmak in public, but she takes it off on dates and hunting, and you have any idea what's going on? Then such an attacked person testifies that he was hit by a catwoman and goes to the tips for observation. The police obviously don't think to take it seriously, and the girl is having a lot of fun. She was not born like this, of course, it is the result of plastic surgery, or rather a whole series of operations. A very skilled plastic surgeon modeled her cat's face and pointed ears in exchange for a preservation. Master Meres Ankh made such a deal with him. And when the girl was 'ready', he preserved her too."

"This is insane!" Oggy exclaimed in shock.

"But absolutely it is. She is crazy about cats, she loves them, and if she finds out that someone have hurt some meow there will be problems. Meres Ankh accompanies him then, and the two of them make the guest regret not having passed away earlier.

"Oh my. There are really many freaks among vampires," laughed Gladiator.

Octavio shrugged slightly as if to show that it could not be helped, and wrinkled his freckled nose.

"What are you going to do now?" He asked.

"Yeah, we'll go back to base," Never answered him. "We have to deliver the bones of these two agents and the hard drive. I already called the general, he was not delighted with our discoveries."

"Seems hard to please him. You know what? Get me in touch with Dr. Pahwass. He's the one who has to report to the police so that they look for those crooks from the hospital, and I know how to convince him to cooperate."

The Indian looked at di Mauro curiously.

"How?"

"I'll just bribe him. There are a lot of old papyri in these catacombs below the Sphinx that will definitely interest him. Besides, I know where he should look for a certain discovery, namely a burial shaft, flooded with water back in the tenth dynasty, and he will be more pleased with it than the skilful multi-million dollar win on the stock exchange."

"Just be careful," Gerard warned. "This archaeologist is a nice animal, I do not deny it, but after all, a human. It can make problems to all of you."

Octavio laughed heartily and patted him on his thin back.

"Beloved," he said with pity. "I am over a thousand years old and I really know how to take care of myself. If Dr. Pahwass finds that I can help him like no other, he will shield me with his breast from the Hunters. I know him. For him, there is nothing but archeology, and nothing is more important than the history of the Egyptian pharaohs, from the fourth, sixth or twentieth dynasty. He doesn't care about vampires, because they don't attack mummies."

"Then deal with him yourself. We go back to the unit before they want us to make report," said Gladiator with military flair.

Everyone laughed heartily. They were after the fourth bottle of Bloody Mary and their moods rose from minute to minute.

Fronda, in particular, was clearly overjoyed and nothing disturbed his thoughts. What should he worry about? They dealt with both matters entrusted to them - admittedly, if not for Gerard, the latter might not have been solved at all. They found Octavio, whose disappearance kept them awake at night. And Oggy was with him again, sitting next to him, still wearing his shirt, clinging to him confidently like a child - what more could he ask for? He did not know what the general would say to her presence at headquarter, but he did not care what he thought. He wouldn't ask him anyway.

It will put him in front of a fait accompli. He will not allow himself to take his beloved friend away, no matter what. Admittedly, some clothes and false papers had to be arranged for her, but that was to be done by Meres-Ankh, who could be proud of her broad connections in the local criminal circles. They welcomed Egypt in four, said goodbye in five, which means that they had a reason to be proud. After all, not everyone could do a similar trick.

THE END

Annex

The Case of the Mysterious Heritage

The lost manuscript of Dr. Watson

I was just filling my pipe when Sherlock Holmes looked at me and smiled.

"Well, dear Watson, you met Miss Maynard this morning."

I was used to my friend's insight, but this time I dropped the tobacco bag in shock and stared at him."

"How on earth...?" I started and stopped. Not more than two days ago, I made a vow to myself not to be surprised anymore, and just broke that promise.

Holmes laughed softly and reached for his cup of coffee. His deep-set eyes shone with triumph, the way he always did when he surprised me with something.

"There is no mystery in it," he explained amused. "I guessed it at first glance.

"You might think I'm a dumb ass, but I don't understand how you could have guessed that I met a woman this morning, and with whom! You will admit that in order to deduce anything, you must have premises, and what could you have had in this matter? I didn't tell you anything that I was interested in Miss Maynard, much less because she is kind to me! Not only that, I didn't tell anyone!"

Holmes sat back in his chair and pressed his fingers together in his favorite gesture.

"And yet you find it trivially simple. First, it has been a long time since your wife died and your grief eased a bit," he began. "Second, Miss Maynard is undoubtedly a lovable person, and you haven't taken your eyes off her in the theater. And she returned you with a tender smile. Third, you've been gone all morning. Fourth, you came back in a state of pleasant distraction. Fifth, when you handed me the Times, I felt your hands smell of the exquisite women's perfume 'Night in Venice'. And sixth and finally, I can see bright red hair on the lapel of your jacket, and Miss Maynard is a redhead. Enough?"

"Now that you've enumerated it, the conclusion is indeed obvious," I admitted.

Always been like that. When Holmes explained to me the ways in which he had come to the solution of one puzzle or another, it seemed to me that anyone could think of it. However, when I tried to use his method myself, I came to completely false conclusions, or even halted.

"I'm glad you started waking up after a period of intense despair," my friend continued. "Though I don't share your admiration for every prettier female. On the contrary, the more beautiful and kinder the lady is, the more alert I am. I would also recommend you to be cautious rather than to the boundless trust that characterizes you every day."

Holmes' misogyny made me laugh, even irritating at times, but I didn't try to convince him. He was chivalrous and protective of women when needed, but he didn't trust them in the slightest. I could not imagine that the delicate, feminine lips would ever touch his sharply outlined lips that the ascetic features of his face would ever soften under the influence of passionate emotion. It was as unbelievable as a man's walk on the moon - the great detective's perfectly balanced mind did not even allow it. And even if his personality was therefore poorer in certain sensations, it was compensated by the benefits of this state of affairs. Feelings never disturbed Holmes's eyes on the mystery and he reasoned coldly and precisely like no one else.

"It wasn't Rendezvous in the strict sense of the word. She asked me for help."

"Oh my... What kind, if not a secret?"

"Leslie, I mean Miss Maynard asked me to come with her to Crane Manor," I said. "She inherited this mansion from a grandfather she didn't even know and he didn't know her. Old Crane was a weirdo in the true sense of the word, idolatrously in love with technology. He devoted his life to constructing clever apparatuses that generally did not work, spent a fortune bringing some strange inventions to his residence, and neglected his daughter altogether. In the end, she got fed up with it and ran away from home. She married Francis Maynard, an American diplomat."

"Ah, the American..."

"Yes, I know what you think about them. She thought his father would be indifferent to it, and he told her so on every occasion that he would rather have a son, because his daughter was of no use. Meanwhile, it happened otherwise. Old Crane was mad with rage, known for his hatred of all American things. He forbade his daughter even to come near the family

Luiza Dobrzynska

residence as long as she was associated with "that Yankee".
Even when she was already dying, he refused to visit her.
However, his conscience moved him, since he wrote everything
down to his granddaughter.

"Some people don't have a conscience. But let's assume that
it was so. So, why does she want you to go with her?"

"Old Crane ordered her in his will to come to Crane Manor
without servants after his death, and then she would receive
further clues as to the family treasure hidden in the mansion.
Leslie is afraid to go alone, and since I am not a servant...
Holmes, would you like to come with us? It does not look good
when the lady make this journey alone with an almost strange
man."

He smiled faintly but with satisfaction.

"Why not? I need a short trip. Lately, I have had no matter
of interest except for the disappearance of Lord Greenshow. It
feels like my brain is screaming for help."

It was nothing new to me. I knew my friend couldn't live
without his mental stimulus, but I honestly doubted that a trip
to Crane Manor would provide him with his favorite nutrient
for gray matter. However, it will be at least a necessary change
of air for him. I have noticed for a while now that Holmes has
lost weight and has become more nervous than ever.

We left as soon as dawn. Already in the carriage, Holmes
began to question Miss Maynard about certain details of his
grandfather's will, and as she answered him, his eyes began to
glow more and more.

"Isn't that strange, Watson?" He finally turned to me. "The
dying old bastard leaves a will, saving everything to a never
seen granddaughter, but on the condition that she comes to the

family residence all alone? This is probably not a normal procedure."

"He was a weird loner... Oh, something shot into his head," I muttered. It didn't escape my notice that Leslie Maynard was looking at my friend with admiring eyes, and I felt a pang of jealousy.

"No, no, Watson. I think he had a purpose in it."

"That's why I asked dear Dr. Watson to accompany me," said Miss Maynard. "I didn't even dare to ask for your company. I did not think that such a famous detective would want to come with me only because I am afraid and have a bad feeling. It's probably just my stupidity..."

My friend, as I have mentioned more than once, was a bit vain and he was visibly flattering to call him "such a famous detective". He kept his face impassive, however.

"Forgive me, but I wouldn't call you stupid," he said after a moment. "First of all, a fool never admits to his stupidity... and secondly, you were not deceived by the flash of gold, you were careful enough to try to get company at the risk of losing your fortune. It was very sensible. However, we must act cunningly so that no one on the spot realizes that you are not alone."

He thought as he looked at the carriage window. His sharp mind was already working on this, but I could find no riddle here. Though I believed in my friend's unfailing instinct, I was of the opinion that he was wrong this time. So, why did I not protest against starting an absurd investigation?

Well, I knew how important puzzles and mysteries he could solve were to Sherlock Holmes. When he missed them, he became lethargic, then went into a nervous state, which usually ended in one way - cocaine. The ease with which he succumbed to this temptation terrified me, and I did my best to prevent it. Among my patients there were people addicted to morphine, opium and hashish. I knew very well what such an addiction did to people's bodies and minds, let alone finances.

As the carriage pulled up by the old-fashioned mansion Miss Maynard clenched my hand fearfully. I wasn't too surprised at her nervousness, as the old building looked downright repulsive. It was a strangely shapeless lump, reminiscent of a huge toad perched in a garden. In fact, it was not even a garden, but a wilderness that the gardener's hand probably never touched. It was nothing like a typical mansion of an old English family.

"Interesting," my friend muttered and put the binoculars to his eyes. He surveyed the building in silence for a moment, then lowered his hand and looked sympathetically at our companion.

"Go over there, Miss Maynard," he said. "There is a man standing outside the door, apparently waiting for you. Don't go home until he leaves and we join you. Come up with something for example that you want to see the garden first. We'll go inside together. It will be safer this way."

"Good," she whispered. "I trust you, Mr. Holmes."

At the same time she looked at him so beautifully that she would have moved the stone with her gaze, so even Holmes smiled involuntarily before we both got to the side of the road. The carriage continued down the road to the mansion, and we made our way through the thick bushes as close to Crane Manor as possible. From where we stopped, we could clearly see the open door and a livery man leaning against the doorframe. He was rather old, as far as I could see from there.

He had quite dark skin, thinning, gray hair and a slightly stooped back.

Leslie walked over to him. Clearly surprised, he looked somewhere beyond her, looked around slightly, finally shrugged as if in resignation, said something to her that we couldn't hear, and walked away, leaving her alone on the doorstep. We waited for the servant to disappear from our sight before joining Miss Maynard.

"Weirdo," she said uncertainly. "He looked at me as if he expected someone completely different."

"Because maybe he was expecting... Let's go inside before someone sees us," said Holmes, looking around carefully.

The door led not in the hall, as we expected, but into a large, gloomy room, furnished like the master of the house's office. Several doors led from it, probably to other rooms. We had barely stepped inside the mansion door when the door slammed shut behind us with a thud. At the same time, the steel shutters fell down, covering all the windows. Miss Maynard gave a shrill cry and ran for the door.

"This is hopeless," said Holmes calmly, watching her struggle. "Someone, probably your grandfather, constructed the clockwork that trapped us here. You have to find out why and think about leaving this place. We can't get anything back by force."

I wouldn't have given my head for it, but I thought he had anticipated the possibility of a similar trap and had entered it deliberately - or at least it didn't surprise him. Unfortunately, the same could not be said of poor Leslie. When she found that neither the door nor the windows would open, she became so hysterical that I had to give her a small shot of morphine. When she fell asleep, I took her in my arms and carried her to one of the rooms, where to my relief there was a wide sofa. I put it on it and went back to my friend.

Holmes was sitting in an old armchair, staring at the table on which stood a sheet of stiff paper, folded in four, leaning against an empty vase.

"What do you think, Watson, does good manners allow us to read a letter not addressed to us?" He asked.

"If it's going to help," I said. "I confess to you that I am confused. What this is about?"

"Let's find out."

He took the piece of paper, unfolded it, and began to read aloud:

"Dear grandson,

As a prudent man, I never trusted banks. I have invested all my wealth in the most reliable currency, diamonds. They are hidden in the inner room, but to get to it, you need to solve some simple math puzzles first.

As you probably know from your mother, I am a man of strict rules. By bonding with Yankee, she lost the right to even a penny from my estate and I did not change my mind.

But it's not your fault, so I decided to give you a chance, albeit after her and her pathetic husband death. I have to be sure neither of them put their hand on my money.

Before you take possession of my property, you must prove that you are a worthy grandson. I don't want it to fall into the hands of some lame.

PS: The locking mechanism for all entrances and exits will automatically turn off as soon as you open the vault door. Otherwise, you'll be in trouble.

Your grandfather, Archibald Maynard"

"And what do you think?" My friend asked with some amusement.

"What a mean, vicious, insensitive old man!" I burst out, unable to cool out.

"I have told you so many times, dear Watson, that you are too emotional and therefore unable to draw the correct conclusions," said Holmes rebukingly. "First of all, we can already formulate a preliminary theory."

"What?"

"Here old Crane was convinced his daughter had borne a boy, not a worthless girl. He must have learned this by accident, since he did not want to hear anything about the ingrate who had abandoned her home. This is clearly seen in the heading "Dear Grandson", not "Granddaughter". How such a misunderstanding came about, we probably won't know, and it's not that important again."

Crane was convinced that his grandson had inherited his scientific mind, and that was the only thing that interested him, not the young man's person. He probably wanted someone to carry on his work, whatever it was. I suggest that we look for this inner room and vault, because I don't think Miss Leslie can figure out the puzzles her grandfather composed. Without insulting this lovely creature in any way, it does not seem like a genius in mathematics to me."

"Probably you are right. And if what they say about old Crane is true, then his rebuses really won't be easy for a woman's head," I admitted.

Indeed, it was hard for me to imagine Miss Maynard, the merry butterfly, being able to concentrate on higher mathematics. After all, we had to save her, otherwise this gloomy mansion could easily become our common grave. Holmes did not seem to care about this at all. He calmly checked all the doors and chose the one that did lead into the house. We followed until we reached some peculiar wall, decorated with a long row of metal levers.

On one of them was another page.

"You must flip down three of these levers to open the passage," read Holmes. "They have to be exactly the right ones and none other, or you'll set off an explosive device that will destroy this house. You have one approach."

"Which right?" I asked helplessly. The levers were completely the same, nothing different.

"Let me think. Take a look during this time," he asked me.

So, I left him alone and started to "look around". The residence was not too luxuriously furnished. It was evident that it was the scientist's seat, because apart from the most necessary equipment, there was only apparatus here, filling all the corner. I couldn't even name most of the devices - I've never seen them and had no idea what they could be used for. No wonder Leslie's mother was unhappy here. I didn't know a single woman who would voluntarily live in such a ghastly place.

When I returned, to my surprise, the next way was already open. The metal plate of the wall was pushed aside, and the three levers were tucked down - obviously the right ones. I opened my mouth, but my surprise was unable to make a sound.

"Oh, it was quite easy," my friend said, catching my gaze. "I just had to take into account the education of our deceased host. He was a mathematician, and from that alone I should have come up with a solution. Together, these levers form a straight line. As you can see, I postponed the beginning and ending and the third exactly to the golden ratio point.

I wasn't strong with geometry, but I didn't want to ask for more explanations now. More puzzles awaited us, and Holmes did not look well. He paled a little, his mouth was dry, and beads of sweat appeared on his forehead. It surely wasn't due to fatigue, so was he sick?

We walked down a winding corridor, leading down like a ramp and ending in another room, except for one bench, devoid of equipment, but equipped with a mechanism, on the front of which there were several double grooves. There were different colored balls in the upper grooves, the same balls in the lower ones, but only a few. Each was connected to the main mechanism by a thin cable. A card attached to some protruding part said:

"If you want to go further, complete the color sequences so that they form a logical whole. You can make a mistake twice."

"What's that supposed to mean?!" I exclaimed, losing my spirit.

"It's a Sharon test," said Holmes with a strange weariness. "I need to concentrate now and figure out the string algorithm, and it'll take a while. Do not bother me."

Even if I thought about a year, there would be no point in arranging these balls, which look like children's toys. I couldn't help so I concentrate on watching the brilliant detective in action. It struck me how he really looked bad, or rather worse and worse. His slim hands trembled slightly as he moved the next marbles, clearly making a heroic effort to concentrate on the work. Finally, he capitulated and leaned against the wall. He was trembling as in an attack of ague.

"Watson," he whispered after a moment. "For God's sake... give me opium or morphine... because I can't take it anymore."

My vague suspicions suddenly turned out to be true, as heavy as a curse. For a long time I had fought with my friend not to take drugs in those moments when he had no case to solve. It seemed to me that I had won, but now it was evident that I had lost, and it was a pain. I took him gently by the shoulders and set him down on the bench.

"No, Holmes," I said firmly. "You know well how much you risk succumbing to this weakness. If you want to commit suicide, accept that I can't help you."

My heart ached at the sight of his torment, but I kept telling myself that this was the only right thing I could do. I knew how much he was suffering, because among my patients I had many addicted to opium, which has been very popular recently, especially in the port areas. I could ease his torment with a single injection, but I didn't want to. As a physician, I had no intention of putting my hand to the destruction.

"John," whispered Holmes, clinging to me like a last resort. "I'm begging you, John..."

He had never called me by name before that alone was a sign of his spiritual condition.

"Calm down and breathe deeply," I replied, trying to be firm. "I declare that you will not get any drug from me, even if you had to kill me."

Holmes pursed his thin lips in a bitter grimace.

"So, that's what you really are!" He blurted out with venomous fury. "You were just waiting for an opportunity to trample me down! You enjoy me squirming here like a bug waiting for mercy."

I knew that he was speaking of suffering and morphine hunger, but nevertheless his words hurt me, they hurt me terribly.

Holmes noticed this, for he rose from the bench and embraced me with a sudden movement.

"Forgive me, my friend," he sobbed in a voice I had never heard from him. "I'm mean, how could I...?"

I hugged him silently and looked at the unfinished "puzzle." I had no idea how I would do without Holmes. He saw this and said:

"There's the last row left. Move the yellow ball down, then black, then blue."

I didn't really believe it would do anything, because in that state my friend couldn't think clearly, but I did what he told me to do. To my relief, and to my surprise, the mechanism rattled and the entire wall slid aside, revealing a corridor with what appeared to be a table at the end. Coming closer, I saw that it was another machine, this time in a chessboard pattern. There were figures standing out on it, bolted to movable booms, and another sheet of paper lay between them.

"In one move you will checkmate the Black King," I read. "You can't go wrong. When you do this, the vault will be open to you."

I looked at the chessboard, hoping to get something into my head. I was playing, but very poorly, so there was no chance for me to discover the right move myself. I was also curious where the treasury was. This time I couldn't see anything to take it as the door.

I left everything and went back to Holmes. He was lying on the bench, and his appearance only depressed me. I knew similar symptoms all too well - a fever, a shivering throughout body, and a severe depression that made it impossible to think logically. In his case it was a real disaster. I sat down next to him and put my face in my hands. I really didn't know how to get out of this situation, and time was pressing and Miss Maynard could wake up at any moment. I wanted some comforting message prepared for this moment, but I didn't have one.

"Do you think about her?" Holmes's weak but conscious voice reached me. "Do you think only as a doctor? Watson, I know you think I'm a machine, you have faith that I have a head, but no heart. This was not always the case. And I used to love, but now I does not show it at all."

I didn't say a word. I let him speak. He needed it.

"Her name was Violet and I called her Vi. She was the half-sister of my friend Victor Trevor, whom I told you about on my first case, you know, Gloria Scott. Even now, I consider myself the most beautiful woman I have ever seen. Moreover, her intelligence was admirable. And she had this unusual charm that made men lose their heads for her. I felt proud that she chose me, neither a rich nor a particularly handsome young man...

When I first heard about the suspicions about Violet, I was indignant. How dare anyone ever suspect... an angel? I took up the matter despite the objections of the local police and Victor's strange reluctance. He kept saying that I shouldn't interfere in the investigation and leave it to the government detectives. It seemed to be a provocation. Three children from the orphanage that Violet took care of for charity, it turned out, died of poison. Suspicion fell on her, because she was the only one among the caretakers who personally gave the little ones candy and it seemed that this was the only circumstance that burdened her.

Ah, Victor was right, I shouldn't be getting involved in this! I was the one who found out that all the children were secretly insured for a large sum by a certain Madame Firefield. As you know, it is not difficult, it is enough to go to the insurance company, provide the details of the insured person, the sum insured and the data of the recipient of the insurance in case of a mishap. Nobody checks who is insured for the insurer...

The devil tempted me to describe her. The color of her hair and dress meant nothing to me, but when the clerk said the lady was left-handed, and when she removed her glove to sign the papers, he noticed that she was missing the tip of her little finger, along with her fingernail... I would never know that what I heard. These minor defects were all too familiar to me.

First, it chilled me to the core. Everything inside me screamed that it must be untrue, but at the same time I knew that the coincidence was too improbable and with the courage of despair I started looking further. If I had at least proved that someone else had bought the poison..."

"So what happened next?" I asked as the pause in the story extended.

"I found everything, all the evidence that the police overlooked. Violet has been arrested. I overcame and went to her. She didn't know yet that I was the one who drove her down, she claimed she was innocent, and begged me for an alibi. I had to tell her the truth. In my life I will never forget her face when she listened to me: as if her mask had fallen off. 'You disappointed me,' she said coldly when I finished speaking. 'I was hoping that you would be useful to me, and in the meantime you betrayed me. And for what? For three brats that were only a burden to society. Nobody care about the loss of their deaths, and I could finally not worry about the future.' And she added contemptuously, 'Do you really think I'd deal with zero like you if I didn't think you'd help me, if not for sake of me then for Victor?'

It was the last time I saw her. Shortly thereafter, she was convicted and hanged, but it was me who tightened the noose around her neck with my own hands. I knew about it. My heart didn't break like romances, but it turned to stone. From then on, I felt nothing anymore, but my mind began to work with the precision that you are so delighted with in your relations. I paid dearly for it, Watson, so dearly, and the price made me never trust women again. Maybe it's unfair of me, but I can't."

I was silent for a long moment, shocked by this confession.

"Do you really think they're all like this?" I asked finally.

I received no reply, and when I looked back, my friend was asleep, exhausted by his efforts.

"Let him sleep," I thought. "It will make him stronger and give him clarity of mind. He will need it if we are to get out of here alive. For now, I have to think about all three of us."

I got up and went to check the room I had left Leslie in. On the way, I found a kitchen where, to my relief, I discovered not only a tap with running water, but also a small gas burner (straight from the laboratory, very out of place in the kitchen) and a box full of pieces of dry bread. Old Crane's orders had all the supplies removed from the pantry, but he either forgot or didn't know about the chest. With water and this bread at my disposal, I could not worry about at least the next few days.

Truth! After all, I also had with me something that was a real treasure in this situation: a flat bottle of cognac, lemon and half a pound of sugar cubes. It is true that they did not belong to the standard equipment of a doctor's bag, but I have found more than once that these unconventional measures work wonders, especially in the case of people who are at risk of apoplexy or an attack of moderate hysteria. I preferred giving it to them than morphine. My experience with Holmes has taught me that it is a very dangerous substance and that it is better to do without it whenever possible.

Formerly a spasmodic lady, or an enraged fat man with apoplectic tendencies, I injected this drug without further ado, but now I preferred to give a glass of water with lemon, sugar and a little cognac. The result was amazing, and I knew for sure that I was not hurting my patient. The fact that I had given Miss Maynard morphine was the result of the belief that the poor girl would be better off getting some sleep - I just wanted Holmes to be able to think calmly. I never thought that I would soon have two instead of one patient.

I heated the water and made some grog for all of us before going to Leslie. She wasn't asleep anymore. She sat upright on the bench and looked around in surprise.

"Are you feeling better?" I asked. "Please drink this."

She dutifully took a few sips.

"I'm fine, really," she assured me. "Where's Mr. Holmes?"

"He's on the sofa in the room he managed to open. He's... very sick and he's asleep now. I hope that he will wake up soon, because the two of us will not solve your grandfather's next puzzle."

Miss Maynard shuddered at the memory of a man she had never seen, who had so cruelly experienced her after his death. Probably she was no longer surprised that her mother had run away from her father to the other end of the world and that she wanted nothing from him.

"Is your friend's illness serious?" She asked, getting up from the bench. "Let's go to him, he shouldn't be alone."

I figured she definitely wasn't like Violet Trevor. Yes, she was flirtatious and liked to play, but she also had, as it is commonly said, a heart on her sleeve. She was kind and compassionate. She certainly wouldn't be able to hurt anyone.

We went to Holmes together. He slept restlessly, throwing himself on the sofa and groaning, and as I put my hand on his forehead, I felt the fever growing stronger. The pulse was fast and irregular, and as I measured it my friend woke up suddenly.

"Drink," I said, handing him a mug of grog.

He did my order, and it struck me that, despite the fever and apparent suffering, he was looking at me alertly, with a hint of old concentration in his eyes.

"What's the inner room?" He asked.

"A chessboard with figures bolted to a part of some mechanism."

"I'll take care of it," he promised, trying to sit up.

"You are sick! Please recover first," said Miss Maynard, stopping him.

Her concern must have amused him, because he twisted his lips into a strained smile.

"I won't recover too soon, Miss Maynard," he said, gently pulling her hands away. "It will be better for all of us if I quickly unravel old Crane's mysteries and we can get out of here."

I looked at him sadly. I had no doubt that as soon as he was released he would run to buy himself morphine, and I knew I couldn't stop him. Here I was in control of the situation, but outside this building, I will be again condemned to the role of a passive observer.

Meanwhile Holmes got up and, swaying with weakness on his feet, went to the inner room. I stopped Leslie from following him. Now he had to be alone, one of us could only disturb him.

"Poor man." Leslie sat down at the table and finished her cold grog. "He's really sick, and I bother him with my affairs... You know, doctor, I'm ashamed that I made such a show of myself. I should be stronger."

"What happened would throw any lady off-balance," I replied. "No wonder you got scared."

She smiled at me, and I thought this girl had a pretty smile. Even with her tousled hair and the rumpled gown, she looked like a princess in that smile.

I made a second batch of grog for us and we ate some bone-dry bread, dipping it in a hot drink. Miss Maynard was really calm now. She told me some funny stories about her childhood in America, and I told her some anecdotes from studies. We tried to keep our moods fairly cheerful, though we were both in our thoughts with Holmes.

We couldn't help but think about him. He was probably staring at the mechanical chessboard now, trying to guess the one and only correct move that would open the vault door. Weak as a child, consumed by fever and pain, he had to use all his phenomenal abilities to make us come out alive. What would have helped him was slowly killing him, and I couldn't, I just couldn't bring myself to give it to him in the name of our escape from hell's trap.

It wasn't the first time that it struck me that this was truly diabolical irony - painkillers, a great blessing for humanity, in irresponsible hands turned into its great misfortune. I mechanically touched the hand of the jacket on my chest, where I hid the bottle of morphine. I did it right after I realized what was wrong with my friend. Though I knew his highly moral course well, I preferred not to tempt. Too often, I have seen people seemingly strong and honest commit the worst crimes to get money for opium.

I just hoped Miss Leslie wouldn't figure out what was really wrong with Holmes - the thought of destroying his opinion I could not bear almost as much as I thought about his addiction.

"Watson, do you have a stethoscope?" My friend's voice from the next room snapped me out of my thoughts.

"What?" I asked absently.

"Stethoscope," he repeated. "I opened the vault, but you still have to guess the combination of the safe. I don't have the strength to do it, so I'll do it another way."

I took the item he wanted from my bag and, out of unstoppable curiosity, followed Holmes to the vault. I saw him kneel by a large metal box and, holding the stethoscope against its door, gently twist the knurled knobs. I have heard about this way of opening safes. Sherlock Holmes, whom nature had endowed with the sensitive fingers of a violinist and the tender hearing of a musician, easily learned the art from a French thief whom he arrested and released. As he explained to me later, he could not bring himself to hand over the brilliant cashier of the Paris gendarmerie, when it was revealed that he was stealing in order to maintain the orphanage where he was brought up. However, he threatened him that if he continued the criminal practice, he would not be merciful a second time. A grateful Frenchman taught him his art because, as he said, a man never knows what will be of use to him in his work.

As if enchanted, I watched the great detective's actions, half believing and half not believing that he would be able to open the safe in this way. At one point, however, there was a slight crash and the door of the safe swung open, revealing an interior full of rainbow-sparkling stones. I heard a choked sigh behind me. Absorbed in what Holmes was doing, I didn't even hear Leslie's soft footsteps as she stood behind me and watched everything over my shoulder.

"Here is your treasure, Miss Maynard," said Holmes, rising from his knees. "And judging by the rumble that comes here, our prison opens."

"Oh, Mr. Holmes," Leslie whispered. "I don't know how I'll repay you... Take half of these diamonds."

My friend answered her with a forced smile.

"Thank you, ma'am, but I don't need them. I rarely charge a higher fee than my flat rate, and never in diamonds. Anyway, that's your heritage. As far as I know jewels, you are now England's richest heiress. I just wish they didn't bring you any misfortune."

He turned and started to leave, and I, despondent at what might happen now, followed him. I vainly explained to myself that I had nothing to reproach myself for, because I did my best. Fear and despair gripped my heart.

At the door of the mansion, Holmes paused and squeezed my arm lightly with his slim fingers.

"Watson," he said softly. "Do something for me. Take me somewhere where you can finish the work, somewhere where I can fight this damned weakness. You were right: If I don't beat it, God won't forgive me for so foolishly wasting the talent he gave me."

Anno 1891